I0586918

Team Alex
'The Russian'

A Saints' team novel

By Ally Adams

Atlas Productions

Team Alex
First published in 2017 and republished in 2019, 2020 and 2021.
Copyright © Ally Adams and Helen Goltz

All rights reserved. No part of this book may be reproduced or transmitted by any person or entity, including internet search engines or retailers, in any form or by any means, electronic or mechanical, including photocopying (except under the statutory exceptions provisions of the Australian Copyright Act 1968), recording, scanning or by any information storage and retrieval systems without the prior written permission of the author or publisher, Atlas Productions.

Atlas Productions
Greenslopes QLD 4102
Web: www.atlasproductions.com.au

NATIONAL
LIBRARY
OF AUSTRALIA

A catalogue record for this book is available from the National Library of Australia

This book is a work of fiction. Names, characters, places and incidents are either the product of the author's imagination or are used fictitiously. Any resemblance to actual persons, living or dead, or to actual events or locales is entirely coincidental. Any medical experiments or results cited in this novel have been fictionalised and any slight of specific people, experiments, research or organisations is unintentional.

Dedicated to the 'Russian'
who never knew that I was madly in love with him

Books by Ally Adams

The Saints Team series:

Team Lucas

Team Tomás

Team Niklas

Team Alex

We're cut from the same cloth, you and me,
made for each other.

Chapter 1

For just one moment I thought I was back in school and I had been pushed into the boys' toilet block – I remember the half a dozen faces that scowled at me, while I grappled with the smell, that huge water trough thing that we don't have in our toilets, and … well, I didn't stay around long enough to notice the other thing that we don't have, before tearing back outside to confront Susan Snowden, the bully that had pushed me in there. Fast forward about twenty years, and I'm almost in the same situation.

I'm due to record a quick interview in the Club Room with a player nicknamed Buzz – a Defender just back from injury and playing for the hottest sports team known to man, well, woman – the Saints. *Room Three*; I check the number, wander in and holy-naked-guys-getting-rub-downs … it appears I'm one of the few with clothes on.

Half a dozen faces turn and smile at me; I see a flash of glowing tight, tanned butts, muscly legs, toned arms, even a groin or two that was just 'out there'.

'Ah, sorry wrong room,' I say, as I stumble backward, trying not to look anywhere but out the door.

'Are you looking for the coach?' a voice from the corner booms.

I put my hands over my eyes, web my fingers a little which sets them off laughing again and look towards the voice. It was 'The Russian' – Alex Renwick.

'No, I'm after Buzz, he said to meet at this time in *Room Three*.' My face was burning red, but I think other parts of my body were enjoying it.

I could see several of the physical therapists shaking their head, smiling, and the youngest answered.

'It's his party trick. He thinks it's funny. Don't worry, you're not the first journo to fall victim.'

'I'll give him funny when I see him,' I muttered.

'Room eight, Carly,' the deep baritone voice said again. The Russian. He knew my name.

'Thank you,' I said, spinning on my heels to leave before I was magnetically drawn to that tall, dark, and gorgeous hunk of a man in the corner. Mm, The Russian.

*****

Yep, it was game day. Not my game day: my basketball team – the Suns – would have to go on without me, I was out of action with a knee injury, but I was reporting on the Saints' game day. Yep, the Saints – a tough gig but someone has got to do it.

After the interview with the very not-amusing Buzz, I settled into the media box, set up my laptop, made sure the WiFi was working and then stopped to look around. Sasha Saxon, the Saints' media officer, was walking towards me with two diet colas. She always grabbed them before the boys in the press box got them. Not that many of them wanted diet drinks, but we wanted them more ... it was our biological right. She looked super stylish as always with her gorgeous blonde hair tied back and her interpretation of the Saints' game day uniform.

'Hey Carly,' she said, sliding into the seat next to me. I noticed she said hello while keeping her eyes on the boys warming up on the ground – one boy in particular. A few months ago she had hitched up with Niklas Wagner, or the Kaiser as he is known – a truly beautiful specimen of German glory and the Saints' Midfielder. Mm. I watched her and laughed when she finally decided to give me her one hundred percent attention.

She flushed. 'What? It's my job?'

'Sure it is,' I agreed. We greeted a couple of other journos who arrived in the box – Dan from radio *K-talk* and Brian from *The Sports Guide*. They grabbed desk space and began to set up their gear.

I had to ask Sasha something, and I wasn't looking forward to doing so. I looked around and lowered my voice ...

'Sash, I wanted to ask you a favor ...'

'Sure,' she said.

I cleared my throat. 'Next weekend I've got the Suns' Gala Ball and Auction Night ...'

Sasha frowned. 'Really? You're cutting that fine if you want a dress made.'

Sasha was a really good part-time designer when she wasn't working with the Saints.

'No, it's not that, but thanks,' I said.

'Well that should be fun,' she continued, 'especially if you're not organizing it. Or do you have to do something?'

'I've been asked to give a speech about the Suns and the importance of the team, given I played my hundredth game this year. Once that's over, I can relax,' I said, taking a sip of my diet cola.

'Right,' she said, and her eyes narrowed with suspicion. 'So, what's the favor?'

'I want to take a date.'

'Oh,' she looked surprised. 'I'm not your type, surely? I mean you're attractive, tall, nice legs, always admired your thick dark hair,' she said fingering a strand of her blonde hair, 'but ...'

I rolled my eyes. 'Not you, you dill,' I said, and she grinned. Funny girl! 'The Russian,' I said, lowering my voice.

She made one of those cringe-type faces.

'What? Why that face?' I frowned. 'I'm not asking him on a date-date, I need a handbag. He doesn't have to fall in love with me.'

Sasha shrugged. 'What's not to love ... he might fall head over heels. But rumor has it that his break-up with Leesa was ugly and he has sworn off women, for a while, anyway. But hey, if you're only after a bit of eye candy ...'

I nodded. 'That's all. Really tall eye candy.'

'I hear you. At least he's in town next weekend since we've got two home games in a row,' she mused. 'Why the Russian?'

I didn't want to let on that I had been lusting after him for a while now, so I played it cool and casual.

'I heard he was single, and he's taller than me which is pretty unique,' I answered.

She smiled at me. 'Ah, you saw him at the press conference earlier this season, I remember now. You asked me then was he single and I think he had just broken up with Leesa.'

I shrugged. The casual act wasn't working when my tongue was hanging out. 'So what's the story with his ex?' I didn't want to know but had to ask, couldn't help myself.

Sasha took a mouthful of her cola before answering. 'I only met her twice, sort of met her ... she came into the office once, and then I saw her at a home game here. She gave me a hard time because she wanted me to get The Russian out of the dressing room to speak to him before a game. As if!'

I laughed at the idea of pulling any professional athlete away from the team before a game unless it was super important. You are really in the zone before a game and the coach and captain would kill you if you went missing in action, especially if it was a LOVE call!

Sasha continued. 'She didn't like it here, too boring for her, not enough partying and stars around. You know, she's Leesa *Hart*,' she emphasized the surname. 'As in Harry Hart, the movie director's daughter?'

'Yeah, I vaguely remember some social media and pics going around at the time, although I was too focussed on getting through the season without an injury to really notice. Plus, no point noticing a guy who's hitched until they're unhitched,' I said, with a shrug.

We stopped for a moment to look out the media box window and watch the guys as they jogged past. Sasha sighed with contentment.

'Sorry where were we?' she asked. 'Oh yeah, The Russian and Leesa. I don't know how they ever got together, though.

From what I saw and heard, you couldn't get two more complete opposites as those two. And she was always in the papers on the arm of some other guy, or at a party with a huge group of hanger-ons. It's lucky The Russian's mild-mannered, or he'd probably be in jail for murder.'

We both looked out at the Saints' stadium, contemplating relationships – well I was, can't really vouch for what was going on in Sasha's head.

'So ...' she said, 'what do you want me to do? What's the favor?'

'Oh yeah, can you put me in his path?'

'That I can do. Can you drop into the office during the week? Come in to do a story, interview him or any of the team, take me for coffee, whatever excuse you'd like and I'll make sure you get one-on-one time,' she said, emphasizing the last few words in a sexy voice.

'What are you two nattering about?' Dan asked, butting in.

'First of all,' I said, rising and looking down on him – often the case with my height – we're not nattering, and secondly it's official girl talk.'

'I love girls' talk,' he said, with a smirk.

'Oh good,' Sasha said. 'I was just telling Carly that I was going to get a wax tomorrow. The Brazilian gets rid of those nasty little hairs ...'

Dan put his hand over his ears. 'Too much information,' he said, moving away.

Sasha grinned at me. 'Come in Monday if you can, he usually doesn't do much but drink coffee and mope around the office recovering from Saturday's game.'

'Thanks,' I said, relieved. The plan was falling into place and right on cue, The Russian ran right past our media box.

Hell yeah, he was definitely a man I could look up to – big, bigger than me ... I think he had a few inches on me; I might be able to get my high heels out ... yes! He needed a haircut, but he could get away with it ... his hair was full and wavy, dark and messy – cute. He had trendy stubble on his face as if he'd just gotten out of bed to come to the game. I couldn't see from afar, but I knew his eyes were dark brown with ridiculously long dark lashes for a guy – almost pretty, but I dare anyone to call him that. I might be tall, but I was thin and athletic whereas The Russian was strong - there was no better word for it. He liked to bench press; I liked him bench pressing too ... The Russian would make me feel like a woman. I wish I had got more of a glimpse of him earlier in all his semi-nakedness – really, where did that thought come from? Disgraceful.

It was Sasha's turn to catch me out.

'Uh, don't forget to report on the game,' she whispered and gave me a wave as she departed the box.

I grinned and dismissed her, getting back to the job of setting up and reporting on the Saints versus the Salt Lake Spears.

Chapter 2

'Well if it isn't Carly Brooker, again,' The Russian said as Sasha and I slowly walked past the open door of his office on Monday, just before midday. I ran my hands down my skirt again for the hundredth time ... it had taken me hours to decide what to wear this morning – yes, I'm pathetic. We stopped and looked in; The Russian looked divine in jeans, a T-shirt, and sneakers. Behind him hung a business shirt, tie and pants, some black boots below them.

The Russian continued. 'Average per game: 19.5 points, 5.3 rebounds, 3.1 assists, and 2.3 steals ... give or take a few points.'

'And if it isn't The Russian,' I returned as we stood in his doorway.

'That's it?' he frowned. 'You don't know all my impressive stats?' he asked with the twitch of a smile.

'Oh, I do,' I assured him, 'but we'd be here all day.'

'Oh please,' Sasha rolled her eyes, 'don't tell him that, his big head will burst out of the room.'

The Russian gave her a look that said he was unimpressed.

'Sorry about the trick Buzz played on you,' he said with a

snarl at the mention of Buzz's name; I had heard there was no love-loss between The Russian and Buzz.

'It's all good,' I said, closing the subject down before Sasha asked questions. 'I've had worse than that thrown at me.'

The Russian nodded. 'So, how's the knee, think you'll get another game?' he asked. 'Actually, don't answer that. I hate that question.'

'Thanks,' I said, it takes a sportsperson to know a sportsperson.

'I can hear my phone,' Sasha said, 'pick me up for coffee on your way out,' she said to me, ditching me there. We both listened ... there were no sounds of a phone ringing. Awkward.

'So, a good game on Saturday, gotta be pleased with that?' I asked, feeling like a shag on a rock – or in a doorway, as was the case.

'Have a seat,' he said, 'Ed, my business partner, is out getting lunch.'

This was looking up. I slid into Ed's chair and swiveled it to face The Russian, making sure I crossed my legs so he couldn't miss them. Hell, you've got to use your assets, it's one of the things the coach was always drumming into us, but she probably meant on the court, I suspect. Sitting at the same level I had the chance to study him; he really was quite exceptional – I itched to run my fingers through his dark, wavy hair. He was shaven today and those high cheekbones gave his masculine face its beauty. He was all arms and shoulders, with a very defined torso – from what I could see covered in clothes, damn those clothes – and very sexy hips. Yep, what an inventory.

'Come to interview me?' he asked, and this time he smiled.

'Uh no, came to take Sasha out for a coffee. Girl talk, you know ... about how tough it is to be a female sports journalist in a man's world,' I said, making it up as I went.

'Yeah, I can just imagine,' The Russian replied, frowning. 'Actually, I can't really, why is it tough? You get to sit in the best seats in the house, don't you?'

'Been up there ... in the Saints' media box?' I asked, grabbing that lead.

'Hell no, you lot would ask me questions if I went there,' he said, a look of mistrust crossing his very handsome, close-by face.

'Mm, that's the idea. You should drop in before or after the game. Nik drops in usually to catch up with Sasha.' I said it before realizing I might be getting Nik in trouble.

'Does he now?' The Russian said, crossing his arms across his chest.

I was just about to backtrack when the door to The Russian's office opened and Captain Fantastic stood there – also known as Lucas Ainswright.

'Ah sorry, didn't know The Russian had company,' he said. 'No one usually visits him.'

The Russian smirked. I rose and offered my hand to Lucas. I'm six-foot-two and I'm guessing, since I had to look up at him, that Lucas was about six-three. Yes, I love a 'tall' office.

'Carly Brooker,' I said, shaking his hand.

'I know,' Lucas said and introduced himself, as if he needed an introduction.

'I know,' I responded, 'great season for you and the Saints, congrats.'

'Yeah, let's hope it continues,' he said. 'Sorry to hear your season got cut short, but you've had an impressive run.'

'Thanks, I would have liked to have seen the season out,' I said, bearing my soul just a little. I was missing the sport and my teammates.

It was definitely warm in the Saints' office and then I realized why – Lucas was still holding my hand. I reluctantly pulled it away. The Russian cleared his throat. I had forgotten he was there for a moment.

'Oh, well, got to go,' I said, reaching back for my handbag. I know most girls would stick around, but I didn't want to make a pest of myself.

'No need to rush off,' Lucas assured me, 'I can come back.'

'Yeah, I can see the captain anytime,' The Russian agreed. The office felt very small with the two super hunks breathing in all the air.

'Thanks, but Sasha will be waiting for me,' I said, lamely pointing up the hallway to her office area, as if they didn't know the way.

The Russian rose. 'Well, see you at the game maybe,' he said.

'Sure,' I said, giving them both a winning smile; I did my best to sashay up the hallway with a walk that said 'so confident' in case they were watching. Who was I kidding? I could barely walk with my tongue dragging on the ground. I think I was having hot flushes. Then I remembered I still didn't have a date for the Ball, but... Houston... we had contact.

✶✶✶✶✶

'You can't wear that,' Josh, my housemate, rolled his eyes as he sat back on our sofa with a red wine in one hand and the television remote in the other.

'Why not?' I said, defensively. 'I love red, and this dress lifts and tucks.'

'It whiffs and sucks, more like it. Next!'

It was my turn to roll my eyes and I stormed off melodramatically back to the bedroom to change. Secretly I was relieved that Josh wanted to vet my Suns' Gala Ball outfit ... not only because I was still holding hope that The Russian would come with me, but given I was speaking in front of about four hundred people, I wanted to look my best when those eight hundred eyes were on me ... aagh, I was just giving myself heart palpitations. I didn't want to buy something new if I could avoid it – my playing fees had stopped, my sponsor fees were on standby and my casual sports writing job didn't pay a lot, but I was applying for full-time roles.

I heard Josh turn the volume up on the television again as he waited for my next appearance. I did have an offer from a couple of local dress suppliers to provide me with a gown for the night, but that was a fallback option. Last time I had taken up the offer, some idiot spilled a drink on me, the stain didn't come out with dry cleaning and I found myself having to buy a dress that I couldn't afford because I couldn't return it. I'd only ever borrow a black dress from now on!

I put on a deep green dress with a plunging neckline and high cut leg that had been given to me after a fashion shoot for one of the team's sponsors. I was sure this would be a winner and I pranced out to show Josh.

'Good Lord no!' he exclaimed.

'Really?' I frowned at him. 'I could have sworn you would love this dress.'

'You look like a harlot,' he said.

I began to laugh. 'No one in the whole world says 'harlot' anymore. Whore, slut, prostitute, hooker, maybe ... but harlot?'

'Harlot,' he confirmed, sighing, 'I think you have no choice, Carly baby ...'

I nodded.

'She did offer,' Josh reminded me.

'But reluctantly,' I said, with a sigh.

I reached for my phone and took it with me when I went in to change. I just hoped that Sasha's throw away comment about making me a dress was a real option.

Chapter 3

Ninety minutes later I stood on Sasha's catwalk while she took my measurements. She had the most amazing apartment – a catwalk right down the middle of the room. I just wanted to put on some music and strut. Plus, she had this platform where she fitted brides or girls getting formal dresses and a whole wall of mirrors. On another level completely, I could see her bedroom and a black cat looking down at me. The best view, however, was in the kitchen – the gorgeous Niklas Wagner was in there. He had gotten home from training early and was now making dinner. I was invited to join them, but I declined. Who could swallow in front of him? I accepted a coffee however and was subtly watching Nik whip that up in the kitchen – sigh.

'Carly!' Sasha snapped at me.

'What?' I looked down at her as she got my waist to ankle measurement.

'Stop wriggling; you're almost as bad as Nik when I try and measure him... almost.'

Nik gave me a sympathetic smile from the kitchen.

'You're just so lucky I like you,' Sasha continued, 'or

there'd be no way you'd be getting this dress made in time.'

'I'm really sorry Sasha… you won't be up late at night, will you?' I felt bad for landing this on her.

She smiled. 'No, I'm just teasing you. I'll have it knocked up in a few days. It helps that you went with one of my designs and I have fabric on hand. I just bought some more when Nik and I went to New York again.' She looked his way and smiled. Mm, can only imagine what went on there.

Nik must have been thinking about it too as he cleared his throat.

'It's a great chance to show off your label Süsse,' he said, using his German nickname for her. They were so cute.

'True,' I said, encouraging that thought. 'There'll be about four hundred people there and I promise to drop your label reference every chance I get.'

'Done,' Sasha said, pushing herself up off the ground. 'You are going to be stunning. The pale gold is really in at the moment, and we'll cinch this at the waist, since you've got a really defined waist, and then let it drop to a full skirt to your ankles.'

'You don't think the split at my chest is too low?' I asked, looking at Sasha's design.

'No, but I'll take it up a little so you're not self-conscious. You can wear it, trust me,' she said.

'I do, thanks, Sash,' I said, stepping off the catwalk. 'We could have the best dance party on this catwalk.'

'Don't let me stop you,' Nik said, 'I could sit here with my coffee and stay out of the way while you two dance.'

Sasha gave him a look.

'Or not,' he said, with a raised eyebrow.

'So, Carly is going to ask The Russian to go to the Suns' Ball with her,' Sasha told Nik. I gave her an alarmed look. I didn't want anyone knowing in case he said no, and I didn't want anyone thinking I was keen, desperate or dateless.

She gave me a barely discernible shake of her head. 'Don't worry, Nik's discreet,' she said.

Nik placed our coffees on the table in the middle of the room and we sat down on the sofas in Sasha's open plan living room. Did I mention he was beautiful? A whole different beautiful to The Russian, but just as good.

'Could be good for him to have a date,' Nik said, putting a hand on Sasha's shoulder. 'I only met Leesa a few times ... strange couple; he's so stable and she was this wild girl. He'd do well to meet a nice lady like you, *Kaa-lee*.'

Ah, Nik – good looking and so charming.

'Want me to tell him to take you?' Nik said.

I spluttered my mouthful of coffee. 'NO, no, but thanks Nik. I better ask him ... I'm not thinking of a date, just friends, sort of,' I said, the last few words trailing off.

'I wonder what he's like in bed,' Sasha said.

'Well, stop wondering,' Nik growled, and she moved closer to pacify him. I grinned at them.

'Big, I suspect,' I said. 'I mean, in length ... I mean in the room he would take up in the bed ... I'm going to stop talking now.' We talked about The Russian for a few more minutes – nothing I didn't know; I finished my coffee and rose from the couch. 'Well, I best go and leave you to have dinner. Thank you Sash for fitting me and fitting me in.'

'Sure, no problem,' she said. She tried to wiggle out of Nik's arms but he wouldn't let go.

She tapped his arm. 'Release me!'

He rose, lifting her with him and planted her on her feet. He kissed the top of her head.

'Got to check our pasta anyway,' he said, with a tap on her butt. 'See you for the next fitting *Kaa-lee*.'

'Or in the media box,' I quipped back. Damn, I meant to tell Sasha I had dobbed her in to The Russian about Nik visiting the media box so that she could be on the front foot. I told her at the door as she saw me out.

'Don't worry, I can handle The Russian,' she said with a smile. 'But about time you did ... I've given you his number, so call him, or email him, or do something but invite him ASAP, in case he makes other plans.'

I nodded and swallowed.

'Seriously, you're going to look gorgeous. He'll be the luckiest guy alive,' she said, boosting my ego.

'Yeah, sure,' I said with a grin. I thanked her and headed down the stairs, out of her apartment block and back to my car. I should just call him or email him and get it over with. Tomorrow.

*****

I couldn't believe my luck the next morning; someone up above was looking after me! I went to the gym; I was only working part-time for *The Sports Daily* and wasn't due back in the office until nine a.m. the next day. I wasn't good at being idle and I still liked to train so I headed to Archer's – it was the best weights gym and there were no pretty boys and girls, it was a serious gym especially for athletes.

I was in the middle of a set of lateral pulldowns when I felt a tap on the shoulder. I turned around and had to look up – that didn't happen much. And wait for it ... I looked up into the dark, sexy eyes of The Russian. Yes! Thank you, God!

Then I assumed a casual pose because I'm so cool, uh-huh, that's me.

'Hey, what are you doing here?' I asked, conscious that I was smelly and sweaty, but so was he.

'Working out ... it's usually why I come here,' he said, with one of his sly grins. 'Good to see you're keeping your fitness up.'

'Addictive,' I said.

'Totally agree. I'd rather do weights than run, but the coach is fixated on running. I'm not a runner,' he added.

I ran my eyes over him. 'Yes,' I teased him. 'As svelte as you are, I can see you're built for things other than speed.'

He gave me the hint of a smile. 'Well, better go shower and get to work,' he said. 'Next time, we could spot each other, even though you're not lifting much there,' he teased.

'Shut up! This is my warm down,' I lied, then I took a big gamble. 'I'm on my last set. Want to get a coffee?' I swear the world stopped spinning. I had never, ever, asked a guy out and if he had said no, then that would have been it ... how embarrassing.

'Only if you're going to shower first,' he said.

I gave him my best 'what do you think?' look and he gave me a real, gorgeous, showing-his-teeth smile.

'Meet you at reception in ten minutes,' he said and wandered off.

Yes! I bet he thought I couldn't be ready in ten minutes; well he was wrong. I powered through the last few in my set with a new enthusiasm I had never shown before in my weights set and headed to the showers.

*****

'What will you have?' The Russian asked as we took a seat at the cafe next to the gym.

'A skinny cappuccino, thanks,' I said, impressed he was going up to order for us. It's not always a given these days.

'Nothing to eat?' he asked.

'I'll grab a banana later,' I told him. Yep, that's me, the poster girl for good health. I was so impressive, I wanted to date myself. I'm sure he could see right through me.

I had the pleasure of watching him at the counter and watching the staff recognize him. One got his autograph on a napkin and the others just batted their eyelashes and flirted outrageously. Good effort girls, worth a try.

He returned and slumped into a seat beside me, winding his legs around mine under the table. We were both tall and had to fight for leg space ... wonderful.

I thought I'd lead with the front foot in case he thought I was putting myself in his line of vision all the time. 'You're not stalking me, are you?' I teased.

He made a scoffing sound and sat back in his chair. 'I'm pretty sure you were in my office the other day, and now in my gym!'

'Oh, your office, your gym,' I said, raising an eyebrow and challenging him. 'Last time I looked, you were playing a team sport ... which means there's more than just you in that office, and I've been going to Archer's gym for years. Longer than you.'

'Want a bet?' he snapped back.

'Yeah, I do, bring it on.' I was pretty sure I could win this one. 'What odds do you want?'

'Okay,' his eyes narrowed. 'If I win, you have to do an exclusive interview with me and get it into the paper, or at worse, online,' he said. 'And I better come off looking good.'

'Done, big head,' I teased him.

He grinned again. 'I have an ulterior motive... we have to do a set number of media interviews a year... you can count as one.'

'Yeah, we had the same at the Suns,' I assured him.

We thanked the waitress as she put our two coffees in front of us and two apple muffins.

The Russian shrugged. 'I took a gamble. If you don't want yours, I'll eat it.'

'You know a muffin is pretty much the same as a cupcake, don't you? It's just clever marketing... you're not going to eat a cupcake for breakfast, but you'll eat a muffin if it's marketed as breakfast food,' I said.

'I disagree,' The Russian said. 'A muffin is bread-based, a cupcake is cake-based. Well that's what I'm telling myself, but if you don't want yours...' he reached for it but I was quicker.

'I can probably manage half,' I assured him, clutching the muffin. 'So our bet, if I win, you have to accompany me to the Suns' Gala Ball and Auction night this Sunday.'

I was watching him carefully and he didn't react at all; no shock, no pleasure, no fear, no panic, nothing. Or he didn't think he was going to lose, so wasn't worried.

'You're on,' he said. He reached for his wallet and pulled

out his Archer's membership card. It was dated five years back. He showed me and smiled. 'Beat that, Brooker,' he said, using my surname.

I gave him a smug look and reached for my purse. I pulled out my membership card and placed it on the table between us. 'Read that and weep, buddy,' I said. The Russian didn't know that everyone on our basketball team had automatic membership with their contract. But I had joined even earlier than that, in the last few years of school when I was training to break into the big league – seven years ago.

His face dropped as he looked at my membership card.

'Right,' he said, 'suit or black tie?'

I grinned at him. 'Black tie. Got one?'

'Naturally,' he said, like he was always swanning around the house in formal wear. 'Better message me your address and what time to pick you up.' He reached for my phone and put his number in. I have his number!

'You're picking me up?' I asked, taking a bite of the muffin even though my stomach was flipping with excitement.

He frowned at me. 'Of course. You're a girl, you'll need every last minute to get ready, won't you?'

I sighed. 'Thanks.'

The Russian laughed. 'I'm not saying you'll need it, but I've never known a girl who can be ready to go anywhere in less than fifteen minutes.'

'Well, you have now,' I said. 'Fussing is not my thing. But it would be really nice to be picked up, thanks. So...'

'So?' he asked as we drank our coffees.

'Should I start calling you by your real name to get into practice since I may have to introduce you to people at our table on Sunday night?' I asked. 'Or I could just tell them your real name is Boris, hence the nickname, The Russian.'

He grinned. 'Either way is fine. I put my phone number in your phone.'

I grabbed the phone and opened my contacts list to see if he had put it under 'A' or 'R'. The second name in the 'A's was new.

'Alex, found you!' I said. Alex … I repeated it in my head. 'It suits you … nice name.'

'Thanks, Brooker.'

'Um, you know my name is Carly, don't you?' I teased him.

'Every time I've seen your name it's written as Brooker, Carly, so I did wonder,' he said, with the hint of amusement on his face.

'Nice to know you're following the stats pages. Is that a hobby or passion?'

'I like numbers,' he said, 'they're logical.'

'I like words,' I said, sitting back after taking the last sip of my coffee.

'Here's some words for you,' he said, 'pick you up Sunday, looking forward to it.'

I gave him a stupid grin like he had made my week – I was so transparent. He actually said he was looking forward to it! Danger, Will Robinson, I was falling heavily in 'like' with my Sunday handbag, and I forgot to ask how he got his nickname.

Chapter 4

Wednesday night was club dinner night with my Suns'
team – my soon-to-be old team – and even though I had to
stop playing mid-season for the Santa Ana Suns, I was still
included in club night. My two besties – Steffi who played
shooting guard and Aimee who played center – always
kept a space for me next to them. I missed them; I missed
playing, the discipline, the excitement, the routine ... the
only thing I didn't miss was the injuries.

Aimee was an Amazon, one of the tallest in the team; I
swear she could look The Russian in the eye. You expected
her to be tough with her size, but she was a big sook; she
cried over sad commercials! She was exotically beautiful –
her mother was originally from Jamaica and her father from
Sweden! Steffi, on the other hand, was a shorty, the shortest
on the team at five-foot-eleven and she was thin like me.
But unlike me – I seemed to sport a tan easily – Steffi was
almost translucent ... I secretly thought she was a vampire,
and she was a little too keen on that idea for my liking. I
hadn't started wearing neck scarves around her yet, but I
was considering it. Me, I was somewhere between the two
of them. One thing we had in common was that we could
all pack away a fair quantity of pasta, particularly during
the season.

'What are you wearing to the Ball?' Aimee asked but didn't wait for an answer. 'I've bought an off-the-shelf, slinky red number ... I won't be able to eat on the night, or I'll bust out of it.'

'I'm going nude,' Steffi said, and Aimee and I gasped. She rolled her eyes. 'Not nude with nothing on, nude in color. It's in, apparently. I have a fitted bodice and flowing skirt ... it's very romantic.'

'Is Wilson coming?' I asked after her boyfriend.

'He wouldn't miss it. He says my cooking is so bad that at least at the Ball he can get a decent feed,' she said, with a smirk.

'I'm bringing my cousin Roy,' Aimee rolled her eyes. 'He's visiting from Jersey City but I reckon he's come knowing the Gala Ball is on and he wants to meet girls ... he's been checking everyone out online. I think he's a bit keen on you,' she said with a look in my direction. 'Anyway, saves me finding a date, he's not bad on the eye and he's worth a fortune ... could be worse.'

'I'm bringing someone,' I said. I took a deep breath and smiled.

'Hold up, girlfriend,' Aimee said, 'is this big news?'

I nodded. 'This is huge news.'

A couple of the girls stopped talking around us and tuned in. I held the floor.

'It's not a date,' I said, 'so no one rush out and buy a hat for a wedding, we're just friends. I'm bringing ...'

Steffi drummed on the table, preparing for my announcement.

'The Russian!' I said.

'Fuck me, no!' Aimee said.

'The Russian as in the gorgeous, huge, Saints player, the guy on the Timex billboard?' Steffi's mouth dropped open.

I nodded enthusiastically. 'That Russian.'

'How did you meet him?' Lia – six seats away from me – leaned over and asked. She must have bionic hearing.

'Are any other members of the team free? I need a date,' Karley asked. 'Can you ask?'

I put up my hand to silence the pack. 'I met him through work and then again at the gym ... we had a bet and I won ... so he has to come with me. Yes, that's him wearing the beautiful sports watch on the Timex billboard,' I said, licking my lower lip like the cat that got the cream.

We got interrupted by a request from the other end of the table to pass the salt and to stop hogging the water jug, and I could hear the news working its way down the table. Eventually the buzz The Russian had created died down.

'So, what are you going to wear?' Aimee said, refocussing.

'I'm getting a dress made.'

'Ooh, I should think so,' Aimee gushed. 'Last week you were wearing the green dress from your closet.'

'Time to retire that dress,' Steffi said.

'Really? I'm clearly clueless then because I thought it had plenty of life in it yet,' I sighed. 'Josh said that dress and all my outfits sucked,' I said, whirling pasta on my fork.

'Josh would know, the man's a style king,' Steffi said. 'Besides, you want to look your best if you're with The Russian. You two will be the 'IT' couple for the night.'

I imagined myself walking in on his arm – one of the hottest players in the league, with me! My whole body was tingling and in some places more than others.

'Lucky bitch,' Aimee said, hitting my arm.

I grinned. 'Yeah, but he's just a handbag for the night. I'd love to move him to the next stage ... body warmer.'

We giggled like schoolgirls; some things never changed, thank goodness.

*****

I know I shouldn't have done it, but who can resist? Josh was spending the night at his boyfriend's place, so after showering and making a cup of tea, I sat in front of my laptop and searched for The Russian and Leesa. If I searched for myself there were years and years of sports reports, action photos, team shots, trophy awards, national team photos, glamorous season launch shots, interviews and fan pages, you name it, but you wouldn't find many of me with past boyfriends.

I'd had a few relationships including one that had lasted for two years – my longest – but never with fellow athletes. The guys didn't have a profile and no one was really interested in who I was dating. I thought back to the last guy I took to the Suns' Ball with me – Sam. I had been pretty wild for Sam; Sam had been pretty wild for Sam too and every other female in the room, so humiliating. Turns out he really just wanted to hang with me to help his prospects for getting a basketball coaching job with his college team, like it would make any difference.

I wondered if the girls were right; if The Russian and I going to the Ball together would fuel a few rumors.

I wished I hadn't looked because there were hundreds

of photos of The Russian and Leesa, and bummer, she was gorgeous. She had this long, wavy blonde hair and was petite and cute. She was a mixture of fashion plate and bohemian, and she looked gorgeous on the arm of the tall, handsome Russian. She was so not me.

There were plenty of stories, too, about her father, Harry Hart, one of the country's most successful and rich film directors. It looked like Leesa had spent her life in the lap of luxury around studios and film stars. She was Hollywood, which begged the questions, how had she met and ended up with The Russian?

She had more followers than my entire basketball team on Facebook and Twitter. There were hundreds of shots of her with The Russian in a hundred poses – none of which he looked really comfortable in considering he wasn't a stranger to getting his photo taken. There were shots of her driving her Mercedes, at openings with gal pals, cutting ribbons, modeling, partying, with her father, with famous actors ... crap. The Russian was not going to be interested in me after partying with a wild child, rich girl like Leesa. I was the gym locker type, she was a socialite.

I closed my laptop and began to coach myself. I didn't need a man to make me feel complete, I was a successful, attractive, and intelligent woman. Friends have told me I have great legs and a good butt, my hair is one of my assets and God knows, I'm funny! Ha, yep ... I was going to enjoy a night out with another successful athlete and then ... move on.

Chapter 5

I got a message from Sasha to say she would be home by five-thirty if I wanted to come around for a fitting – my final fitting – so when my shift finished at *The Sports Daily*, I went straight to her place. This time it was just Sash, me and Prada the puss; her gorgeous live-in-lover Saint Nik was at training. Seriously, could the week go any slower ... bring on Sunday night.

'Righto, do a lap for me,' Sasha ordered after she had pinned up my hem and pulled herself up from her knees.

'Love to,' I said, and took to the catwalk. I walked down and back, head high, shoes high, just like you see in the fashion shows. I watched my reflection and how the dress moved in the mirrors.

'Oh Sash, it is truly stunning, you are a miracle worker,' I gushed, and she grinned with pleasure.

'It has come up a treat and you do it justice. It's like having a model wearing my designs.'

'It's just so fluid and glamorous,' I said, twirling again and watching the skirt kick out from the bottom. The fitted bodice and hips were just perfect and not so tight that I couldn't eat, drink or breathe, and the neckline was flattering, showing off my assets without putting them in anyone's face if you get my meaning.

'I love it,' I said. 'You should be charging more and doing this full time.'

'That's the dream,' Sasha said, 'but for now, a few social pics and label dropping will be much appreciated,' she assured me. 'Okay, you can slip it off.'

I was both relieved and excited ... I knew it would get the Josh nod. I disappeared into Sasha's changing room and returned five minutes later, with the dress over my arm.

'I have a few finishing touches to do and then I'll bring it hanging but wrapped to the media box on Saturday and you can sneak it home after we finish work. Okay?'

'That's perfect, thank you. I can't wait to wear it,' I said, watching her lay it out carefully, ready for hemming.

We exchanged air kisses and I headed home. I was terrified that The Russian would pull out; that he would find some reason to get out of the bet and I'd be embarrassed in front of everyone I had told. I had to keep coaching myself to put the thought out of my mind so it wouldn't become a reality.

Just as I entered my apartment my phone rang; I didn't recognize the number.

'Carly, hi, it's Deidre Carmichael, personal assistant for Karen Meares,' the mature female voice said.

Karen Meares ... my brain was sifting names ... Karen Meares was the Head of Production at the Cable TV station where I had applied for a basketball commentary job!

'Deidre, hi, how are you?' I said, trying not to sound insanely excited.

'Well, thank you,' she said, then cut to the chase. 'Karen would like you to come for an interview for the women's basketball commentary job on Monday. Would you be available at ten a.m.?'

'Absolutely, thank you,' I said. 'Should I bring anything in particular?'

'No, just yourself. So we'll see you Monday, at ten at the studios. Just ask for me at reception when you arrive.'

I thanked Deidre and hung up. I looked at the phone … yes, that really did just happen … I leaped for joy. I had applied for this job several weeks ago; I wanted it so bad I could taste it, and it tasted sweet. If I got the gig, I would be working with former competitors – Lynx's Captain Suzie Ellis and Storm's recently retired goal shooter, Catherine Allan. Since I couldn't play, it was the next best thing to attend women's basketball games around the country with the commentary team, doing interviews and calling the games for home viewers.

I couldn't believe it – after coping with major injury and not being able to play – now suddenly this was the best week ever! I was going to the Ball with The Russian on Sunday in a gorgeous new dress, and now an interview for my dream job on Monday. Thank you, universe!

I dropped my gear on the table, opened the fridge and saw a casserole dish with a note on it reading 'Eat me'. I lifted the lid - fantastic - dark, rich, beef casserole. I put it into the oven to heat up - thank you, Josh. He must have cooked it earlier then gotten a better offer; we were great housemates - he liked to cook and I liked to eat.

I changed, slipping on some fitted Lycra running pants

and a long-sleeve Suns t-shirt and headed to the couch with the remote to watch *Sports Week* on television. They were interviewing a gridiron player and I waited patiently for the discussions around this weekend's major league games including the Saints and Suns. My girls – the Suns – were playing the Firebirds and it wasn't going to be pretty. We had lost to them more than we had won. Imagine if The Russian and I got together – a Saint and a Sun – well, a retired Sun. Mm ...

I can't believe that I was so busy swooning that I forgot to send The Russian my address to pick me up for the Ball Awards on Sunday night. I reached for my phone and messaged him.

Hey Alex, hope the tux still fits. My address is 2/14 Scarborough Street. Starts at 7pm. See you Sunday at 6.30pm here? Carly.

I thought I'd better write my name since I had his number and he didn't have mine ... I didn't want him to confuse me with anyone else he might have been dating this week. I put the phone down and waited. *Nothing.* Maybe he was still at training. I rose, poured a glass of wine – I could do that now that I wasn't training – and returned to my program. *Still nothing.* Maybe he was trying to think of a way to get out of it. I was pleasantly distracted by the review of the Saints and Suns pending games, and then I realized it was forty-five minutes since I had sent the text and still nothing. A churning feeling rose in my stomach ... maybe he had forgotten already about the bet and the date. What would I do if he never texted back? Crap, that was a drama I could do without.

Then my phone pinged, and I almost leaped off the couch reaching for it. So uncool, lucky I was home alone. Crap again, it was from Aimee asking if I was coming to the Suns' game on Saturday. I shot back a response that I was working in the Saints' media box but would be following scores online and told her to break a leg.

I got up to serve myself some casserole and glanced at the clock. It was nearing eight p.m. *He must be out somewhere, with someone, because training would be over by now.* Sasha was expecting Nik early because they had started early. *Whatever.* Men sucked. I wished The Russian would suck me. Seriously, where had that come from? My apartment buzzer went off and I jumped again ... so jumpy lately. I lifted the intercom phone.

'Hello?'

A deep male voice spoke up. 'Brooker, open up.'

Oh my God, he was there. *Play it cool.* Deep breath.

'Who is it?' I teased, knowing full well who it was.

I heard him clear his throat while he swallowed his impatience.

'It's your Sunday night date. Were you expecting your Thursday night date?'

I laughed. 'Hello *Alex*,' I accentuated his name. 'Come up, second floor, first door on the right.' I hung up and raced to the bathroom. I patted down my hair ... Lord knows why, it didn't make any difference. I raced back out and opened the door. He was coming up the stairs with several suits covered in clear plastic, draped over his arm. I loved how easily he took the stairs like the athlete that he was.

I drank him in – what an Adonis. He was wearing jeans, a black T-shirt and sneakers, and he looked so very hot that I couldn't take my eyes off his huge arms and chest and ...

'Nice location,' he said, stopping in front of me as I stood in the open doorway. 'I hope it's okay I came over unannounced, but I figured you'd be home preparing for your date with me.'

I smirked at him. 'It's only Thursday.'

'I know, but you want to be perfect.'

'Shut up and come in,' I said, trying to hide my smile as I stood aside to let him in. He grinned as he passed me. The Russian knew how to relax a situation. I glanced quickly at his butt and got caught in the act. He gave me a suspicious look and then turned his eyes to appraise my apartment. It was a decent size with a good view – the apartment that is; I had gotten it the first year of my contract when the area hadn't been so trendy and now I owned it and it had increased in value a lot. I was super lucky.

'This your place?' he asked.

'Yep, all mine but I have a housemate. He's out somewhere.'

'Why didn't you take him to the Ball?' The Russian asked. He put the suits down over the back of the sofa.

'You want out?' I asked, challenging him.

'I never renege on a bet. But I wouldn't mind a coffee.' He wandered around the room looking at my things. 'I like your minimalist style.'

'Mm, I like space. Are you a minimalist too?' I asked.

'No. Probably more of a 'leave it where it falls' guy,' he said, picking up a photo of me with my parents. 'You were a cute kid.' He said matter-of-factly.

'Still am cute,' I said, filling the kettle. He looked up and smiled at me. OMG he was beautiful; I loved the way he filled the lounge room and just looked so good in something so simple to wear. He noted the collar on my father in the photo.

'Your dad's a reverend? Wow, that must have been an interesting upbringing. What's your mom do?' he asked.

'She's a reverend's wife,' I said.

'Did you have one of those rebellious periods where you went against the church and your dad? Got a tattoo, went out with a bikie?' he teased.

I laughed. 'Not yet, but I'm still planning to.' I pulled two mugs out of the cupboard then changed my mind and reached for two water glasses. 'I was about to have some of my housemate's beef casserole. Have you eaten? Want some?' I asked.

'Don't want to impose,' he said, putting the photo down.

'Trust me, you wouldn't be imposing. I've done nothing, Josh cooked, all I have to do is serve it.' I reached for two bowls without waiting for his answer and placed them on the counter. I kept sneaking glances at him. I couldn't believe The Russian was in my living room – all six-foot-five of him, I just wanted to knock him to the ground and press all my bones against his.

I lifted the casserole out of the oven and opened the lid. The Russian came into the kitchen area to join me; be still my very loud beating heart. He sniffed the steam rising above the casserole.

'That's good, really good.'

'Yeah, Josh loves to cook. I should reduce his rent for all the meals he's cooked,' I said. 'So, what's with the suits?'

'Ah the suits,' he said, with a glance towards them.

I held up my hand. 'Before you answer, grab a drink,' I nodded to the glasses. 'Wine, water, cola, et cetera, in the fridge. Napkins top drawer, cutlery below, we can eat on the balcony' I said, issuing orders.

'Yes ma'am,' he saluted. Fuck, that was sexy too. The way his arm flexed when he saluted, I could just imagine him in a uniform. I forgot what I was doing for a moment and almost ordered him to give me five.

He rattled around in the drawers and cupboards, gathering everything we needed.

'The suits ... well, I can't decide which one to wear, so I brought the three tuxes I have over to let you pick,' he said. He filled our glasses with cold water from the fridge.

'Who on earth has three tuxes?' I asked, pausing from serving the casserole long enough to frown in his direction.

He shrugged. 'I've had to do a few appearances. I liked one of the suits so I bought it; the other two were given to me. But I don't know if the cuts go out of style or whatever.'

I grabbed our plates, leaving The Russian to follow with the cutlery and water glasses. I wondered if he was checking out my butt – I wouldn't have missed the opportunity if the situation had been reversed. He followed me onto the balcony.

'This is great,' he said, again, taking in the view.

Oh yes, it sure is, I thought. As for the other view, it was of the district – high and airy with plenty of twinkling lights. A balmy breeze made the night just perfect. We sat at my large outdoor timber table, both on the same side, facing the view. I raised my water glass and clinked it against his.

'To wins for the Saints and Suns,' I said.

'To wins,' he agreed, tapping his glass. I tried the casserole first.

'Yep, you're lucky I didn't cook,' I said.

He smiled and tried some. 'That housemate is a keeper,' he agreed.

'So what's your place like? Got a housemate?' I asked. I was finding it really difficult to eat and breathe with The Russian less than a foot away from me. I could smell him; musty, masculine and manly.

'I live by myself ... I like to come home and not make small talk. It's a big apartment, but I have a cleaner who comes in once a week and keeps the place in good condition. Besides, occasionally my sisters crash with me so I have spare rooms ready. Ana's eighteen; she sometimes stays over when I'm at an away game ... gives her some privacy to see her friends, although I suspect there's a boyfriend in the mix too,' he said, in a not-so-happy voice.

'How many siblings have you got?' I asked.

'Three younger sisters,' he said.

'Ah,' I said, with a nod.

He turned to look at me. 'Ah ... what? What does that mean?' His eyes narrowed suspiciously.

'Sasha said you were one of the girls; now I know why ... you know how to talk to girls. I bet you were spoilt rotten being the only boy,' I said, feeling sorry for his sisters.

'Brooker, you can't spoil a good thing,' he said. I rolled my eyes accordingly.

'Suits,' I said, bringing the conversation around. 'I wouldn't have a clue what's in and what's not, sorry.'

The Russian turned to look at me like I was an alien.

'Is there something you're not telling me? You are a girl aren't you?'

I grimaced at him. 'I have other interests besides fashion. It's like art ... I know what I like, not necessarily what's in.'

The Russian raised an eyebrow in my direction. 'Let me get this straight – at the gym you managed to shower and be ready in ten minutes, now you're telling me you don't know a lot about fashion ... how do you feel about social media?'

'Take it or leave it,' I said, with a shrug. 'I hate that I have so little control over what gets posted about me.'

He didn't say anything for a minute and I reached for my water, sipped and then asked, 'you prefer your female friends to be really girly and into shopping, make-up, and selfies?'

'No, definitely not. I've been there, had enough of that to last me a lifetime,' he said. 'I was just shocked by your revelations ... I think I've met the female version of myself.'

I laughed. 'At least our mothers can tell us apart.'

'Never said you weren't an attractive, feminine woman,' he added, and I didn't know where to go with that. He had touched a sore spot with me – my mother was always saying I was too independent, feministic, a tomboy and add my height to that, I'd never attract a man.

' ... who can't take a compliment,' he added after a minute.

I chuckled. 'Sorry, I just got distracted by something you said.'

'What's that?'

'Another time,' I suggested. 'So, your suits, you can try

them on and I'll see if I can narrow it down to the one you should wear ... I'm a Libran though ... we're known for being indecisive. Maybe you should ask Sasha or that other girl in your office, the pretty little one who is dating Tomás Carrera.'

'Alice,' he said.

I was watching to see what he thought of her, but he gave nothing away.

'Indecisive huh ... and what are these other interests?' he asked.

I told him about my job interview Monday and he was really pleased for me. That was a good sign, too – he didn't have any caveman notions that a woman's place was supporting a man. I suspect being raised by a pack of females has helped a lot. Plus, he didn't seem jealous or competitive which often happens to couples in similar careers ... or maybe he didn't care enough about me to be competitive.

Then, I froze – I heard the door open; Josh was home. This was going to be interesting – Josh was very effeminate, and The Russian was, well, very alpha. I couldn't bear it if he was rude to Josh or disliked him, I couldn't be with a man who wasn't accepting; it was a deal-breaker. I turned and looked through the glass sliding doors and waved to Josh. His eyes widened in surprise and then he gave me a thumbs-up which I hoped The Russian hadn't seen. Josh came out to the balcony.

'Hi Carly,' he said, with a special smile in my direction. He offered his hand to The Russian to shake.

'Josh Turnbull,' he said. I held my breath, worried – I was scared for Josh and just as scared for myself – I didn't want to have to stop liking The Russian.

The Russian stood to shake hands with Josh; he looked about two feet taller and wider.

'Alex Renwick,' he said. 'I think I just ate your dinner.'

Josh laughed. 'Lucky I've eaten and you're welcome.'

'Great casserole,' The Russian declared, sitting down again. 'If Carly ever raises your rent and you want out, look me up,' he said, with a sly glance in my direction. 'I've got beach views.'

I hit his arm. 'Don't try and tempt my roomie away.'

The Russian smiled. 'Just putting it out there,' he said.

'Good to have fall back options,' Josh agreed.

'Stop talking immediately you two,' I ordered them in fun. I breathed out. Thank the Lord ... The Russian was just getting better and better.

'Given Josh cooked and I set the table, surely you can make coffee at least? I'd offer to make it, but I don't know your kitchen yet,' The Russian said, with a glance at his watch. 'Then I'll have to bolt.'

Yet, he said *yet*. OMG ... did that mean he was going to get to know my kitchen?

'Carly makes a terrible coffee,' Josh said, 'but I'm about to brew a pot.'

'Hey!' I exclaimed, 'it's not that bad.'

'Can you cook anything?' The Russian turned to look at me. 'Toast?'

'Toast is my specialty,' I said. We rose and grabbed plates, following Josh inside.

'It's actually cereal,' Josh said. 'She's really good at pouring that from the box.'

The Russian laughed and returned to the balcony to get

our glasses. I watched from the kitchen with Josh as The Russian went to the balcony edge to observe the view.

Josh's eyes widened and he mouthed the word 'divine'.

'I know,' I said.

'Sorry to crash, want me to leave?' he asked.

'Definitely not, I'm glad you got a chance to meet him. Besides, he clearly won't be sticking around ... tonight anyway.'

'Get out there,' Josh said, pushing me to the balcony. 'I can make coffee for three, go, go, go.'

Then I had a brilliant idea – yeah I was full of them; Josh could check out The Russian's suits and tell him what style was in ... Josh was a fashion guru after all.

'Know anything about tuxedos?' I asked.

'Is Chanel timeless?' he said.

I gave him a grin, left the dishes in the sink and went back out to the balcony to appreciate the view of The Russian. He turned as I rejoined him.

'You've done well, Brooker,' he said, 'I like a self-made woman.'

'Thanks. I like to be independent, have my own assets, you know a girl has to these day,' I said, not letting on that I'd checked out his ex-girlfriend and knew she was living off daddy – but hey, who wouldn't in her situation?

'Good on you,' he said.

'I have a suggestion.'

He looked at me with raised eyebrows as if I was going to suggest he stay the night. *I wish.*

'Josh is a bit of a fashion guru, he's been helping me with my dress selection for the Gala Ball. I think you should put the tuxes on for us both, and let him tell you what's in vogue.'

He narrowed his eyes. 'Anyone would think you just want to see me in a tux,' he said.

'Hell no, I've got other things I could be doing,' I teased him. 'There's the sock drawer which needs sorting by color and I usually polish the silver once a week.'

He gave me one of those melt-your-insides smiles that he turned on so effortlessly.

'But,' I continued, 'given I'm a guest speaker on Sunday night and I'm going to look pretty fabulous, well, you need to step up.'

'I'll give you step up in a moment,' he said and moved to tickle me. Yes, seriously, tickle me! Clearly he had sisters. I fought him off laughing and then I grabbed his hand – mine felt small in his – and pulled him inside. I picked up the suits and pointed to my room. 'You can change in there.'

He and Josh exchanged looks like they were two men who put up with me – I was so pleased they had bonded, even at my expense, and I watched The Russian's sexy butt as he went into my room and made a point of closing the door. Thank the Lord I was a minimalist and I knew my room was pretty clean. Plus, years and years of my dad, the reverend, boring into me that 'cleanliness is next to godliness' had worked – not that the Holy Scriptures actually said that but try telling my father that.

Josh brought our coffees and a plate of chocolate biscuits over to the coffee table in front of the sofa and we sat waiting for The Russian's fashion parade – I would have paid to see that. Five minutes later he walked out of my room in the first tux to find us both sitting on the sofa, staring at my bedroom door waiting for him. Josh gasped louder than I did, the Lord keep him for that. The Russian shook his head at the two of us.

'Shh, Russian,' I said, 'we're working here.'

Josh gave me a look.

'Okay, Josh is working here,' I shrugged.

'Armani? A Giorgio tuxedo?' Josh asked.

The Russian's eyes widened in surprise. 'Got it in one.'

My jaw dropped open. 'How do you even know that?' I said, momentarily tearing my gaze away from The Russian to look at Josh, but returning immediately to The Russian.

'I know quality,' Josh said.

'He's a fashionista and makeup artist,' I said, explaining Josh to The Russian.

'Mm, turn around,' Josh said.

I love Josh, did I mention that? The Russian did a full turn, and was not at all uncomfortable with the instruction.

'Nice,' Josh said. 'Lightweight wool, satin accents, peak lapels, single button close. Nice, very nice. That's very much in vogue. Next.'

'Maybe you shouldn't watch, Brooker,' The Russian said. 'It will ruin the impact when I arrive Sunday night looking resplendent.'

'Wild dogs wouldn't drag me away,' I said. 'It's okay, I promise to be impressed Sunday night as well.'

'I feel cheap,' The Russian said to Josh and he shook his head.

'Women,' Josh agreed.

The Russian went back into my room to change. I fanned myself with the TV program.

'Oh my, was that hot or what?' I said.

Josh nodded. 'I'm going to need some water with my coffee.'

'I'm onto it,' I said. I rushed to the kitchen, grabbed two glasses of water and got back in time before the second showing. We snuggled back next to each other. This was better than porn, or so I had heard – I wouldn't know, honest.

Five minutes later, the door opened again and then The Russian appeared in all his glory in another tuxedo.

'Magnificent,' I whispered. I wished Josh wasn't there and I could run at The Russian, knock him back on my bed and lick him. Right, focus.

'Dolce and Gabbana,' The Russian said and turned full circle, without prompting this time, while looking to Josh for approval.

Josh nodded. 'Another classic. Tailored three-piece tuxedo suit with blazer, peaked lapels and satin detail. Solid wool,' he said, with a glance at me like that meant something.

Gorgeous, sexy, dream-worthy. 'Very nice,' I said, restraining myself.

'Just very nice, Brooker?' The Russian challenged me.

'Superb,' Josh raised the bar. 'Both of those tuxedos are first class.'

'First class,' I said, nodding and agreeing. The Russian gave me a small smile and ventured in to try on the final suit.

'Wipe your mouth,' Josh said.

'I'm not drooling, I'm salivating,' I said. 'Tall, dark and handsome, my dream man is in my bedroom in a tux.'

'I hear you,' Josh said. 'It's my fantasy too.'

We both giggled. This was the best night ever. Finally, The Russian came out in the third tuxedo and my jaw dropped open.

'Beautiful,' I said, without thinking.

'Thanks Brooker, hope you can match it,' he said, his eyes twinkling at me.

'Magnificent,' Josh agreed. 'Is that a Tom Ford tux?'

'You're good,' The Russian said, looking impressed. 'Very good. It is indeed; got it at a photoshoot recently.'

'Turn around please,' Josh ordered.

Well done, Josh.

'Magnificent,' Josh said again and I nodded. He rose and went over to The Russian. He felt the coat fabric between his fingers.

'Slim-Fit Mohair and Wool-Blend, the suit of Bond, James Bond,' Josh said.

'Is that so?' The Russian asked. 'Then this is the suit for me.'

'It most certainly is,' I said, admiring the lustrous satin.

'That's the one,' Josh agreed. 'Easy. Are you right for cufflinks, a bow tie, white shirt and shoes?'

The Russian nodded. 'Got all that. Thanks for the help, I'll get it off.'

'You could leave it on while you have coffee,' I suggested.

The Russian shook his head. 'Brooker, you'll just have to wait to see it again.'

I gave him a disappointed look and he disappeared behind the door to change.

'You two are going to be beautiful together,' Josh said, turning from the closed door to look at me.

'Wait until you see my dress,' I said, 'seriously, Sasha has made it for my figure, I never thought I could look that good,' I lowered my voice.

'I never doubted it,' Josh said. I squeezed his arm.

The Russian came out a few minutes later in his jeans and t-shirt again, carrying the three suits. He thanked Josh again, grabbed his coffee and remained standing while he sipped it.

'Better get going,' he said.

I looked from him to my bedroom and back to him again. At least I could dream tonight about him being in there, half undressed.

But an hour later I found out that the idea of sleep was just a fantasy. I didn't get one wink – I imagined opening the front door to The Russian, kissing those lips, stripping off his tux and making slow love to a man who confessed to not moving too quickly. I kept cautioning myself – I was not his type, especially after his Hollywood blonde girlfriend; it was just a friendship.

But it was too late. I was a goner and I had set myself up for heartbreak, I just knew it.

Chapter 6

I sat in the Suns' physical therapist's room waiting room for Serge – the head PT – to summon me. My work commitment to report at the Saints' game for *The Sports Daily* meant I couldn't go and watch my Suns play, which was sort of a relief. I knew that was selfish and unsupportive of my team, but it was painfully hard to sit on the sideline when I wanted to be amongst it. Especially when it was an injury that forced me to step out for the rest of the season and not my choice. Even though I had said I was looking at retirement, I hadn't made it official. The team was still hoping I would be able to play again before the end of the season and Coach, my physical therapist and I were pretty confident I'd at least be able to play in the last game before the final series began. That would be my swansong – management wanted to see me off in style and I knew our marketing manager, Maria, thought plugging it as my last game would help ticket sales. I was hoping I could play in it too; Serge sounded positive.

I rose and gave him a smile as he waved me into his PT room.

'Before you ask, yes, maybe,' he said, with a grin.

I gave him a smirk, and dropped my handbag on the chair while he closed the door. I sat on the table; we knew the routine ... he'd manipulate, massage and work the muscles in my leg for half an hour and I'd groan with the pain.

'I was going to say 'hello' before I asked,' I said.

Serge grinned. He was nuggetty and a good head shorter than me, which wasn't uncommon. He had muscles on his muscles and the biggest hands – probably why he had chosen to be a PT. He began working on my injured leg, especially around the knee area.

'You're moving better,' he said. 'I watched you when you walked in. If you strapped your knee and didn't play the whole game, I'm pretty confident we can get you on the basketball court for one last game ... maybe the end of season game.'

'Fantastic,' I said, combining a smile and a grimace. Serge was brilliant but tough. 'So when do you think I can let the coach know?' I pushed him.

I waited while he pondered the question, drawing it out ... killing me.

'Well,' he said, 'about now probably.'

'Really?' I squealed in delight.

'But only if you don't do anything stupid before then, or I'll be calling your coach personally and pulling you from the game,' he threatened. 'Stick to the gym, no running, no sneaking in for a friendly basketball game, no wrestling any of the Saints.'

I twisted around to look at him.

'What do you mean?'

He smiled a sneaky sort of smile. 'I heard you were going

to the Ball with that big guy from The Saints, the one they call The Russian.'

'Wow,' I said, turning back around and trying not to sound so pathetically excited. 'News travels fast. Who told you that?'

'Aimee was in here this morning,' he said. 'Was it supposed to be a secret?'

'Not at all. I can always count on Aimee to spread the news though ... she's a walking news bulletin.'

We made a bit of small talk for the rest of the session and then I was 'released'.

'Thank you Serge, you're a magician,' I said, putting my weight on my leg, feeling it getting better and better each time.

'I look forward to seeing you two all over social media the day after the Ball,' Serge said, and flicked me with the back of the towel.

'You'll be there, won't you?' I asked.

'Wouldn't miss it,' Serge confirmed. 'You're good to go and remember—'

'—no wrestling Russians,' I grinned.

I left the physical therapist's office and called Coach. I knew this day would come – when I had to face my last game, but most of us tried not to think about it. She answered on the second ring.

'Carly, how are you darling?' she asked.

'Good Coach, and you?'

'Fine. You've been with Serge?' There wasn't much she missed.

'Just left his office. If you can use me and if you want me

to play, I can play the final game before the finals series,' I said, holding my breath. We were both assuming the Suns would make the finals.

'Wonderful,' she said, and sounded almost relieved, 'of course I want to play you. We're short on experience and need you back.'

'Thank you, Coach,' I said, but it will be my last game ... Serge and I agree that will be all I have left in my body.' I just got the words out before my voice hitched.

She sighed. 'I understand darling, I've been there, it's a day that comes for us all. But we'll make it a day you won't forget.'

I chuckled with a throaty sound as I tried to swallow my tears.

'So,' she said, 'you better get back to us next week then and join in some light training.'

'Can't believe I'm going to say this,' I said, 'but I can't wait to train!'

This time it was Coach's turn to laugh. 'Can I get that in writing?' she teased.

I was back! Even if it was for just one game – my swansong.

Chapter 7

Game day – Saints and Suns game day that was, and I was due at the media box for the Saints' game at eleven o'clock. Sasha and I had organized to meet in the parking lot fifteen minutes earlier than usual to transfer the dress from her car to mine. I couldn't wait to wear it; I was nervous just thinking about the night – nervous-crazy, excited that is. Plus, I was kind of hoping The Russian might find his way to the media box to say 'hello' today. That would mean he was thinking of me and I wasn't just a bet he had lost, making him go to the Ball tonight.

I drove into the parking lot and saw Sasha there, waiting by her car. She always looked so eccentric – a classic car, a mod haircut, she was an original. She waved, opened her car boot and pulled out a long dress covered in a white plastic sheet ... at least I was hoping there was a dress in there. I pulled my car into the parking spot next to hers and turning it off, I leaped out; I couldn't see the dress itself but I couldn't wait to slip it on.

'Sorry, were you waiting long?' I asked.

'About a minute,' she assured me. 'Ta-da!'

I grinned at her as she carried the dress to my open back door.

'Sash, I can't wait to wear it, what would I do without you? Thank you, thank you,' I gushed.

She grinned and we settled the dress across the seat.

'I've transferred the funds to your bank account,' I assured her.

She waved her hand. 'All good. Now I want the scoop ... the least you can do is send me a photo of the two of you before you leave home and let me have the first tweet ... I am the Saints' media officer after all, as well as the designer.'

'The least I can do,' I agreed, excited that she even wanted the shot. 'I'll have my flatmate Josh take the shot and send it to you straight away. Plus, I'll promote your label, I promise. Thanks again Sash. If I can ever return a favor ...'

'The pleasure is all mine,' she said, then she narrowed her eyes. 'There is one small thing, a favor sort of ...' she said.

'Sure, anything.'

She moved to her car, locked it and leaning on it, crossed her arms across her chest. 'I want to know how The Russian gets to the coffee van before the rest of us. He always knows when it is coming and beats me every day in the office.'

I laughed. 'Seriously?'

'Yeah, I bet he gets a message in advance from Wendy our coffee van lady, but they're both saying nothing,' Sasha said.

'I'm onto it,' I said, assuring her that my investigation would be intense. 'Just call me Scoop.'

'Thanks Scoop,' she grinned, and moved away from the car. 'I'll see you in the media box soon. I've got to go meet a journo in the training rooms.'

'Sure,' I said, giving her a wave as my phone rang. It was my boss asking if I'd do a few TV crosses as well as my newspaper and online pieces. Our sister company's journo had called in sick. *Yes!* Well bad for them, but good for me. A few pieces-to-camera would be good to mention when I had my job interview for the basketball commentator role. I raced up the stairs to the media box, and found Dave, an online reporter setting up. We made a bit of small talk as I set up my laptop and then I quickly freshened up my makeup and raced downstairs again to meet the television camera crew. They wanted the first piece to be a generic story before the game, then an update at half-time and a wrap at the end of the game. Easy.

I found the crew, we picked a location that showed the crowds pouring in behind me and the cameras rolled. I swear I must have done something good in the world, because Karma caught up with me. Just as I started to wind up, someone approached me – that was pretty normal, people always ran up to cameras and carried on – walking within a foot of me on his way to the training room was Captain Fantastic – Lucas Ainswright. The cameras caught him and he greeted me by name. Go my CV!

'The Saints Captain himself, Lucas Ainswright,' I said, grabbing him, talking to the camera. 'How do you feel about today's game Lucas?'

'We're in good shape, we've got our Defender, Eddie Mosley back from injury, and our track record against the Chicago Cats is solid.'

'Thanks Captain,' I said, as he squeezed me on the shoulder and kept walking. 'That's the Saints Captain Lucas

Ainswright. Today's game starts at one p.m. and you can watch it right here on the Sports Channel.'

'And we're out,' the cameraman said. 'Nice one. Friends in high places, huh?'

I grinned. 'All in the timing,' I said. I looked around, no sign of The Russian yet; I just needed to see him, a glimpse would do. I organized a time to meet the camera crew at half-time for a rundown on the game thus far and returned to the media box. Sasha was there when I got back, along with Dan from *K-talk* radio, and a few of the other online journos that I had seen at our Suns games but not met yet. We introduced each other. They asked me all the inevitable questions about my injury – if I was going to return, did I think the Suns would make it to the finals, blah, blah, blah.

I couldn't focus; I just wanted The Russian to drop in. Or Nik to come up and see Sasha and maybe The Russian would come along with him. But in my heart of hearts, I knew he wouldn't come to the media box – I wouldn't either. If I was playing that day, I would be totally in the zone; I wouldn't allow any distractions, there was too much at stake. Damn him. But at least it would make tonight even more special ... I'd be dying to see him by the time he came to pick me up for the Ball, if I hadn't died from withdrawal symptoms by then – I was so not dramatic at all.

My laptop was open, I had the Facebook and Twitter pages open for the media groups that I fed and I had the Suns' Twitter page open so I could watch the results from my team as they came through ... well, I hoped the girls would win, it would make for a better night at the Ball. I looked at the clock – fifteen minutes until the game started so no hope of seeing The Russian now. Thank God Sasha wasn't a girly-girl and didn't ask me a whole lot of questions, I was already on that thin wedge of love, fear and loss. I was totally taken by The Russian and I knew I was up for the biggest fall if it wasn't mutual ... and I was pretty sure it wasn't.

*****

By half-time there was good news, great news and brilliant news. The good news – my beloved Suns were well in the lead and looked like they were going to bring the game home ... it relieved my guilt that I couldn't be there, but also made me feel a little superfluous. Such is the life of a professional athlete I guess. I hated not being there but the team understood work was work and we weren't paid the big salaries like the male sports stars, we had to take it when we could.

The great news was that the Saints were comfortably in front ... in soccer, a couple of goals was super comfortable, and the Chicago Cats were in bad form. I did look at other players besides The Russian, honest, but he was having a great game so I was forced to look at him a lot – just one of the things you had to endure as a sports journo. It also meant he would be on high tonight if they won ... a win-win all around.

The brilliant news – I know I saved the best for last – is that The Russian acknowledged me. It might not sound like much but it was huge ... really huge. At the end of half-time as the team went to their respective tunnels and training rooms, he glanced up at the media box. I swear he looked right at me, right through me and gave me just the hint of a smile. I almost forgot to tweet the halftime score I was so excited. Once I stopped blushing and my breathing returned to normal, I raced downstairs to meet the camera crew and do the half-time piece. The day was looking up – even in the middle of a high-pressure game, Alex was thinking of me. I would feed on that for hours until he arrived at my door that night in that mind-blowing tux and we would make some more unique memories.

Chapter 8

Josh stood back and looked at my eyes. He was doing my make-up and just knew how to do it so perfectly so that I looked natural – my eyes sort of popped and my lips looked luscious – I was hoping that would be how The Russian saw it.

'Okay, I think you are done,' he said.

'Josh, you're the best, thank you,' I said, glancing in the mirror. 'It looks brilliant.' I jumped up from the chair in front of the main balcony windows – Josh liked to have plenty of light when he was working – and folded up the makeup clothes protector he had draped around my shoulders.

'I am dying to see this dress on,' he said, 'then we'll get a pic, send it to Sasha and let the online sharing begin. And another with Alex when he arrives,' he added almost as an afterthought. The Russian was my every thought at the moment.

With a glance at the clock, I raced in to change; The Russian would be arriving in twenty minutes. The only time I could remember feeling that excited was playing in our Suns grand final the year before. I had bought new underwear during the week too ... not that I necessarily expected to be sharing it with The Russian – it was officially only our first unofficial date, but I wanted to be prepared.

I slipped on the cream and lace brief and matching strapless support bra; they were a gorgeous set and felt beautiful on my skin. I slipped my feet into my strappy, high heel, silver sandals with just a hint of bling, and then the dress. I unzipped the long zip at the back and removed it from the coat hanger. I carefully stepped into it and slid the smooth and slinky gown up my body, placing the thin straps over my shoulders. It was beautiful, absolutely beautiful. With Sasha's dress and Josh's make-up, I felt like I was the best I could be ... this was me, highlighted. Does that make sense? I might never be as good as I was at that moment ever again.

I grabbed my small, matching clutch bag and checking I had a compact, tissue, lipstick, comb, mirror, credit card and house keys, proclaimed myself 'ready'. I opened the door and Josh gasped.

'Oh my, just stunning,' he said, clasping his hands together.

'It feels amazing, Josh, and with your make-up too, I'm blown away,' I said. 'Zip me please?' I asked, turning around. I felt the zip close the dress snugly around me, and I turned to swirl the skirt as the generous layers of fabric swelled out from my hips down. 'What would I do without you and Sasha? I feel like a million dollars.'

'You look gorgeous,' Josh said again. 'Quick, a couple of pics of you in the gown first so Sasha can put them up on her designer website.'

I glanced at the clock again; the closer it got to The

Russian's arrival time, the more nervous I became. I wondered if he was nervous at all or if he would be like he always was ... cool and calm.

Josh snapped a few shots with me doing glamour-type poses, front and back, and then, the intercom buzzed.

I breathed in and moved to answer it. I could see the small image of this beautiful man in a tuxedo in my doorway. *He's here, thank you God, thank you* – I said my silent prayer of thanks.

'Hi Russian, come on up,' I said, and buzzed him through.

Josh went to open the door to The Russian while I raced back into my bedroom to fuss a bit more, check my hair, dress and make-up once again. I heard their voices outside, and taking a moment to prepare myself – seriously I was more nervous about going to the Ball with The Russian than I was about getting up on stage later and making a speech.

I walked through to the living area. I saw his face light up, really light up. He'd had a haircut – super sexy short back and sides which showed off those beautiful high cheekbones and chiseled jaw, and he was holding a dozen long stem red roses ... he knew how to take a woman on a date.

'Wow,' he said. 'You look absolutely beautiful.' He just said it so naturally, no spin, that I heard myself laugh.

'Thank you, Russian. You look gorgeous too.'

'You do,' Josh agreed, 'you both do. Now photo, come on, Carly promised Sasha the scoop.'

I saw The Russian wince.

'She made a dress for me in four days and she is the Saints media officer, I kind of promised her,' I said.

'She's a pain in my butt,' he said, good-naturedly, 'but she's done a mighty job on the dress.' He handed me the roses.

'They're stunning, thank you.' I inhaled the roses, they were perfect, just past the bud stage and almost ready to bloom.

'I'll put those in water,' Josh said, taking them off me and putting them down on the kitchen counter. 'Let's get a quick photo, and get you two out of here,' he said.

We found a neutral wall to stand against and as I went to place my hand on the Russian's arm, he put his arm around my waist instead and pulled me in closer. Forget going out, I could just stay there. He smelled beautiful, he was groomed to within an inch of his life, his haircut really suited him, although I liked the longish hair on him too and that tux ... I was hoping I would get a chance to get it off him. Josh framed up the shot.

'Alex and Carly dressed by ...?' Josh asked.

'Tom Ford and Sasha Saxon, make-up by Josh Turnbull,' I said, with a grin.

'Done,' Josh said. 'Now have fun kids and behave,' he teased. 'Have her home by tomorrow?'

The Russian smiled, opened the door for me and I stepped through. My dream night was finally here.

*****

The Russian opened the car door for me and I slid into his silver Mercedes sedan, well it felt like I slid in my slinky dress. He leaned down and tucked my skirt in ... so gentlemanly. As I waited for him to join me, I inspected his car. Very luxurious, very big and the back was half-full of sports gear – at least it wasn't smelly. He slid into the driver's seat looking so gorgeous it took everything in my control not to throw myself at him. The fact that I was so nervous and was a bit rooted to the spot helped. He turned on the ignition and then, before belting up he turned side-on to look at me.

'You okay?' he asked.

I nodded. 'Sure. Why?'

'I thought tonight might be a bit hard on you ... the end of a very impressive era,' he said, gently.

'Thank you,' I said. Tears welled in my eyes and I blinked them away, turning away from The Russian so he didn't see. He was right but I hadn't allowed myself to go there. I lost myself in the excitement and euphoria of going with The Russian and not the reality that tonight was my swansong event.

He squeezed my hand, kissed it and released it as I heard him turn to belt up. For a big guy, he was hugely sensitive. I pulled myself together. The Russian started the car and we headed off.

'Big car,' I said.

'Yeah, well, I hate those small cars that you have to fold yourself up to get into,' he said. 'Plus, I ferry my sisters around a bit so I want them to be safe. Nikki thinks I'm an on-call taxi service, Ana did too until she got her license thankfully.'

'Has she got a car?' I asked, remembering my first car bought on my first basketball salary which hadn't been much.

'I bought her one just to get her off my back.'

'Aren't you the sweetest brother?' I grinned at him,

knowing full well a new car wouldn't make a dent in one month of his contract fee. 'I'm surprised Nikki's not hitting you up for driving lessons.'

'Oh that's started but I'm not sure I have the patience,' he said.

'You come across as a very patient, methodical type,' I said, studying him.

'I am with things I can control. Nikki driving is not one of them unless I get dual controls.'

I didn't realize I was biting my lip and tapping my fingers until The Russian's hand wrapped around mine.

'You're nervous? What time is this speech?' he asked.

I drew a short breath and looked at him. 'To be honest, I'm nervous with you.' I didn't know why I'd said it ... I'm a reverend's daughter and I guess Dad had always pushed me to be honest about my feelings.

'Of course you are, I'm gorgeous,' he said.

I wasn't expecting that; I laughed aloud. He gave me a grin.

We traveled on the roads I knew like the back of my hand to the Suns' grounds where the Ball would be held in the VIP club area. Five hundred tickets had been sold so it was going to be a big night, plus there would be dancing.

'You know as well as speeches, there's going to be a fund-raising auction and dancing tonight?' I warned him.

'I assumed as much. I've been to a few club Ball nights and Best & Fairest Award ceremonies in my time.'

'Won any?'

'Two,' he said. 'One for the Saints and one for my first club when I first went pro.'

'Bravo you!' I grinned at him.

'And you've won four,' he said.

'Good job, stats man.'

He grinned. God he was beautiful. Even his expensive watch looked gorgeous on his wrist, somewhere between where the white cuff of his crisp shirt finished and his beautiful hand began.

'Do you dance?' I asked, pushing my luck.

He threw his head back and scoffed. 'Do I dance? Are you kidding? Just wait and see ... but it won't be a tango like Tango,' he said, referring to the team's Latin lover Tomás Carrera.

'I was at that lunch when you and Tomás were the guests of honor and he tangoed with his sister.' I stopped myself just in time before I said he was hot! 'I'd love to hear you on your guitar doing some rock,' I said, remembering that he played but wouldn't do it that day.

'Yeah, well I've got to have a few rums under the belt before I do that,' he said, looking uncharacteristically uncomfortable. 'I didn't see you at the lunch, where were you?'

'On a table right over near the windows ... I was a guest of Sasha's, and the media always get bad tables at those events because they're freebies.'

'Fair enough you freeloader,' he teased.

The Russian turned the car into the Suns' large parking lot and word did travel fast – there were photographers lining the entrance and on the road.

'Do you always get a media turn out like this for your Ball? Impressive,' he said.

'No, never. Um, I'm thinking Sasha's tweets and Facebook posts might have done the trick,' I warned him. I wasn't sure how he would react to being hassled and his photo and mine appearing everywhere, especially when we had both agreed earlier that we were a little social media shy, and I was very conscious of not taking up where his ex-girlfriend had left off in that regard.

'Seriously, for us? Wow, must be a slow media night,' he said and shrugged.

That was it? Totally unphased. I breathed a sigh of relief. The Russian pulled the car into a parking space and I could see several of my teammates heading inside with their dates on their arms. The Suns' coach had stopped for an interview in the doorway – she looked very glamorous; it was weird seeing everyone dressed up when we were more used to seeing each other in sports kit and gym gear.

The Russian was around my side of the car before I had barely reached for the door handle. He opened my door, extended his hand and I took it as he helped me from the car. I grabbed my clutch bag and squinted as the flashes went off. He closed the door and locked it behind us. The Russian hooked his arm and I slipped mine in.

'You look beautiful,' he said, again. 'Ready?'

I nodded and smiled at him. 'Thank you again for coming with me,' I said, while I had the chance. If nothing else happened, this would be a memory I would never forget and The Russian would have helped make magical a night that might have been terribly depressing.

'The pleasure is mine,' he said, as he looked me over.

So sweet, so smooth. Let the night begin.

Chapter 9

We hadn't gotten a few feet away from The Russian's car when the media circus began.

'Russian, Carly, over here,' a photographer called out and then more and more requests to look this way or that. It was lucky we came early because it took us close to fifteen minutes to make it to the door. We both blinked to clear the bulbs from our eyes and then once inside it was magical – we were inundated with my teammates and their partners wanting to say hello, telling me they missed me and wanting to meet The Russian, too, of course, especially the guys so they could talk sports.

We didn't have much time to catch up with everyone before the announcement came to find our tables. Aimee waved me over, we were at the same table as she was. I don't know how she had pulled that off because usually the marketing team made sure every table had a Suns player on it and we were all circulated; she must have had some dirt on Maria our Marketing Manager. On the way to our table, I stopped to introduce The Russian to my other best friend, Steffi, and her boyfriend Wilson. We promised to catch up with them later.

Aimee rose and gave me a hug and then shook hands with the Russian, who was to sit between the two of us. I could see him studying her with her exotic looks – a Jamaican mom and Swedish father make for a beautiful mix. Plus, they were eye to eye in height ... I bet that didn't happen much for either of them. Just as I thought that, The Russian confirmed it.

'Wow, I don't meet many people that can look me in the eye,' he said, giving her one of his sexy smiles. I was so busy showing him off I was prepared to lose a few of those smiles to close friends. Aimee's cousin leaned over and shook hands.

'Roy,' he said introducing himself.

'Roy's very upset you're here Alex,' Aimee said to The Russian, 'he was hoping to meet a single Carly.'

Roy nodded. 'But lovely to meet you regardless.'

I was holding my breath, dreading The Russian's response ... that *we weren't officially partners*', or '*you go for it Roy*' but something else wonderful happened ... I think he growled. I can't be sure but he stiffened and made this guttural sort of noise that I think only I heard, like a territorial lion. So sexy.

'Good to meet you Roy, and yeah sorry but Brooker's out of action, to use a sporting term.'

'Lucky there's other single Suns,' I said, sweetly. I wasn't used to attracting the interest of two men – hell, my last date that I had brought to the Ball hadn't even been interested in me, but let's not go there again. It was so exciting to be with a man who made me feel protected and feminine and desirable. Even if it was just for one night, it was worth it ... worth any potential pain, I think.

The meal was being served and straight after I would

have to make my speech; then there would be the chance to socialize and dance, followed by dessert. After that the club would announce the results of the silent auction – it was where all our sponsors donated big prizes for free and any money made went back to the club – it was one of our biggest fundraising events, especially since a lot of our wealthy sponsors were with us that night and often spent up after a few drinks.

The Russian and Aimee were chatting about the benefits of having parents from different cultures and where they could go on their respective passports, while I was running through my speech in my head. Then the meal appeared and was alternated for every second person, which was often the case in set menus, and they placed an entree of scallops with shrimp, served with noodles and what looked like a light soy dressing in front of me. The waiter put a chickpea, zucchini and ricotta green salad in front of The Russian. Sasha had warned me not to get between The Russian and his food; he was a big boy who needed to eat and I knew the green salad was not going to excite him ... besides, I wanted it.

'Swap?' I asked him.

I barely got the word out before he'd happily agreed and swapped our plates. Guess he was keen on that idea. I didn't even have to ask him when the main course arrived; I swapped the steak placed in front of me for the chicken dish placed in front of The Russian.

'You know me so well already,' he said.

'What I really want to know is how you get to the coffee van first,' I said. 'I probably should have asked you that before I swapped plates.'

The Russian narrowed his eyes at me and gave me a cheeky grin. He leaned closer. 'Tell Sasha she's going to have to work harder to get that information,' he said, as if it was some sort of girl conspiracy.

'I'm just starting,' I said. 'I thought I'd open with the obvious question in case you coughed up the answer, but I'm not a journalist for nothing. I will find out.'

He scoffed. 'My sources are loyal, and I won't be spilling. But I look forward to the interrogation.'

I gave him a smile and then I had time to dart to the ladies and make sure my nose wasn't shiny and I didn't have spinach on my teeth before my speech. As I came out of the cubicle, Lia, one of my Suns' teammates was there washing her hands.

'He's gorgeous, isn't he?' she said.

'Who?' I asked, which just went to show my head had moved to speech phase.

'Your date!' she almost squealed.

'Isn't he?' I said, nodding enthusiastically. 'I know most guys look good in a tux but talk about taking my breath away.'

'Not fair to the others,' Lia agreed.

We stopped talking for a moment while we both touched up our lipstick.

'Love your dress Lia, you look gorgeous,' I said, admiring her black shimmy cocktail dress.

'You too, that is a classic,' she admired Sasha's work. We heard the sound of the master of ceremonies, Jenna, and we hurried back to our seats with a promise to catch up later.

The Russian half stood and pulled out my chair for me. So gallant.

'Ready Brooker?' he asked me all business-like.

'Ready Russian,' I confirmed with a nod.

'Go get them kid,' he said, as Jenna called me up. She kept talking as I walked up to the stage; I was praying and hoping that I wouldn't fall over or get tongue-tied.

'As you know our current Best & Fairest champion Carly Brooker will be retiring at the end of the season, and we are delighted to welcome her tonight to offer the opening address and talk about the Suns and the importance of our club.'

I got a rousing welcome, the flashes went off again and I got a loud whistle.

'Thank you for that Aimee,' I said, and everyone laughed. I took a deep breath and looked out over the crowd of five-hundred strong and some media and photographers at the back of the room. It wasn't the first time I had got up to speak, I had done it many times, but it was still scary.

'I would like to start by thanking everyone for their messages of support since my injury, it meant a lot, and a special vote of thanks to my date tonight for his support ... you may know him as The Russian.'

The Russian gave me a smile and nod – big ham, he was accustomed to being in the limelight – and he got a huge cheer and a lot more whistles.

I continued. 'You know you are at a female Ball when the men get more whistles than the girls.' Everyone laughed again, I was on a roll thus far. I spoke of the season, the team, the pride in winning last year's Best and Fairest, and thanked our sponsors and patrons present for all they did for keeping our team alive. I called on them again to help us this year. Then I introduced the coach to say a few words and waited while she came up to the stage. She was there in no time – it happens when your legs are that long – and we gave each other a hug as we passed on the stairs off the stage. The Russian rose and helped me down the stairs in my dress and high heels – so charming – and we sat and listened to the coach. She praised my efforts and contribution to the club over the years and I struggled not to cry, again. Then our M.C., Jenna, reminded everyone to bid on the silent auctions and dobbed me in again ... it felt like the Carly show, enough already!

'I'm excited to announce that our PT has given Carly the all-clear to play in our last game of the season before the finals, assuming we make the finals of course ...but let's assume that's a given,' Jenna said, and everyone gave me a roaring clap again. I felt tears welling in my eyes and I really didn't want to cry, my mascara would run!

Jenna continued. 'So this will be a special game, because Carly has also advised it will be her last game for the Suns and she will be retiring before the finals series.' An audible moan rose from the crowd, which was kind of funny.

The Russian whispered in my ear. 'You didn't tell me that, congrats.'

I turned to smile at him. 'Thanks ... one more game. Weird, huh?'

'For sure. But not if you're busy and still involved in the sport, right?' he assured me.

'Right,' I nodded.

Jenna continued. 'Given it is Carly's swansong, one of the prizes in our silent auction is the ultimate home game experience – 10 VIP seats front row courtside at Carly's last game, VIP catering before, during and after the game and an open bar of course. Plus, there are a dozen more great lots to bid on, so enjoy some dancing and bidding and we'll be back here in thirty minutes for dessert and the auction results.'

The coach came over to my table to meet The Russian and then we had a quick chat; The Russian wasn't short of company, everyone wanted to talk with him. When the coach left, I turned to face him and he gave me a smile that would melt any female with a pulse.

'Well done, Brooker,' he said.

'I'm so glad that's over,' I sighed. 'Dance?'

The dance floor was already full and I wanted to see The Russian's moves.

'I'm waiting for the right song,' he said, 'can't just dance to anything.'

'Oh, of course,' I said.

'Come on,' he took my elbow and led me away from the table. 'I'd better make a bid on the silent auction to help the club.'

'I think you've already done your bit for the club,' I teased him, 'I know one Suns' player who is pretty happy.'

'That so?' he teased and took my hand; I swear I was floating. He did this thing where he rubbed his thumb over my skin – I could barely concentrate it was so distracting.

I felt like every eye in the room was watching us, and as we arrived at the long table of auction items, The Russian put his arm around my waist and I was right up against him as we read the auction sheets.

'Got a dog?' I asked.

'My folks have ... Brodie is his name,' he said looking at the sheet I was pointing to.

'A year's dog grooming ... Brodie will love you,' I suggested.

'Brodie will eat me if I do that to him,' The Russian said, as we moved along the line and moved past people bidding. 'Here's one ... a couple portrait ... what about a nude drawing of the two of us?'

'The world's not ready for that,' I assured him. 'Ooh, a signed shirt from Saints' Captain Lucas Ainswright! Did you know he was donating that?'

'No. I should bid and get it back for him,' The Russian joked, 'give it to him for Christmas.'

We continued along the line and then my PT, Serge, came over for a quick chat. I introduced The Russian and then let him keep looking while Serge and I had a brief chat. The Russian look towards me and Serge a few times ... funny, like he was sussing out if Serge was any competition, so I excused myself and caught up with The Russian again as he put a pen back in his suit.

'What did you bid on?' I asked him suspiciously.

'Never you mind, but I had better win it. I'm very competitive,' he said.

'Me too, funny that given we're both playing professional sport,' I reminded him.

Then Eric Clapton's *Wonderful Tonight* came on and The Russian sighed. 'Great song, would you care to dance, Brooker?'

'I would, thank you, Russian,' I said, a silly grin on my face, and he led me to the dance floor. I was not sure technically that you could call it dancing, but he pulled me close and we moved. I had one hand on his shoulder and the other under his jacket, on his hip. He wrapped his fingers around my hand pressed to his shoulder and held me tightly, his face nestled into my hair. I tried to remember every detail of that perfect moment and when I looked at The Russian's lowered head, he had his eyes closed. Was he thinking it was perfect too? Or was he thinking of someone else? He opened his eyes momentarily and caught me looking at him.

'I'm not thinking about anything,' he said.

I laughed. 'What? How did you know I was even thinking that?'

'You're a girl. I grew up with four of them ... aren't you always thinking 'what are we thinking'?'

I looked a bit sheepish and shrugged. 'Maybe.'

'Mm,' he said, 'if you must know, I was thinking you smell and feel good.'

'Really?' I said. Yep, that was the best I could come up with after that compliment, sad wasn't it?

'Really Brooker, now be quiet, I'm dancing here,' he said, and closed his eyes again.

'Okay, sorry,' I whispered, and closed my eyes, but not for long. I wanted to see him as well as feel him; I kept my eyes open and kept catching the eyes of my friends with their encouraging looks. I was in heaven. The lyrics were so beautiful too that I was hoping he had picked it for that reason ... maybe just a little anyway.

Damn Eric Clapton, he finished too soon and damn that DJ who then invited us to take our seats for dessert and the results of the silent auction. This time they placed the fruit salad in front of me and sticky date pudding in front of The Russian. I didn't know if he had a sweet tooth, but I wanted his and reading my mind – or from the experience of growing up with four females – he swapped our bowls and I grinned my thanks.

The Russian shook his head. 'The sacrifices I make for you, Brooker.'

'You're the best for sure,' I said, taking a large bite of dessert and groaning.

'Well, don't rub it in,' he said.

I put a taste on my spoon and offered it to him. I saw some flashes go ... seriously, now I was being snapped feeding him dessert? He was pretty cute though when he let me feed him.

Jenna, our master of ceremonies, called for our attention and began reading out the highest bid for each prize, and then the winner.

'The winner of the year's worth of dog grooming with a value of $1200, is a bid for $3000 from Allen Stapelton,' Jenna announced. 'Where are you, Allen?'

Allen waved from a table near the door and one of our marketing team ran over with his prize certificate.

'Give Allen a big round of applause, and thank you to Furry Friend's Dog Grooming and Allen for the donation to our club.'

I turned to look at The Russian who sat behind me as we faced the stage. He leaned forward and I whispered in his ear. 'I'm telling you, Brodie would have been the better for that,' I said, and The Russian grinned. 'Promise me you

didn't bid on the portrait drawing on the basis it was nude?'
I grimaced.

The Russian shook his head. 'I can't promise anything ...
sorry, but if it comes through, I expect your one hundred
percent support and participation.'

I gave a concerned moan and turned back around to face
Jenna on the stage. I was so conscious of The Russian behind
me; I wanted to lean into him, or for him to put his hands
on me, but he didn't. I could barely concentrate for sensing
his presence and feeling his warm breath on my neck.

Jenna announced the winner of the Lucas Ainswright
signed Saints' shirt with a bid of $500, and the winner of
a $4000 bid for a VIP pamper weekend. Now that one I
would have been prepared to share with The Russian, the
caring-sharing girl I am.

Jenna worked through the other prizes – dinner for two,
a trip to Hawaii for a family which went for $8000 to one of
our sponsors, a Suns framed and signed winning grand final
photo, a month worth of physical therapy from Serge, until
she came to the last lot. I began to wonder if The Russian had
actually won his bid since he wouldn't tell me which one he
had bid for, and now we were at the end of the auction.

'Now for our major auction item,' Jenna continued. 'Ten
VIP seats front row courtside at our end-of-season game
and now tribute game featuring Suns' star Carly Brooker,
along with VIP catering before, during and after the game
and an open bar. Valued at $4000, we have a winning bid of
...' Jenna stopped and gasped. She showed the envelope to
Maria our Marketing Manager who read it and nodded, a
look of shock on her face.

Jenna cleared her throat and returned to the microphone. 'Sorry for that, I just had to check I wasn't seeing too many zeroes. Valued at $4000, the winning bid for the VIP package is TWENTY THOUSAND DOLLARS!' she yelled it out.

The room went ballistic with people gasping and cheering. Jenna accepted a piece of paper from Maria and read it out.

'That brings our fundraising efforts from tonight's silent auction to $65,000.' Again the cheering continued. 'And the VIP lot was bought by Alex Renwick. Where are you Alex?'

Everyone looked around except for a few who recognized or remembered The Russian's real name. I caught Jenna's eye and nodded to The Russian.

'Or you might know him as The Russian.' Maria came over and gave him his prize voucher. The Russian was trying to keep a low profile behind me; he thanked her and tucked it inside his tuxedo.

'Enjoy your dessert and more dancing,' Jenna called over the crowd noise, and left the stage.

I swung around to face The Russian with a big grin on my face.

'Do you even have ten friends?' I teased him.

The Russian laughed. 'I'm sure I can rustle up enough people to fill the seats or rent some friends.'

I squeezed his hand. 'Thank you. It's turned out to be a very expensive night for you.'

'You're welcome Brooker,' he said, lifting my hand and kissing inside my palm. I was so gone. It was nearing midnight and The Russian had put in a valiant effort.

'Want to get out of here?' I asked.

'Whenever you're ready,' he said.

'I'm good to go.'

He rose and I grabbed my clutch bag, and we said goodbye to the people remaining at our table. I waved to a few of my friends, including Aimee who was on the dance floor with some of the girls.

We got outside and The Russian opened the car door for me and I slipped in. He came around to his side, slid in and started the car. We turned out of the grounds, still subject to a barrage of flashes, and headed to my house.

Here came the sticky bit – to invite him in and risk rejection or not to invite him in. Don't get me wrong I wanted to bed The Russian more than I wanted oxygen at the moment, but I'd never slept with a guy on the first date and technically it was a first date.

If I never saw him again, then I wanted to have sex – it would top off the perfect night and be a night I'd never forget. I was going to be in pain anyway that it had just been that one night, so might as well go the full morose than the half morose. However, if there was a chance he might ask me out again, then I didn't want to have sex because I wanted us to build to that. I wanted a relationship, not a fling. So tough.

'You're quiet, are you okay?' he asked.

I looked over at the gorgeous man driving me home.

'Is that your way of asking what I'm thinking?' I eyed him suspiciously.

He gave me a smile.

'Okay, caught out. What are you thinking?' he asked.

I sighed. 'I'm thinking I had the most perfect night ever and thank you for making it so, and not a tearful night as I expected.'

He gave me a smile. 'It was fun ... your friends are great girls, especially Aimee, she's direct isn't she?'

'Oh God, what did she ask you?'

'I can't repeat it,' he teased. 'It's all good, she's a bit of fun and so was your coach ... an impressive lady.' He pulled up outside my apartment block and turned the car off. Well, that answered that question. Again he was at my door offering his hand before I got out. So charming.

'I'll see you to your door,' he said, not being presumptuous.

'You're welcome to come in for tea or coffee if you like,' I offered. So awkward.

'Sure, that would be good,' he said.

I think I heard the load falling off my shoulders. I opened the door and saw Josh had left a lamp on in the corner; he'd made a point of saying he was staying out for the night. The Russian removed his jacket and undid his bow tie.

Just as I moved to the kitchen to put on the kettle, his phone rang. I heard him groan and turned to see him look at the screen and frown.

'Sorry Brooker, got to take this,' he said, with a sigh.

'Sure,' I said.

Mm, ex-girlfriend, new girlfriend?

'Nikki,' he said, in a not-very-happy voice. I listened in. Nikki was the middle sister from memory.

'Can't you call Mom or Dad? ... Well, what about Ana, where's she? Get her to pick you up? ... Nikki, there's such a thing as a taxi ... fine, where are you? Stay there. Don't leave, don't talk to strangers, and don't talk to anyone male. I'll be there in fifteen minutes.'

He hung up and came over to the island where I stood.

'So, you best be going,' I said.

'Sorry, Brooker. That's my sister. Long story, but she's somewhere where she shouldn't be and now she's freaking out because her friends have left ... and so on ...' he sighed.

'It's all good. I remember doing something similar ... you're a good brother,' I teased.

'Walk me out?'

'Sure,' I said.

We got halfway down the stairs when The Russian stopped and turned. Standing one step above him, my face was aligned with his. What a beautiful face, I could kiss it all night.

'Sorry the night ended like that,' he said, as I studied his beautiful face to memory in case this was the last time I saw it close-up.

'Don't be. It was a great night,' I said.

He placed his hands on my waist.

'What time is your job interview tomorrow?'

'Ah, nice of you to remember,' I said. 'Ten o'clock.'

'Call me after and tell me how you think it went, yeah?' he asked.

'Sure, thanks,' I said. *Yes!* A chance for another contact ... I was building this house of love slowly, contact by contact.

I placed my hands on his shoulders since I could reach them comfortably from my higher step. 'Go rescue your sister, you good guy.'

'Yeah, I bet you're probably thinking I'm pretty perfect right now,' he said, with the hint of a grin.

'Yeah, too good to be true really,' I agreed. 'I look forward to you falling off that pedestal.'

He laughed. 'Now go inside so I can hear you lock the

door, and call me tomorrow after the interview.' The Russian ordered me.

'Yes Sir, I will,' I snapped at it. 'Thank you again.'

I went to move away and he pulled me back. He looked at me for what seemed like an eternity, then pressed his lips quickly to mine.

'Goodnight,' he said, and gently pushed me towards the door.

I went back up the stairs, opened the door, and with one final look his way, I went inside locking the door.

Holy mother of all things good, I was going to self-combust. And if my father knew I'd used that term I'd be on my knees saying 'Hail Marys' until I died an old spinster.

*****

I washed off my make-up and crawled into bed. It was close to two a.m. I grabbed my iPad and looked at the social media which was going crazy with stories about us. I swear they had made a mountain out of it – there were photos of The Russian helping me out of the car, the two of us posing near the entrance to the Ball, looking at the auction items together, and shots where I hadn't even seen a flash going off, including the two of us dancing close and me feeding The Russian dessert. We were being called the 'IT' couple and there were plenty of out-there headlines including a play on The Russian and American relationship 'No Cold War Here'; or 'When Sports Collide', 'Saints Preserve Us', 'Sun shines on Saint', and on it went.

On other sites, there was plenty of talk about Sasha's gown and its design with photos of me wearing it, with and without The Russian. I was so glad she'd had hits from it. I put the iPad down and snuggled into my sheets. I knew it would be impossibly hard to get to sleep, but I was happy to lie in bed and dream of the manliness of The Russian. What a package, and I had 'permission' to call him tomorrow. I knew what euphoria felt like.

Chapter 10

I didn't feel tired the next morning; I was still running on excitement and adrenaline. I wanted The Russian, I wanted this job so badly, I wanted it all! Before I left home for my job interview – at about nine o'clock – when I knew Sasha would be in the Saints' office, I gave her a quick call.

'Well, hello belle of the ball,' she answered, and I laughed.

'Hello to the hottest dressmaker on the west coast,' I said, and she laughed. 'Hey, just a quick call to thank you again for making me the most amazing dress, I felt just beautiful in it.'

'Hey, my pleasure, you were a beautiful model and thank you for all the promotion, my website has had so many hits and I've been returning email queries already.'

'That's brilliant. On the downside, I haven't cracked the coffee lady secret yet, but I'm not giving up.'

'I think you've cracked The Russian though,' Sasha said.

'Really?' I said, my voice sounding way too thrilled. 'What makes you say that?'

Sasha lowered her voice. 'Well, this morning he came in and I said you two looked beautiful together and asked did he have a good night, and he gave me this sort of satisfied smirk that said volumes.'

'That's it?' I asked, disappointed.

'Are you kidding? That's huge for grumpy bum ... the few other times I've caught him out with dates and asked him about it, he snapped and shut me down immediately like the whole thing was stupid. Not this time ... he looked, well, happy.'

'Oh, well that's good,' I brightened. 'Anyway, got to run, but I just wanted to say thank you again. See you at the game.'

'Look forward to it and don't give up on the coffee secret,' she said.

'Never,' I assured her and hung up. Hmm, so The Russian smiled – big deal ... well maybe it was, I'm running with it.

Forty-five minutes later, I took a deep breath and entered the cable television station foyer taking in the photos of their stars on the wall; I could be right at home there ... please! I greeted the receptionist and asked for Deidre Carmichael in relation to a meeting with Karen Meares –then I felt nervous having said it out loud. She indicated that I should take a seat while she rang through to let them know I was here. I felt my phone buzz with a text and took the opportunity to put it on silence. It was from The Russian wishing me good luck – so adorable. If I hadn't been so nervous I would have been swooning ... fine, I was still swooning.

'I loved your dress at the Suns' Ball,' the receptionist said to me, 'I loved your date, too.'

I gave her a 'couldn't-agree-more' smile. 'It was a brilliant night and thanks, Sasha Saxon made the dress, the date I picked up from the Saints.'

She laughed. 'Stunning, both of them. He's the guy on the watch billboard isn't he?'

'That's him,' I agreed. I would have loved to have that billboard as wallpaper in my bedroom. I didn't say that out loud did I? No, phew, thank goodness for that. Mm, therein lay my future if I partnered up with The Russian – women would be ogling him everywhere we went. It was a burden I would have to bear.

The door behind the receptionist opened and a more mature woman stepped out and said my name. She invited me to come through and I thanked the receptionist as I departed. She introduced herself as Deidre and we walked up a long hallway where both sides of the wall were covered with framed photographs of every celebrity that had ever worked at the station, from sport to weather to soap stars. Luckily, Deidre walked in front of me so I could get my head in the right space for the interview instead of making small talk. She showed me into a boardroom where I could look down on the journalists and a bank of television screens below.

'Would you like a glass of water?' she asked.

'That would be appreciated, thank you,' I said.

Deidre disappeared and returned within a few minutes with a jug and three glasses. I poured and waited and then Karen entered with a middle-aged, slightly overweight man. I rose and shook her hand.

'Good to meet you Carly, and this is the Head of Cable Sport, Gerard Threlfall.'

We shook hands and I wondered if Gerard was a journalist or from a sports background; clearly he worked too much and didn't participate in sport enough.

'Well, you know how to make an impact at a Ball night,' Karen said.

I gave her a smile, but kept professional – I didn't want to be too girly. 'It was a great night,' I agreed, 'I'll miss being part of the team.'

'Aimee Nilsson has had a great year,' Gerard said, referring to my best friend.

'She has, so has Lia Cartwright,' I said, and we talked a bit about the Suns. Then Karen took over and the next hour flew by as they asked about my interests, passions and future plans. They had seen my pieces on camera from The Saints games and knew of my work with *The Sports Daily*. Karen liked my sporting pedigree as she put it, and Gerard said the publicity I had been getting wouldn't hurt the ratings either if people tuned in to check me out. I didn't want to get any favoritism based on a relationship that might not happen, but I guess profile-boosting and publicity was all part of the media game, sadly.

I thanked them for the opportunity to be considered and was back in the parking lot feeling exhausted but satisfied I had given it my best. I decided to drive back to my favorite coffee shop and call The Russian from there, rather than sit in the parking lot on the phone. I couldn't wait to hear his voice. That would be our last contact though ... I was hoping he would ask me out or make the next move. I hoped he wouldn't just say 'well good luck' and that'd be that.

I waited until I had a coffee in front of me before calling him, and then I rang. I think I was holding my breath ... it rang once, twice, three times and he picked up. What a rush ... nerves, excitement, lack of air ...

'Brooker,' he said, in his sexy baritone voice.

'Russian, how are you?'

'Great,' he answered. 'Did you get the job?'

I laughed. 'Not that quickly. They said they'd let me know by Wednesday.'

'Who interviewed you?'

'Karen Meares and Gerard Threlfall,' I told him. 'Know them?'

'I know Gerard,' he said.

'And, more importantly, the receptionist bailed me up before I entered the interview to tell me she thought you were stunning. Not handsome, but stunning ... like a sunset,' I teased. I couldn't help myself, it was a bit of a test. I was hoping he wouldn't say *did she now, what's her number?* or *I'll have to drop in* or something equally as flirty and horrendous. I couldn't stand a flirty man. But the gorgeous Russian didn't. Instead he said: 'Stunning, well that's a new one. And what's the potential sports commentator for cable TV think?'

I stirred my coffee, grinning from ear to ear like a totally love-smitten teenager.

'Well, she thought you scrubbed up pretty well,' I said.

I heard his deep chuckle.

'Mm, high praise. Hold a sec for me?' he asked.

'Sure,' I answered. I heard him talking to someone in the background, he must have been in his office. He returned to the phone call.

'Sorry about that, I'm always in demand,' he sighed.

'It's a curse,' I agreed. *Please, please, ask me out again.* My brain was urgently debating whether to say I should let him go since he was at work or make some other pointless small talk when he took charge.

'I'm going to the gym tomorrow morning. Going to be there?' he asked. 'We could spot each other on the weights.'

'We could do that if you think you can manage the weights I'm lifting,' I teased him.

I heard him chuckle again. 'I'll do my best. Six?'

'See you there at six,' I agreed and hung up.

I loved my life! How funny it was ... one month before I had been in the throes of depression, unable to play, getting more PT than the entire Suns team, my career crashing down on me and then, two months later, I was in the running for my dream job and getting another chance to see the man of my dreams.

You never knew what was around the corner, but it was worth waiting for.

The next morning I would get to see The Russian lifting weights, his muscles bulging and rippling, his sexy waist and hips bending and stretching, those long legs ... where was I? Oh yes, The Russian looking gorgeous ... and I might even get a coffee and muffin with him afterward if I was lucky.

Chapter 11

When I got to the gym at 5.45am the next morning – nothing was going to keep me from that gym – Ken, one of my fans or some might say resident stalker, was there. Ken was harmless I think, and I had had a few over-zealous fans over the years who had found out where I was working out or came to where I was reporting sporting events and just hung around waiting to see me and be acknowledged.

Luckily, I'd never had a bad experience, but one of my teammates, Latoya, had. She had started talking to a guy online and they had begun exchanging photos. After a few too many drinks one night, they were exchanging raunchier photos and he put them online – my worst nightmare. The police and club lawyers had stepped in and it had been shut down pretty quickly and he was charged. It came out that he had done that to half a dozen other women as well, but Latoya was mortified; it had really taken away her confidence.

My stalker, Ken – or I should say fan – was carrying a bit of weight, a smoker, in his mid-forties at a guess, just a bit odd. He was a taxi driver so he was often in the taxi zone after our games and I had once seen him at the Saints' when

I was reporting there, but he usually just said a few words and departed. I gave him a hesitant wave and headed in.

My eyes swept the gym and, of course, landed straight on The Russian. He was spotting for some other guy; I loved that he never seemed to flirt even though there were girls lifting weights nearby him; he was so solid in every sense of the word – well, from what I'd seen to date that was. He looked up and saw me and smiled; be still my beating heart. I indicated the lockers and went in to put away my car keys, phone and wallet. When I came back he was waiting for me by a set of weights, just doing hand lifts.

'Brooker, looking good,' he said, with the hint of a smile.

'Russian, looking pretty good yourself,' I said, and swept my eyes over him.

'I saw that,' he teased.

'Feel cheap?' I ribbed him.

'I would prefer you liked me for my mind,' he teased, and then we got down to business, because I knew somewhere in my psyche that The Russian didn't need another pretty girl who looked and talked the part.

The Russian – if he liked me at all – might have been liking me because I was real, I was an athlete, I was a driven person. Well, that was what I was counting on and if I was wrong, then so be it. I did a work out with intensity; I didn't care if I sweated or groaned or didn't look pretty – okay, I did care a little that I might not have looked pretty, but I was turned on by The Russian straining, not posing, so I gave him the same ... and I wanted to beat him, not that I did, not once ... I came close with the number of sit-ups, I did. I think it paid off because at the end of the workout when we both stopped and breathed in, he looked at me with what I think was respect.

'Well done, Brooker, you're not a pussy,' he said.

'I beg your pardon?' I said, shocked.

I think my reaction unnerved him.

'Sorry, I meant, you worked hard, poor choice of words,' he stumbled. It was good to unhinge The Russian every now and then, he was so confident.

I grinned at him and gave him a wink and he shook his head at me. He grabbed a plastic cup of water from the dispenser and gave it to me while he poured his own.

'Thanks,' I said, drinking it like a woman who had been working out for an hour with a super fit, gorgeous Saint.

He swallowed his cupful and refilled us both. 'Got time to grab a coffee?'

'I'd love one. Can you give me the number?'

He looked confused.

'For the coffee lady? I need her number,' I said, trying to sound casual.

'Brooker, Brooker, Brooker, that the best you got?' he asked, and then he laughed. 'Keep trying.'

I sighed. 'Fine then.'

'So, coffee now?' he asked again. 'Ten minutes enough to shower and change?'

'Sure, I'm a natural beauty,' I said.

'Five minutes then?'

'Don't be ridiculous. I'm not that natural, see you in ten.'

I heard him chuckle as I headed off before he could renegotiate. This was going so well; I think The Russian liked me. God knows I tried to show him the few good angles I had that day while working out. A girl's got to use what she's got, when she can, and I don't have long blonde wavy hair, I'm not Boho and my daddy is rich in faith only.

*****

He was waiting for me when I returned, but I hadn't taken much longer than ten minutes. We headed to the cafe that we had frequented last time.

The Russian went to order and when he came back and slid into the booth opposite, I forgot for a moment to raise my eyes from his torso and he caught me checking him out.

'Okay?' he asked.

'Just checking that gym session is working for you,' I said, sheepishly.

'Good of you,' he said, with the hint of a smile. The Russian sat back in our booth and looked around. There were a few other people from the gym and some guy trying to take a subtle photo of us on his phone.

'Should we just smile and wave?' The Russian asked.

'We could, or we could put glasses on and hats and try and look more cloak and dagger. He might make money from that shot,' I suggested. Then my friendly stalker, Ken, went past the window and waved to me and I waved back.

'Who was that?' The Russian asked, checking him out.

'Just one of my friendly stalkers,' I said. I swear The Russian grew a foot taller if it was at all possible.

'What do you mean?' he said.

I told him I had a few regulars – Ken, Alby and Ron, and a female called Liz – and I assured him they had never caused me any trouble.

'What's he doing here then?' he asked, still tense and watching Ken walk through the parking lot.

I shrugged. 'I don't know, he often comes here. I've seen him before and after some of my workouts.'

'I don't like it, Brooker,' The Russian growled. 'Next time you see him or any of the others, including the female, you're going to introduce me as your boyfriend and I'll be moving them on. Okay?'

I frowned at him. 'I appreciate ...'

'Not up for discussion,' he said, closing it down.

I swallowed and stayed patient. While I appreciated his concern for me, was even pretty turned on by it – sadly – I had been pretty good at looking after myself up to that point.

'Russian, I appreciate it but ...'

'No, Brooker. I protect my own ...'

'And I'm your own?' I asked, with raised eyebrows.

He placed his hands palm down on the table and took a deep breath. 'You keep forgetting I'm in security. These people seem harmless until they're not ... how many times have you seen news reports where the neighbors say 'he was such a nice man, quiet and wouldn't hurt a fly'. We're shutting this down.'

I stared at him and he stared at me and then he reached for my hand.

'Let me at least do what I can, while I can, to protect you. You'd do the same for me if the situation was reversed and it was your area of expertise, wouldn't you?' he asked. God he was good. I took a deep breath and smiled.

'Thank you, but you can't hurt them,' I said.

He scoffed. 'Wow, you don't think much of me, do you?'

I looked at the disappointment on his face.

'I don't really know you, Russian,' I said, truthfully.

He nodded. 'Fair enough. I'm not going to hurt them. I'm just going to make it clear that I'm with you now, and I'll be the one looking out for you, so their work is done here. Okay? Put this number in your phone.'

'What number?' I asked.

'The number I'm about to give you,' he said, rolling his eyes.

'Oh that number,' I said, with a smile and picked up my phone ready to key in. He dictated a number and I entered it.

'That's Saints' security,' The Russian said. 'If you can't reach me, call that number, it's 24-7 and someone will always answer and respond to you. I'll put you on the list of our clients.'

'Thank you Russian, that's very kind and weirdly reassuring ... like having a bodyguard on call.'

'You mean 'thanks Russian, you're my hero?" he said, and smiled.

'Don't push your luck,' I said.

'Speaking of pushing my luck, I've got a bit of a problem,' he said, and sat back as our coffees and two muffins were delivered.

I think I stopped breathing; I just stared at him. A problem ... *is his ex-girlfriend back? Does he not want a relationship right now? Does he want to focus on his sport? Crap, I hate men.*

'What?' he asked. 'Don't look so freaked out.' He broke his muffin in half and began to eat it.

I breathed again. 'You know, saying 'I've got a problem' for a guy is akin to a woman saying 'we need to talk'' I said, and he grinned at me.

'Brooker, you think too much. My problem is that my delightful sisters – namely Ana and Nikki – showed my mother all the social media photos of our night at your Ball. Now Mom is insisting you come to dinner.'

'Really?' I brightened. I took a bite of my muffin now that the problem was actually a good thing and I could formulate saliva and swallow again.

'So, will you?' he asked, looking down on me with his big chocolate eyes.

Hell, try and keep me away.

'I'd be delighted,' I said, 'thank you. Who would miss the chance to see where you sprung from?' I laughed at the thought.

'Hmm,' he sort of snorted. 'Tomorrow night, Wednesday?'

'Tomorrow?' I gulped.

'Too soon?' he frowned. 'I can tell Mom that another date might be better.'

'No, I'm free, tomorrow night is good. Thank you.' *Make my day, make my month, make my ... you get the idea.*

'I can pick you up after training, around seven?' he said.

'Where do you live?' I asked and he told me.

'I have a better idea,' I said. 'I'm working at *The Sports Daily* tomorrow which is closer to your place than mine and I don't finish until 6.30pm. Why don't I come to your place straight after work and you drive from then?'

'So you're not going to go home and spend two hours beautifying yourself for me?' he said, surprised. I narrowed my eyes at him, lucky I knew him well enough to know he was joking.

'I'll powder my nose,' I assured him. 'Might even spray a bit of perfume around.'

'Yep, you're completely taken with me,' he said. 'Give me your phone and I'll put my address in.'

I think I had an orgasm as I handed over my phone and watched that beautiful man enter his address. Is that possible without being touched? I had now seen him Sunday night, spoken Monday, worked out together Tuesday and we were having dinner with his family Wednesday night.

I think maybe, just maybe, The Russian might like me too.

Chapter 12

About midday the following day, Sasha gave me a call. I stepped away from my desk, and headed to *The Sports Daily* kitchen to chat.

'Hey you,' I said, 'how're things?'

'Good,' she said, 'very good in fact. Just checking you're coming to the media box for the next game?'

'I haven't got my weekly roster from *The Sports Daily* yet, but assume yes and I'll confirm ASAP,' I said. 'They've sent me to everyone this season, so the odds are good. Why, short on space?'

She sighed. 'The national league magazine is going to be in town and wants four places ... it shouldn't be a problem, but I just want to look after our regulars first.'

'Thanks, appreciate it.'

'So, what have you done to The Russian?' she asked.

Last time I had heard he was okay. My breath hitched.

'Nothing, why?'

'Because when I dropped in on him before, he was watching one of your old games on his computer ... hmm ...' she said, 'sounds like someone's a bit keen.'

'Really?' I asked, with a bit of a squeal, unfortunately.

'From what I could see before he paused it and glared at me, it was the finals against the New York Sparks,' she said. Sasha knew her sport.

'Good, I won best on the court for that game,' I said, a big smile on my face, which fortunately she couldn't see.

'Did you do a gym wear photoshoot too?' she asked.

'Yes! A couple of years ago for *Planet Fit Sportswear*, paid off half my car. Don't tell me ...'

'Yep, your *lover* was checking that out too, I saw the tab open. Don't tell him I told you, just thought you'd like to know he was perving on you,' Sasha said.

'You're right, very happy about that. Thanks for calling, you wonderful source of good news.'

Sasha laughed. 'See you at the game unless I hear otherwise,' she said.

So The Russian was watching me play and checking out my modeling work ... The Russian liked me enough to go on YouTube and find my last finals game and watch me play. Yes! I wondered if he'd bring it up.

*****

That evening, just after seven p.m., The Russian parked kerbside outside his parents' house. Their house was big, but not obnoxious ... it was stately but didn't stand out. I suspect regardless of the money The Russian made and could have – and most likely would have offered them – they liked to keep their feet firmly planted on the ground. The house was in a new estate with wide streets and other similar-sized big homes, that all shared a communal park; it had a nice vibe about it. I relaxed a bit on seeing it – I don't know what I had been expecting, a mansion maybe. My family home was attached to the church ... a reverend usually got it as part of his package so I'd lived in churchyards all my life. Sometimes with cemeteries out the front too, which other kids thought was weird, but when you didn't know any different ...

I felt The Russian's hand cover mine for just a moment before he turned off the ignition.

'You're not nervous, are you?' he asked with the hint of a grin.

'No, more curious to find out what sort of superior beings created this perfect specimen,' I said, playing into his hand. 'I'll be okay, I've met a few parents in my time.'

'Have you now,' he said, undoing his seatbelt. He made a sort of unimpressed sound as if I should have been a virgin, at home waiting for him.

I unbuckled and opened the door; The Russian was on my side before I finished stepping out; he closed the door for me. As we made our way up the driveway, the door opened and a young girl and a beautiful cream Labrador came bounding towards us.

'Alex,' she screamed with delight, her braids dancing as she looked from me to Alex and back. So did the dog. Not sure where to go first, she ran headlong into Alex, wrapping herself around him, and the dog jumped on me with his tongue at the ready for an affectionate lick. Good thing I loved dogs.

'Brodie, down,' Alex ordered the dog, 'Tia, Tia, Tia,' he

spun her around as she squealed in delight. He put her down and she raced up to me and wrapped her arms around my waist.

I laughed with surprise.

'Carly, I would like you to meet my sister Natalia, she's the one attached to you,' The Russian said, and bent down to give Brodie some rough-and-tumble.

'Tia,' she corrected him and then looked back at me. She was a cutie – the opposite to The Russian in coloring; as dark as The Russian was, she was as fair as snow with blonde hair in braids, blue eyes and pale skin.

'Hello Tia and ...'

'Brodie,' she said, introducing me to the family Labrador.

'Ah Brodie, of course,' I said.

She released me from the hug and took my hand. 'Mom's been cooking and cleaning all day, but you can't tell her I told you that because she said we had to make you feel welcome and we weren't allowed to ask you any nosy questions.'

I laughed again and The Russian just shook his head as we started up the path, Brodie racing in front and Tia taking both of our hands like our love child ... I wish.

'Do you like my brother?' she asked.

'I do, most of the time,' I said.

'Me too, except when he tickles me,' she said.

'I thought you loved that,' The Russian said, and grabbed her and began tickling. She squealed with delight and he lowered her to the ground as his mother and father appeared in the doorway. I could see traces of The Russian in both of them – his mother was tall, thin and fair; his father was tall, of solid build and dark.

He embraced them both and then introduced me.

'Good to meet you Mr and Mrs Renwick,' I said.

'James, please,' his father said, shaking my hand.

'And you must call me Lana,' his mother said. 'Come in, please Carly, you are most welcome.'

His father sounded very much American and with a surname like Renwick, I suspected he was. His mother's accent was still very noticeable in her clipped words and I guessed from The Russian's nickname where she came from.

We stumbled in with Tia and Brodie trying to push through the door at the same time. Inside, the house was spacious but full of family clutter ... photos, trophies, drawings, games – a large unfinished jigsaw puzzle sat on the snooker table and the game *Twister* was spread out on the floor; I swear I hadn't played *Twister* since primary school.

I would have liked to play nude *Twister* with The Russian ... really, where had that thought come from in this wholesome family moment?

Framed photos of the family at many different walks of life adorned the walls and I intended to spend some time looking at the young Alex on Santa's knee and in other poses as soon as I could get to them. Yep, that would be stored away for later teasing.

'Don't even think about it,' he whispered in my ear, following my gaze.

'What?' I asked innocently and he narrowed his eyes at me.

The Russian's dad, James, busied himself getting us both a drink and within a minute two more girls – both in their teens – came down the stairs. The family was split ... Tia and one of the other girls looked like their mother, Lana; The Russian and the eldest girl looked like their father, James.

'Alex has a girlfriend,' Tia teased. 'Carly these are my sisters ...'

Lana re-entered the room after checking on dinner, which was filling the house with a mouth-watering scent. 'Tia, I'm sure your brother can do the introductions ... Carly is his guest.'

Young Tia sighed as if her skills were not appreciated.

The eldest of the two girls stepped forward and offered me her hand. She was a very attractive female version of The Russian, only shorter, shorter than me too, with long dark hair and large dark eyes.

'Hello Carly, I'm Ana,' she said.

'Anastasia,' Tia piped up.

'Quiet please, *Natalia*,' she said, putting Tia back in her place. We shook hands.

'Good to meet you,' I said.

'You too. I'm always surprised when someone likes my brother,' she said, giving him a smirk. He grabbed her in a hug and kissed her roughly on the cheek. She pulled away and made a show of wiping her face, but I could tell she loved it, she was grinning from ear-to-ear.

'And I'm Nikita, but everyone calls me Nikki,' a teenager who liked like an older carbon copy of young Tia, with the blonde hair and blue eyes, said.

'Nikita,' I repeated her name. 'Such beautiful names – Anastasia, Nikita and Natalia.'

'Beautiful Russian names,' The Russian's mother agreed.

'Since we moved to America before the girls were born, we compromised by giving them Russian names to keep a little of my history alive. They were names of women in my family.' She gave her husband an affectionate look.

'And Alex, is that Russian?' I asked, frowning.

'Alexei,' Lana said, looking at her son.

I turned my eyes to him and grinned. And thus, I worked out how The Russian once got his nickname.

'Alexei, that's beautiful,' I said.

The Russian winced. 'Yeah, I'm starving,' he said, in a bad attempt to change the subject. His mother laughed.

'Come on then, let's eat. Nikki, can you help me with the salads, please? James, will you serve the stroganoff, Ana please top up our glasses, Tia if you can turn that music off and Brodie eat your dinner,' she said, directing the dog. 'Alex, you make Carly feel at home.'

'Can I help at all?' I asked, following everyone into the large open plan kitchen and dining area.

'Yes please, Carly,' Lana said, 'you can keep Alex away while we serve, so he doesn't pick.'

'I'm always ganged up on here,' he grumbled good-naturedly.

'Come then, you can walk me through the photos and I'll make sure you stay away from the plates.'

'This dinner was a bad idea,' he mumbled, following me back over to the wall of framed photos, not far from all the activity in the kitchen. He pulled me away from the photos of him and started at the end with the older family photos. The Russian photos from Lana's side were severe – somber subjects looking into the camera, looking less than happy.

'Russia and its people have not had a happy history,' The Russian explained as he pointed out Lana's parents.

'Is Lana a Russian name too? It doesn't sound Russian?' I asked.

'It's short for Svetlana,' he said. 'And here's Dad's parents and grandparents.'

I looked at the subjects all suited up and the women with their hats and dresses covering every inch of their body.

The Russian pointed out a great shot of his parents on the crumbling Berlin Wall.

'That's where my parents met. Mom was traveling around Europe, Dad was there working as an engineer.'

I loved watching The Russian as he told me about his family. His deep voice warming me, his strong presence beside me sending sparks through my whole body.

The Russian's father piped in from the open plan kitchen. 'I had only been qualified a few years, but the company I was working for won a contract to do a project in Berlin,' he said. 'The moment I saw Lana on the wall, waving her banner, it was love at first sight. I wasn't going back to the States without her, and luckily she was so charmed by me that she agreed.'

Lana blushed and shook her head at him. Yep, like father like son.

'Did you love him at first sight too, Mom?' Tia asked.

'Of course, you know that story,' she said, shutting the discussion down. Clearly Lana wasn't one for expressing emotions out loud.

'Did you love Alex at first sight Carly?' Tia said, turning to me.

'Tia!' Her mother shook her head.

'Of course she did, she's smitten,' The Russian said to Tia. His two other sisters Ana and Nikki groaned, and I laughed.

'He is handsome,' Tia said, smiling up at her big brother with a look of adoration.

'Very handsome,' Alex agreed and she giggled.

I moved to the next set of photos. 'And look at that cutie.' There was a great shot of his parents out the front of what must have been their first house, holding baby Alex, along with a series of shots of the four children from school days all the way through.

'Yeah, I was a cute kid, not much has changed,' The Russian agreed.

'Alexei, you were a beautiful boy,' his mother agreed, embarrassing him this time. 'Ladies on the street would stop me to look at you.'

'You should have stopped at perfection then,' he said, teasing his sisters.

'They did,' Nikki added. 'One boy broke the mold. After that, Mom and Dad only wanted girls, far less trouble.' She made a face at her brother.

Lana placed the large dish of steaming stroganoff in the center of the table and James began to serve it. Next to her Russian specialty, she placed some homemade corn bread. Nikki followed with two large bowls of salad. I was ravenous and it looked delicious.

'Please be seated,' Lana said, and The Russian pulled out a chair for me and then sat himself down beside me. The table was nicely set with a navy blue tablecloth and white dinner set. The family didn't say grace like my family always did, but I said my own few words privately. Then the bowls began to fly around the table.

'This is wonderful Lana, thank you. I haven't had a home-cooked meal since I went home after last season.'

'We've checked you out,' Nikki piped up, 'you're an amazing basketball player. You could beat Alex at it.'

'I'd hope so,' Alex said, 'since I play soccer.'

'Thank you,' I said, sheepishly. 'Although this is my last season.'

'That's sad about your injury,' Ana agreed. 'Do you have a degree to fall back on?' I noticed Ana – the eldest daughter – glanced at her parents as she said this ... given she was college age, I suspected there had been some debate about her continuing on to study.

I nodded in the affirmative. 'I'm a qualified journalist. I'm doing some sports reporting at the moment, including reporting the Saints games.'

'Always good to have a qualification behind you that you can fall back on,' James added in the way you'd expect parents to do and with a glance to Ana.

'Yes, that's what my father says,' I added. 'What are you studying, Ana ... I'm guessing you're at college?'

'Law,' she said, 'but I'm only in my first year.'

'That will be very handy, especially for Alex with his contract,' I said.

'If she hurries up and gets enough skills to be useful,' he said, teasing her. 'At the rate Ana's going, my career will be over before graduation.'

'Alex won't be able to afford me, but I'd love to do sports law, particularly basketball contracts,' she threw back at him with a grin.

I felt so at home even though the family was three times the size of my small family unit. Lana asked about my family and James asked about my remaining basketball season. The Russian looked at me with what looked like pride on his face ... like we were boyfriend and girlfriend and he was proud of me. I wondered when we'd officially become that.

I smiled and looked away before I self-combusted with passion and desire, and set the table on fire at the same time. His hand touched my knee under the table and I swear I nearly shot up to the roof. Luckily Tia was holding court at the time and no one noticed. Then she turned her attention back to me.

'Will you marry Alex?' she asked.

Everyone laughed, except Lana.

'Tia, what did I tell you about asking personal questions?' Lana asked her daughter.

'That it's rude and I am not to do it,' Tia said, with a sigh again.

'That is correct. Apologize to Carly please,' Lana said.

'Sorry Carly. But I want to be a flower girl ... if you marry Alex, have you got a little sister or will you need a flower girl?'

'I will need one if I ask your brother to marry me,' I teased.

'But he has to ask you!' she said.

Her mother gave me a smile that said she approved of a strong, independent woman.

'Not anymore,' Ana told her little sister, 'girls can ask anyone we like.'

'But I'll be doing the asking,' The Russian said, going all alpha on me.

'So if Carly asks you, you'd say no?' Ana studied him.

The Russian nodded and I raised an eyebrow in his direction. 'But then I'd ask her right back straight away,' he said. 'And probably do a better job of it.'

'You are such a big head,' I said with a smile, shaking my head at him.

Tia giggled. 'So I can ask a boy to marry me!' She sounded way too excited about it, like she had someone in mind.

'When you are grown up and I've approved of them,' Alex added. 'Speaking of which, Dad tells me you've started seeing someone from College, Ana ... when do I get to meet him?'

I chuckled beside him at his overprotective ways.

Ana smirked at him. 'I think that's Dad's job, Alex, and he's met Tyler.'

'I'm happy for Alex to take over the role,' his father said. 'They might be more worried about the consequences of not looking after my daughters then.'

'There you go,' Alex said, grabbing the serving dish of stroganoff, offering it to me first and then helping himself to seconds. 'What does this Tyler character do?'

'I'm not telling you,' she said. 'I may let you meet him at some point and time. Actually, he was keen for tickets to your next home game ...'

'Ah, well that's easily done,' Alex said.

'Thanks,' Ana grinned at her brother.

'Once I've checked him out and approved him.'

She groaned. 'Did your brother check out Alex, Carly?' she asked me.

'I don't have a brother, but Dad's yet to meet Alex. My dad's a reverend,' I said.

'Lord help us,' James added and I giggled beside him. 'Your father's got his work cut out for him with Alex.'

'Miracles do happen,' I said, and Alex gave me a look that said he was unimpressed. Ha!

'Don't worry Son, I'm really on your side,' James said. 'I'll tell you how I won over your mother's father, and he was a very fearsome Russian politician.'

'My father died before you met him,' Lana said.

'And that's how it's done,' James said and we all laughed. Lana shook her head at him. I could see where The Russian's dry humor came from.

'Nikki's just broken up with her boyfriend,' Tia said.

We all turned to look at Nikki who then got a bit teary-eyed. I heard The Russian groan ... I don't think he was comfortable with tears.

'Shoosh Tia,' Nikki snapped at her.

'Don't worry, Nikki,' The Russian said. 'Whoever he was, he's clearly a loser with no taste, and you were too good for him.'

She gave her brother a grateful smile.

'Hear, hear,' her Dad agreed.

'Anyway, you're too young at fourteen to have a serious boyfriend, Nikki,' her mother said.

'How old were you when you got your first boyfriend, Carly?' Nikki asked me, as she wiped her eyes.

'I'm the wrong one to ask,' I said. 'Boys were scared to ask me out because my dad was the reverend; you know, he might send them to hell or something, so no one asked me out for years and years.'

Tia lightened the mood that she had previously darkened.

'Want to play *Twister* after dinner, Carly?' she asked, putting the spotlight back on herself.

Oh yes I did, but a private game only with The Russian.

I shook my head. 'I have to warn you Tia, I am very, very good at *Twister* because I am hugely tall. My legs stretch easily from the green dots to the pink dots and I can still reach the blue dot at the far end with my hand while stretched out.'

Tia took this in, biting her lip as she thought.

'Are you any good at *Monopoly*?' she asked.

'Carly has to go straight home after dinner unfortunately, because her handsome date has to be at training at six in the morning,' The Russian told his little sister. 'But next time we come over, I'll find out what she's not good at and let you know,' he said with a wink in her direction. She clumsily returned his wink – so cute.

I was in a mixed state of euphoria ... there was going to be a next time, but probably not a bed session with The Russian that night ... man, my hand was going to drop off if I had to perform any more functions on myself while picturing Alex in the act. I wasn't even at deep kiss stage with him yet – what would it take to get laid by The Russian, even an intimate kiss, for crying in a bucket?

*****

On the way back to The Russian's place, where I had left my car, The Russian looked over at me and smiled.

'Well you were a hit,' he said. 'Mom really likes you.'

'That's kind of her,' I said, 'I really liked your family, too. Thank you for taking me to meet them.'

'She'll give me a hard time now about making sure I follow you up and do the right thing, and she'll be giving me all the reasons I should be seeing you or someone like you ...' he said, thinking out loud.

I was a bit taken aback. So, was this a good thing or a bad thing? Did he want to be encouraged to see me or was that going to be a pain in the butt?

'You sound like someone your mother likes wouldn't be someone you would want to date,' I said, after a few moments.

He glanced at me with a look of surprise as if he hadn't meant to say all that out loud.

The Russian turned his eyes back to the road. 'I just meant that ... um, she's only met a couple of my female friends over the years and she never liked my ex-girlfriend.'

'Leesa?' I asked.

'Yeah. She didn't like her from day one when Leesa and I met at school ... always said she was a spoilt troublemaker, and Mom was right, but still ... I just meant that she's got a look at you and is probably breathing a huge sigh of relief.'

'Oh well, she may change her mind when she gets to know me better,' I said.

The Russian glanced over, gave me a frown and looked away again.

'Why would you say that? Are you hiding something?' he asked.

'No,' I laughed. 'I was just kidding. What would I be hiding?' I think I had trodden on very dangerous ground there, I could almost feel The Russian bristling beside me. I wished I had known something about The Russian to be a bit forewarned ... no one seemed to know him. Sasha could tell me how dry his sense of humor was and how all the office girls liked him, but she didn't know a thing about The Russian in love other than he and Leesa had seemed so unsuited ... had he been hurt to the point of no return? Did he treat women well? All I knew was what I had read about his ex-girlfriend and her high profile party life which hadn't told me much except he had been part of it or had tolerated it.

I looked over at him as he seemed to be thinking about my comments and after a few minutes, he pulled himself out of whatever dark thoughts he was having. He looked at me and smiled.

'Sorry, I guess you could call me gun-shy. I've had years and years of relationship lies and games ... I'm not up for it anymore, I'm trained to be suspicious. If we, you know, get serious ... do you believe in monogamy?'

I turned to look at him front on. Did I give some indication that I slept around?

'Are you seriously asking me this?'

'Sorry,' he said. He ran a hand over his face. For a normally laid back guy, the Russian was sweating it.

'If you need to hear it, then yes, I am a one-man woman. Good grief, just because you sporting guys tart around and get offered plenty of skirt, don't assume the sporting women sleep around as well.'

Wow, how did this conversation go so off track?

We pulled into his street and he breathed out a sigh of frustration. I could almost hear his brain ticking, trying to work out how he had gotten himself into this situation and how to get himself out of it.

I was also a bit cranky by then; he'd ruined a good night with silly comments. I know he didn't know me that well, but from my upbringing, from our talks, from my actions towards him, did he really think I was the flirty, sleep around type? That I was just hanging with him for a quick roll in the sack? And was it so bad that his mother liked me, or might give him a hard time to follow me up? How insulting.

'Carly ...' he started, after pulling his car past my parked car on the curbside, and into his driveway.

I cut him off. 'Hey, thanks again for taking me to meet your family, and I hope your mother doesn't give you too much of a *hard time* about having to like me,' I said, quoting him back. I opened the door and was out before he had his seatbelt off.

For a big guy who professes to be slow, he moved pretty quickly, intercepting me before I got to the back of his car. He grabbed my hand and pulled me to him.

'Hey, I've insulted you somewhere along the line there and I didn't mean to ...' he said, looking down on me.

I shook my head. 'It's all good, really. Anyway, you've got training early, so thanks again.' I pulled away. 'We'll talk soon, yeah?'

Men! I'm not interested in being a prospect just because I'm different from Leesa; and do I look like I'm a charity case that is looking for a date? Well, I am, but I'm not desperate, I've got my stalkers.

He walked down the driveway following me, only a few inches behind me; he said my name again and was clearly uncomfortable with handling an emotional female. 'Carly, stop, please.'

I turned around to face him.

'About training, I just said that so we could leave after dinner and not have to stay all night. I have got training early, but that doesn't mean you have to rush off,' he said. 'Come up for a while.'

I've always had too much pride, and now I was cutting off my own nose to spite my face. Since the day I had met The Russian, I'd been dreaming of getting closer to him, tasting those lips. Now, I just wanted to smack him – he really was an insensitive ass.

'No, I've got an early start too. Another time, huh?' I said, throwing the comment over my shoulder as I continued my walk to my car. But as long as my strides were, The Russian's were longer and he beat me there, opening my car door for me. I lowered myself into the front seat, started the engine and the sexy beast he was, lowered himself down to squat next to me in the open car doorway.

'Brooker, I'm a bit rusty at dating,' he said, 'I'd been with my last girlfriend since school, and anyone since has just been ... well, short-lived by mutual agreement. You'll have to cut me some slack,' he said, with the hint of a smile. He looked divine squatting there in front of me, his dark eyes scanning my face, his muscular arm resting on the steering wheel.

I cocked my head to the side and studied him. 'I thought you were the expert on women, having been raised with four at home,' I said, tongue in cheek.

'Apparently I've still got a few things to learn,' he said, raising an eyebrow. 'I want to see you again,' he continued.

'We've got a bye this weekend, will you come over Friday night and let me cook for you?'

'Can you cook?' I asked, lightening the moment.

'Can I cook!' he scoffed and then reached for his phone. 'Can I get Josh's number before you go?' he referred to my excellent cook of a housemate.

I laughed.

'I'll make it up to you, okay?'

'There's nothing to make up, we're all good,' I said. 'Friday night.'

'Friday night,' he repeated, and gave me a smile. He rose and leaned in long enough to brush my lips with his and then he pulled away and closed the car door. He stood back as I drove off.

Served me right for being an idiot. Now I was going home alone, horny, desperately wanting The Russian and it was all my own fault for being so high and mighty! Just kill me now.

Chapter 13

I got the job. I got the J-O-B! I had made an idiot of myself on the phone when Karen – the Head of TV Production – had called me herself to tell me. I gave an almighty cheer, and then I got off the phone and did some more high leaps and cheering. Josh raced out of his room, pulling a T-shirt over his chest as he dressed for work.

'What? What's happened?' he asked, scanning the room for clues.

'I got the commentating cable TV job,' I said, still jumping.

He gave a loud whoop and raced over to hug me. We jumped around in a hug ... he was so supportive of me.

'When do you start?' he asked.

'Two weeks, so I've got to go in and give *The Sports Daily* notice today. My first commentary game will be here when my Suns play the Minnesota Leopards. I can't believe it,' I said, stopping my jumping to get some air into my lungs.

'Everything is working out as it should,' Josh said. 'It's a new start.'

'It is, my next chapter,' I agreed. 'Thanks for being happy for me.'

'Of course, we have to celebrate in style!' he said, planning a gathering already. I swear he loved a get-together. Josh squeezed my arm and went to finish getting ready for work.

I looked skyward to give thanks. I thought finishing playing was going to be the end of me ... that I'd be lost in the world. It was all I had known for almost a decade and everything I had ever worked for. Now I had this opportunity to keep using my skills but in commentary and to still be associated with the game I love. I was overwhelmed with joy. I wanted to call The Russian and tell him but a quick glance at the clock told me it was not yet eight a.m.; I'd leave it an hour or so and catch him at work. I made a cup of tea and plonked myself on the couch; I'd call Mom and Dad, and then I'd text Aimee and Steffi, and my coach, and Serge, who had all asked me to let them know. Then I would get dressed and go into *The Sports Daily* and do the deed!

I was now a cable TV sports commentator; *Carly Brooker for Sports Network One*, I said aloud, practicing using the call sign. I'm such a dick, but it sounded so cool.

****

Half an hour later Josh had left for work and I had made all my calls and texts, plus got heaps of good wishes, bless them all. I was dressed ready to drop into *The Sports Daily* even though I wasn't rostered to work today, but I needed to give notice right away to start at Network One in two weeks' time. I had one major thing to do before I left the house and it was all I could think about.

I moved onto the balcony, took a deep breath, and finding The Russian's number in my phone, dialed it. I breathed in, my heart rate always went through the roof at all points of contact with him and after our frosty departure, I really wanted to smooth things over. It rang three times and I debated if I should hang up ... maybe he was in a meeting and was frowning at his phone and my name on his screen; maybe after our last talk he thought it was all too hard; maybe he was with someone ... *don't go there, that's stupid, it is nine in the morning after all.*

Suddenly a male voice answered and it wasn't The Russian.

'Oh, hello,' I said, surprised. 'It's Carly here, I was looking for The Russian please?'

'Hi Carly,' a very smooth voice said. 'It's Eddie here, The Russian's business partner.'

'Hi Eddie, we didn't get to meet when I was in the office the other day,' I said. 'You were clearly out working while The Russian was entertaining.'

He laughed. 'And that's the story of my life,' he agreed. 'Good news that you can play the big end of season game, pleased for you.'

'Thanks Eddie,' I said, surprised he knew. 'It's a much nicer way to go out than just finishing abruptly mid-season. Anyway, sorry to bother you, I'm guessing The Russian is missing in action?'

'He's in with the coach,' Eddie said. 'Probably getting dropped,' he teased.

I laughed, knowing full well that The Russian was one of their A-list players and they had just re-signed him for three years.

'But I'll get him to call you when he surfaces,' he said.

'Thanks, that would be great. See you at the game sometime.'

'For sure,' he said.

I hung up and realized I would only be reporting at one more Saints' games now before I started my new job. But if the Saints games were on different days to my basketball games, I could go and actually sit in the grandstand and watch with the other wives and girlfriends, if I was officially The Russian's girlfriend. I could be a WAG and The Russian could be a HAB ... husband and boyfriend, well at least at my final game. I didn't know if HAB was actually a term, I'd have to research that.

I grabbed my bag, locked up my apartment and headed to my car. I just slipped in behind the wheel when my phone rang – The Russian!

'Hey there,' I answered, on top of the world, and now The Russian was calling. 'Did the coach give you homework?'

'Brooker,' he said, in his lovely baritone voice, a sound of a laugh in his tone. 'He wanted to congratulate me on a great season,' he teased.

'Of course he did,' I said.

'Well you saw right through that, I forgot you were an athlete,' he teased. 'Okay, he just wanted to point out areas I could improve in ... coaches are never happy, are they?' he sighed.

'Never,' I agreed. 'Even after winning our grand final, Coach made us watch the game and work on our weaknesses!'

'Tell me about it,' he agreed. 'So how are you, beautiful?' he asked. *Beautiful. I would ride on that one for hours. Sigh.*

'I am so good I could explode. I got the job!'

'Brooker, you legend!' The Russian exclaimed. He sounded genuinely excited for me. 'I didn't doubt it for a moment, so when's your first broadcast?'

'In two weeks' time, when the Suns take on the Minnesota Leopards, here.'

'That's brilliant. Having your own team for the first game will help ease you into it too since you know all their moves and their names,' he said.

'True, probably why they picked it,' I said. 'I hadn't stopped to think about that.'

'I'd better get some good champagne for Friday night then, so we can celebrate,' The Russian said. He was adorable.

'Speaking of which, what can I bring?' I asked.

'How about dinner?' he said, then laughed. 'Just joking. Just bring you, I've got it sorted. About seven-thirty?'

'Done. See you then and thanks for calling back.'

'Really pleased for you, Brooker, this is the beginning of something big,' he said.

Didn't I know it, big was all around me at the moment!

Chapter 14

I never thought Friday night would come ... seriously, the longest Thursday of my life and Friday daytime dragged on ... what the ...? I was dreaming, hoping, desperately praying that The Russian would be my first really serious relationship – maybe my last, if you get the drift. But, no matter how mature, clever, independent and successful you might think you are at laying out your future, you are never too old for a major serve from your parents, and they timed that right before my date.

In fairness, Dad was a gentle soul, not one of those fire and brimstone type reverends; Mom was the tough one, but I guess she'd had a few hard knocks in life. Dad sort of fell into the religious life ... he was working as a counselor in a hospital and often gave patients comfort or helped their families. After a while he wanted to do more than work with the sick and dying, he wanted to work in the community. So he decided to combine his faith with a job where he could help people every day.

Mom was the church warden at the first parish that Dad got assigned to. Her job meant that she organized pretty much everything from keeping order in the church to organizing the maintenance of the grounds. It wasn't long before she was organizing Dad, and they've been together ever since. They really were perfect for each other; they just fitted together.

What I most loved about Mom was that she told it to me straight, I could always count on her for that. Dad on the other hand was so supportive which was great, but sometimes you just want someone who says 'go for it' or 'dumb idea'. You know what I mean?

Anyway, I was in the bathroom blow-drying my hair for said big date when my phone rang. I didn't hear it at first, and only just answered in time to find Mom on the line. She got stuck into me because it had been several months since I had come home for dinner, and really, as she pointed out, they were only a couple of hours away by car. I could even stay the night if I wanted to – no thank you, I loved my folks but that ship had sailed, besides I liked driving. Then like good cop, bad cop, Dad got on the phone and did the soft sell – how much they were missing me and how the family was important. Sigh, of course they were right. Then came the crunch ... they wanted to meet The Russian; Mom had seen him in the media, which meant her nosy neighbor had told them all about it and she hated to hear anything about her daughter second-hand, which I understood.

I assured them I would definitely be coming home for dinner, but if they could just give me a couple of weeks to wind up my old job and settle into my new one – read between the lines, settle into Alex – I'd definitely sort something out and be home to tell them all about it. That pacified them for the moment and I got them off the phone.

I did the final check – no lipstick on my teeth, my butt didn't look big, no stray hairs, perfume not overbearing – good to go. I wished Josh a good night and he asked me if I had a condom. I gave him a look that initially said *'that's the man's job'* and ended with *'do you think I should take one?'*

I headed off, keen to check out The Russian's place inside since I had only seen the exterior – it was one of four white condominiums scaling down the hill on the beach front, each condo boasting a huge balcony that faced the ocean and in touching distance of the beach. When I had dropped in the other day after work so he could drive us to his parents, I hadn't gotten the tour; The Russian had been outside waiting for me. It must've been an amazing view, Sasha had mentioned Lucas lived in the same area.

I was big on punctuality and it was just nearing seven-thirty when I drove into his street. I brought some divine creamy brie and crackers, plus liquor dark chocolates; I figured if the main course was a disaster, at least we had a starter and dessert.

My stomach was churning with excitement and nerves, and maybe desire too; hard to tell with that much churning going on. And, I was going to work really hard at not doing anything that caused tension between us like the other night. I wanted the night to end on a high.

I stopped at the security gate – it was a gated community – and the guy on the gate checked me off the list. He welcomed me and told me The Russian's place was the second condo. I thanked him and drove on. Each of the condos had a private entrance, a level of their own –seriously! The Russian was pretty gracious to rave about my place compared to where he was living. I parked on the street outside and, juggling the chocolates, cheese and crackers, I made my way to the front door, adjusting my clothes one final time. Deep breath. As I approached I heard voices; I looked behind, but I was alone. I moved closer and the door to The Russian's condo was ajar and the voices were coming from inside. I was just about to knock when I heard the female raise her voice. I stopped in my tracks. Had he a girl in there? I didn't know what to do now. I bit my lip, standing on the doorstep like a groupie.

'I came back to see you,' I heard her say.

'I didn't ask you to come back to see me,' The Russian sighed. 'We're over. That's it ... you go and live your life, I'll live mine. Good luck and all that.'

It was Leesa; his ex-girlfriend was there on my date night. Fuck, fuck, fuck it. All my dreams for the night were just fading in front of my eyes.

'I didn't mean to call it off,' she said, 'I just thought we needed time out.'

'And you were right,' The Russian said. 'The first time, the second time and the subsequent ten times you called it off.'

'So what is this? Payback? Now you're calling it off?' she demanded, with a raised voice.

'You, me, whatever. Leesa, it's over. We gave it a fair go but we're different people, it's amazing we've lasted this long.'

'We're not that different. We both love sex and partying, and we have a brilliant time together. '

I pulled the knife out of my heart at the thought that they loved having sex together, and took in a small breath. I was frozen to the spot.

The Russian's voice remained calm, but I could tell he'd had enough, his sentences were becoming clipped.

'I don't like partying. You love fucking partying, that's why you can't take my lifestyle. In fact, I don't know anything we have in common.'

'Why do we have to stay here though?' she whined.

'Because I've got a three-year contract that's just been renewed – a huge fucking contract ... this is my career, this is what I do, what I want to do,' he said, voice raised.

'Doesn't mean you have to stay home all the time.'

'You don't get it. I'm in training, I'm playing professional soccer. This is my career.' Again his voice was raised and filled with disbelief.

'It's frigging boring. You don't need to work, you know Daddy said he'd give us ...'

'Leesa!'

'Well he will, we could travel and party,' she whined.

'I want to play professional soccer. You want to party. Go party. Go screw around every night like you were doing anyway. You're free to do whatever you like.'

'So, are you serious with this bitch?'

My eyes narrowed.

'Don't speak about Carly like that, and yes, I'm serious about her. Unlike you, she gets the need to train and perform, we have things in common ... and she'll be here in a minute, so time you headed off. Thanks for dropping in.'

'So a sweaty athlete turns you on now?'

'A champion,' The Russian corrected her.

I didn't hear anything for a moment, but she must have looked upset because The Russian spoke again in a softer voice.

'I don't mean to hurt you, Leesa, but we've flogged this horse. There are so many more men out there better suited to you than me, you'll know that the minute you find one that you click with, and you'll wonder why you wasted so much time with me,' he said.

'Because I love you,' she said.

'Love or habit?' he asked.

I heard her scoff. I took another breath; I'm sure I had forgotten to breathe given the ache in my chest. I loved what The Russian had said about me but I imagined the pain of being in Leesa's shoes and having those words spoken to her about some other woman. I would just die.

I heard her voice again, this time raised and a little hysterical. 'You don't even give a fuck about ... forget it, you're weak, you're just a fucking weak asshole,' she was yelling now.

'Fine, happy you've said that? Time you left,' The Russian said.

'I'm really pleased I slept with Jason, because you're a loser,' she continued.

I heard a loud thump, like The Russian had punched the wall, and she screamed.

I raced in – Lord knows why, you would think I would run the other way, but I couldn't leave her alone in there if he had hit her. I'm sure he wouldn't have hit her. Would he hit her?

Then I saw her slap him hard across the face; The Russian was a big man but that even knocked him back with shock more than impact. His face was red with the imprint of her hand, and then he saw me.

'Carly,' he said, turning to face me, his eyes wide. Behind him was a huge hole in the plaster wall. So that was what he had thumped.

'So this is Carly,' Leesa said, taking me in. 'Nice to meet you, I'm Leesa. I'm sure you've heard a lot about me,' she said, smiling.

'No,' I said, 'I haven't. Are you okay?' She had a bruised cheek and a large scratch down the left side of her face; it was red and raw and recent. But surely The Russian hadn't been part of that, had he?

I saw The Russian look at me with shock, then to the wall and to Leesa as he put it all together.

'I didn't do that to her, you can't seriously think I'd hit a woman?' he said, his voice hurt. 'Tell her, Leesa.'

Leesa just gave him a smirk and then turned to look me over.

'Tell her,' The Russian thundered, well out of patience. I stood there with my cheese and chocolates, caught between the two of them, my romantic night gone for good.

She rolled her eyes. 'Fine, he didn't do it, but he could go after whoever did it,' she said, and turned to face him again. 'You're a fucking pussy.'

His lips thinned, his eyes narrowed and I saw how she really pushed his buttons.

'If you want to tart around and party with every guy who has a joint to offer you, then this is what's going to happen. Get daddy to rescue you.' He hissed.

Oh yeah, we're really going to be able to get tonight back on track after this. I started to move back towards the door and The Russian ran his hands over his face. In the background,

I could see the ocean through the large glass doors of his balcony, and a table set for two with champagne glasses.

'Don't go,' he said, to me. 'Leesa was just leaving.'

' I'm not going anywhere yet, we haven't finished talking,' she said, and then glanced in my direction. 'But you can leave anytime you like.'

'Carly's not leaving,' The Russian said through clenched teeth.

'Neither am I.' She sat down on a chair in his lounge room and kicking off her shoes, she wrapped her legs around her. 'We've been together since high school, we're not just throwing it away on some whim.'

I held up my hand to get their attention. 'I'm just going to leave you to it,' I said, gazing at the hole he had made in the wall and the mad woman in front of him. I turned and headed out the door, hearing his deep voice call me back. I got to my car, unlocked it, and throwing my offerings onto the passenger's seat, I sped away. When I got far enough away I started to cry.

I knew he was too good to be true. I believed he hadn't hurt her and wouldn't, plus she confirmed that, but he had put a hole in the wall. Was he capable of more? But she ruined our night, our lovely romantic night.

I didn't go home; Josh and Spencer were having a night together. I rang Aimee and luckily she was home for the night and told me to come straight over. I took my cheese and chocolates to her place, where she promised to have a good red open and breathing when I arrived. The disappointment overwhelmed me. I had been waiting for that night since dinner at his family's house, and now, I had entered someone's soap drama.

I took a deep breath. I'm okay, I'm going to be okay. Thank God for my new job. I would just throw myself into that, I'd be fine, in fact I was so excited about it that I was going to be more than fine. I might get a cat for company. Yep, that was my future sewn up.

Chapter 15

Thank God for Aimee and her box of tissues. She was such a sensitive soul that she used as many as I did while I told her the story. Luckily her flatmate was out to dinner, so we sat on her sofa – Aimee in her pajamas, me dressed up to see The Russian – and I told her the whole miserable story. She reached over to top up my wine glass and I waved her off, reaching instead for some of that great brie I had bought to eat with The Russian.

'I have to drive,' I said, explaining my lack of hitting the bottle.

'You can crash here,' she offered.

'Thanks Aim, but I'll go home, wash my make-up off, crawl into bed with my Kindle and just pretend it didn't happen.

'It doesn't mean it is over,' she said. 'He said some lovely things about you, and defended you to her ... you just have to put it all in perspective.'

'I know, you're right, but if he puts a hole through the wall every time he gets angry or that ex keeps hanging around trying to persuade him to get back together, I don't know if I want the drama ... you should have seen her, she was beautiful.'

'So are you,' Aimee said, loyally. 'The Russian said it was over with her, so maybe just give him some time and let him move her on for good.'

'I haven't given up on him,' I said, 'I'm just disappointed, pissed off, flat ... tonight was our night. Why can't I just have a normal relationship? How hard is it to find an available guy who does normal things like dating without the ex dropping in?' I sighed.

'Honey, tell me about it. Do you see a boyfriend here?' she said.

*****

When I pulled into my driveway just after ten-thirty, my breath hitched; The Russian's silver Merc was there, parked in my car spot. *What a cheek!*

I parked him in and with a glance upstairs, I could see the living room lights were on so I guessed Josh and Spencer were entertaining him. I quickly checked my face to ensure there were no tear tracks or smudged mascara, did a quick compact powder improvement job and made my way upstairs. As I opened the door all three men turned to look at me; they were on the sofa, watching soccer, a beer in their hands. The Russian looked like a lion sitting next to two meerkats.

Josh and Spencer rose and I gave Spencer a quick kiss hello; I hadn't seen him for a few weeks.

'Well we're exhausted, better turn in,' Josh said, with a

raised eyebrow and a look in my direction that said 'good luck'.

'Thanks for the beer and company,' The Russian said.

'Our pleasure,' Spencer assured him as he followed Josh, and the room was suddenly empty ... just The Russian and me.

He walked towards me as I put my handbag down on the end of the kitchen island, and moving into my space, he put his hands in his pockets and we looked at each other. I wanted to say something; I just hadn't had time to prepare what my next conversation with him was going to be. My thoughts jumbled with a thousand words: *Did he hit back? Has he ever hit her? Does he want her back? Where do we fit in? Is there a 'we'? Should I get a cat and forget about men forever? Why the hell does he have to be so frigging gorgeous? Does he have to fill out those jeans and black t-shirt so damn well?*

He was going through the same dilemma; The Russian held my gaze and ran his tongue along his bottom lip as he thought. He put his hands out and reached for me. I must have flinched, I didn't realize I did, but the expression on his face said he was hurt and a bit worried.

'I won't hurt you,' he said, and I let him pull me into him. I looked up at him. 'I know that.'

'Do you? I think you're a little scared of me now,' he said. 'I'm sorry you were caught up in that.' His presence was overwhelming but I wasn't scared of him, I was scared of how I felt about him and what was going to happen next.

'Can we talk about it?' I said.

'Of course,' he said, his chest rose and fell heavily as if he knew a discussion was inevitable. But then we didn't talk; we just looked at each other. My hands sat on his hips and he played with my neck and rubbed my back. Neither of us spoke. He raised a hand to cup my cheek, his other hand threaded into my hair at the back of my neck. He leaned down and his lips touched mine. It was so slow, so sublime that if I hadn't been pressing against him, I would have slid down to the ground and melted. I felt something else pressing against me; his desire was obvious. Our lips parted and our kisses got deeper; my heart was beating so loudly I'm surprised Josh didn't yell out to keep the noise down.

Then The Russian slowly pulled away, took a deep breath and opened his eyes. 'You want to talk?'

'About what?' I said, and The Russian smiled.

I nodded. 'I do.'

'I want to go back to my place,' he said, 'with you. We can talk then if you like.'

I glanced at the clock – it was nearing eleven p.m.

'I know it's late,' he said, following my gaze. 'But I haven't got training tomorrow morning because of our bye, and if you're free?'

'I'm free,' I said, probably a bit too quickly. Way uncool me.

'I want to show you something.'

I narrowed my eyes.

'Not that,' he said, and rolled his eyes. 'Yeah, well maybe that,' he countered. 'Tomorrow, I want to show you a sunrise over the beach ... I planned it.'

I looked at him with surprise. The Russian continued to surprise me – who would have thought he'd be so romantic?

He also assumed we'd be staying the night together ... I think that was a good thing.

'And then,' he continued, 'I thought maybe we could go to the gym and do a workout together ...'

'Love to,' I said. I know that probably sounds weird but I love starting the day with a workout; my body buzzes all day and my mind is sharp yet relaxed. To workout with The Russian was even better ... watching him flex was the most amazing foreplay.

'Then ...' I took over, 'we could come back for an ocean swim to finish it off.'

'Perfect. Then do brunch,' The Russian concluded. 'There's a great place beachside. What do you think?'

'I think that sounds perfect,' I agreed. 'I've parked you in since you took my spot,' I said, with attitude.

'I'm surprised you haven't organized me a parking space and entry key yet,' he teased. 'We'll swap cars and I'll drop you back tomorrow. Grab some gear.'

I nodded and raced into the room to throw my gym gear, swimsuit and a cafe outfit into a small bag. I grabbed my traveling toiletries bag – the spare set I kept permanently packed and updated for our away games – and headed back into the living room. The Russian looked impressed.

'That was quick,' he said.

'I travel light and I wasn't kidding when I said I was a natural beauty,' I said, with a shrug.

'That you are,' he agreed, and I gave him a 'thanks for the compliment' grin.

'At away games I always shared a room with Steffi because she took forever to get ready. It worked well, I was done in about ten minutes and she could take over the bathroom for the rest of the time until we were needed downstairs.'

'Lucas is the same,' The Russian joked about the Saints' captain. 'I've had to share with him a few times on away trips. Try getting in front of that mirror.' He shook his head.

I laughed at the thought of the two beautiful Saints men fighting for bathroom space.

The Russian grabbed my bag and opened the door as I ran around turning off the lights. I grabbed my handbag and keys to swap cars and we headed downstairs. My night was back, my romance was back on track and life was brilliant again. I offered a prayer of thanks to God, the universe and the Patron Saint of Lovers ... who was that?

Chapter 16

On entering The Russian's house again, I held my breath. I sort of expected Leesa to be back, but the place was quiet. The only evidence of the former drama was a hole in the plasterboard wall. The Russian looked a bit sheepish as he saw me looking at it.

'Here's the plan,' he said. He was so like me, I always had a plan.

'Let's go for a beach walk and do our talking there, then come back here and crash for the night. First light is at quarter-to-seven, sunrise at just after seven o'clock ...' he stopped, catching my expression.

'I'm impressed,' I said.

'I hope so. I've got some other impressive things to show you too, if you can be any more impressed by me,' he teased.

'Does seem impossible,' I agreed.

He put my bag down in one of the bedrooms ... I didn't know if it was his, *hmm, interesting*, and he grabbed the keys and then my hand. We went out through the balcony glass doors and he locked them.

He kicked his shoes off and suggested I did the same; we

left them near the door. I turned and breathed in the salt air and the view. Even at night by moonlight it was stunning; I could only imagine what it was like to live there when you could see it all the time. We took the stairs down the side of his condo and within a minute were on the beach. There were people around even at that hour and we made our way to the harder sand on the water's edge and began to walk. It was the most magic of settings. The moon lit the water, it was quiet and balmy and The Russian took my hand. It was so private – most people on the beach wanted their own space so no one was there to witness us, ask for autographs or get photos. *Magic.*

He cleared his throat. 'I don't know what you want to hear ... I've never hit a woman and I never will, ever. Leesa just knows how to rile me.'

'But why did you stay together this long if it was so wrong?'

The Russian sighed and looked out to sea, as we continued to walk along the beach.

'I know this will probably sound stupid, but I guess we didn't know how to leave,' he said, with a shrug. 'We were together from our school days and I knew it wasn't a great relationship, but we had invested so much time, it seemed futile to throw it away – like it just should work or it once did, so let's force it,' he tried to explain it. 'But once I got contracted and couldn't give her the time she wanted, things got worse. It's one of the reasons I signed with the Saints.'

'To move here? To get away from her?' I asked.

'More or less. It was running away, or running home – my family moved here when I started middle school ...

Dad got a transfer here. That's how I met Leesa because her father kept a house here, he wanted Leesa schooled away from the city lights. As soon as we graduated, she was out of here. When I came back to play for the Saints, I knew Leesa wouldn't want to come back, she wanted the Hollywood lifestyle. She needs to be in the party scene and I hate that scene.'

I nodded, not saying anything in case he stopped talking. I'd never heard him say so much.

'Did you want to ask me anything?' he said.

I bit my lip, thinking. I wanted to ask him a thousand questions but I wanted the night to be about us too, what was left of it. 'Do you want to get back with her?'

'Never.'

I loved that word, it was so 'forever'. His wary eyes watched me as I prepared my next question.

'Do you want some time out to ... you know ... play the field, have a break from relationships, just have some fun? Because I'm not interested in a fling but I'll understand if you need to do that.' I stopped breathing while I waited for his answer.

He shook his head. 'I've played the field during the times we've been off and there's been a lot of times. The ex has been playing the field on me for years. I hate that; I won't live with that kind of relationship again.'

Just what I wanted to hear, my stomach settled down again. The Russian was ticking all my boxes, I was getting the security I needed to think we had a chance.

Then he brought it home beautifully.

'I wish you and I had met earlier, years ago,' he said, and

my heart went straight to my throat. I swallowed, holding back tears. 'I know it's really early days, but we get each other and what we need to do.' He turned around, spinning me under his arm like a dance move and put his arm around my shoulder as we walked back in the moonlight towards his place.

I nodded. 'The partner of an athlete is not an easy role.'

'But if the partners aren't competing or jealous it can be great,' he said. 'I've seen it around the club, like Lucas and Mia. She's a physical therapist, she loves the game, loves him, gets what he has to do and he needs her. So far, you seem calm ... no tantrums, no demands, you even make me want to work harder at being better.'

I smiled up at him, flattered he would say that. I felt the same; in fact, I was hoping my last game was going to be super impressive if The Russian was going to be watching me from one of the ten seats he had bought at the auction.

'What about Nik and Sasha?' I asked about our mutual friends, curiosity getting the better of me.

'They're solid, but different. They're both ambitious but not competing, so they help each other. Nik needs security and Sasha has that in buckets. Not sure about Tomás and Alice though.'

'Why?' I asked, even though I'd only met Alice once.

The Russian shrugged. 'Just a feeling they won't make it.'

I smiled at him and gave him a poke.

'What?' he grinned at me.

'Sasha said you loved to be amongst the girl gossip.'

'Hard not to be,' he rolled his eyes. 'Right next door to my office is Kay, Sasha and Alice; I go home to visit and

Dad and I are outnumbered as you know. If you can't beat them – metaphorically speaking,' he added quickly, 'might as well join them.'

'Hmm, that so?' I studied him. 'So what do you think about that potential new couple ... The Russian and that gorgeous Suns' player he's met, Carly Brooker?' I asked, tongue-in-cheek.

'Well,' he said, and gave a long sigh. 'Luckiest girl alive, I'd say.'

I laughed and poked his muscled chest again and he grabbed my hand and kissed it.

'Careful, Brooker. Don't work me up,' he teased. He kissed the top of my head and tucked me under his arm. His condo was close now and our beach walk was going to be over in moments. He must have thought the same thing and suddenly got very serious.

'The thing is, Brooker I want you to have all the success in the world, because like you, when I finish my contract – and I've got a few more years to go yet, knock on wood – I'm going to be trying to stay in the game somehow ... in sport administration, coaching or business. It's my life. So this existence, these hours and the routine, they are not a passing phase,' he said.

'Exactly, it's our passion; it's what I want to stay involved in, I've worked hard at it, so have you.'

We arrived back at his place and headed up the stairs. He unlocked the sliding glass door, we left our shoes outside still and entered. The Russian locked the door behind us and turned to me.

'Are we good?' he asked.

'I have one more question,' I said, trying to look as serious as I could.

'Okay, shoot,' he said, a frown appearing on his handsome face.

'What did you make for dinner?'

He grinned. 'The best lasagne you have *never* tasted. It was superb. Still in the fridge ... really, you would have been impressed.'

'Your mom made it didn't she?' I asked, narrowing my eyes at him.

'Fine, yes she did.'

I laughed.

'So, are we good now?'

'We're good,' I agreed. He smiled and looked relaxed for the first time that night. He leaned his forehead against mine and we breathed each other in, and then I yelped as my feet disappeared from underneath me and he swept me up.

*****

I wrapped my arms around his neck as he carried me into the main bedroom and wow, The Russian was an alpha in every sense of the word – it was a room for a king: a huge king bed, a huge room, ocean views, a huge ensuite that I could see through the door and a walk-in-closet that you could live in.

The Russian placed me beside the bed, standing me in front of him, but he didn't let me go. He reached to beside the bed where he hit a button and the bedroom blind went down. Then he looked at me again – his dark eyes scanning my face.

'We don't have to do this if you're not ready.'

'I'm ready,' I said. 'Are you?'

He made a scoffing sound as he pressed against me, his body was so hard – in fact, everything about him was hard except for the look in his eyes. His hands went down to my legs and he lifted the skirt of my dress, slowly pulling it up and over my head. I stood in front of him with a pale cream lace and satin lingerie set on. I had bought it for that night and I had started thinking I had lost the chance to show it off. I was pretty sure The Russian appreciated it; he made this growling sort of sound and his hands ran down my body; I broke out in tingles all over.

He stopped long enough to pull his T-shirt off over his head and then it was my turn to be tongue-tied. Actually, my tongue just wanted to trace that six-pack. I ran my fingers along his arms, feeling his muscles, his built arms. He undid his belt and slipped his jeans down and off. He stood tanned and muscled, in a white pair of fitted boxers. I wish I could have gotten a photo for the nights I was alone.

'You okay?' he asked.

I nodded with just the hint of impatience and The Russian read that too – take me right now! He took both of my hands in his and then watching me, he slowly lowered me to the bed and followed, holding his own weight above me with those magnificent arms.

Then he began a slow exploration of my body, touching, kissing and trailing his hands over my skin.

'Russian' I groaned.

'Mm?'

'So good.'

He chuckled. 'Beautiful, you're beautiful, Brooker,' he said, moving his gaze from my body to my eyes and back. Then he returned to my lips and began to kiss me slowly; I'd never thought I could orgasm from kissing but holy hell, with the kiss and his rock-hard desire pressing against me through the fabric of our underwear, I was dangerously close. Then his kisses moved down my body and my breathing took on a life of its own. My hands began to do their own exploring and I felt him shiver from my touch; I loved having that power over this huge hunk of a man.

I swear I was so close I was going to come before he even got me naked, but that thought went out the window as he began to remove my lingerie. My stomach lurched; this was so intimate and he was working his way down my body. I wasn't really ready for him to go down there, I just wanted vanilla to begin with, very, very vanilla ... kissing, missionary, hands only, that sort of thing. I know that sounds silly but the tongue below is so ... well not in your face.

'Russian?' I said, trying to grab him and pull him back up by his impressive arms. I was so tightly wound and I didn't want to be a tease, but could we go slower, just a bit slower or was I being stupid or childish?

'Russian!'

He stopped, looked up and crawled back up me, his still underwear-encased body holding pride of place alongside the taut arms that held his body over me.

'What? What's wrong?'

'I want you to come inside me ... now,' I stuttered. 'I'm not ready for ...' He looked a little confused. I don't think

The Russian was used to a woman taking over when he was in charge in the bedroom and I didn't mean to, I just didn't want to be totally opened up to him yet.

'You're beautiful, Brooker, and I want to touch every inch of you,' he said, looking at me intensely. 'What's going on in there?' he lightly tapped my head and pulled me hard against him.

'Nothing, I'm just going slow.'

He bit his lower lip for a moment as he watched me, and I tried to squirm away, but he wasn't having it.

'You're not a virgin, are you?' he asked.

'No,' I laughed. 'I just want to get to know every inch of each other, slowly ... does that make sense?' I'm sure it didn't but I wasn't used to doing everything so soon. I'd only had two real relationships and one of those guys hadn't liked doing some things and the other guy hadn't done it well – it scared the hell out of me. How did I say that without killing the moment?

I reached for his boxers and began to slide them down. The Russian helped.

'For someone who is going slow, you're in a hurry to get those off,' he said, reaching into the top drawer of the dresser beside the bed and grabbing a condom. I giggled like I was love drunk and enjoyed the view. The reaching for the condom process had given me a perfect close-up view of him and 'wow' said it all.

The Russian groaned as I softly ran my fingers over him. He breathed in and seemed to hold it before remembering to let it out and take another breath.

'Slow is just fine,' The Russian agreed. 'Is this okay?' he

said kissing me again and I nodded, unable to form words, but I did manage a pleasure moan. Then he worked his fingers down below.

'That okay?' he whispered near my ear.

'So okay,' I said, barely able to get the words out. I heard him chuckle.

'Come inside me,' I begged.

'Just wait for it, Brooker. No wonder you play forward, so bossy and defensive,' he joked.

I laughed then stopped suddenly as he hit a spot that took me to a whole new level of ecstasy. I moaned with pleasure.

'Yeah, and that's why I play forward, I know how to score,' he teased me.

'Oh my God,' I muttered, 'Russian ...' I felt the sensation everywhere – inside, outside, it was overwhelming and I think I cried out his name a few more times as the build-up took the tension to a whole new level. I could smell him, feel, him, sense him. Then, thank God, I exploded in relief and release, taking it for as long as I could before I tried to pull his hands away from me.

The Russian repositioned me underneath him and, keeping his weight off me, he slowly worked his way inside me. So tight and painful and good.

'Going slow,' he said in his low, sexy baritone voice as he inched in. His breathing became more erratic, sometimes stopping. Finally, he was in completely.

'Holy fuck,' he whispered, and I might have made a joke about how it kind of was since he was doing the reverend's daughter, if I could have formed words.

I didn't want him to think I was a total missionary-position dud on our first session, so I tried a few tricks – I tightened my internal muscles around him and felt him react.

'Fuck, Brooker,' he said, stopping completely still. 'Don't move for a minute,' he ordered me. The Russian swore a lot more during sex than he did during normal conversation – yep sexy, everything he did was sexy.

'Why?' I teased him and tightened my muscles around him again. His eyes opened and he frowned as he fixed a hazy glare at me, before closing his eyes again. He began to move slowly inside of me, with each move his arm muscles flexed. He began to pick up the pace and even though I don't orgasm that way, it felt so good to feel completely connected to The Russian.

As he quickened, he seemed to fill every part of me and I cried out with pleasure and pain. Then he came in a loud growl of pleasure; so hot. He seemed to come forever, and then he settled down holding me.

We remained attached, breathing heavy, looking at each other and I was gone –truly, madly, deeply lost in the 'L' word that was too early to say.

*****

We did manage to get some sleep somewhere between one a.m. and sunrise. I stirred before The Russian and just watched him sleep. He was so beautiful – long dark lashes, the most kissable mouth, high cheekbones and chiseled jaw ... just beautiful. And even though he joked about being a great catch, I don't think he really knew what a great catch he was. Then there was the body I could study every day for the rest of my life and never tire of it. I ran my eyes down his chest, down to the sheet at the edge of his hips. When I returned my eyes to his, he was watching me.

'Brooker,' he said my name softly and with affection, and then he reached over and touched my face with an expression in his eyes like he was home. I was in heaven, kill me now, this will do me; I can leave the earth happy.

'Did you sleep or have you just been studying me all night?' he teased.

'I tried to stay awake to gaze upon you, but in all honesty, I was completely out of it until about ten minutes ago. And you?'

'Same,' he said.

I ran my nails lightly over his chest, watching as his skin broke out in goosebumps and his desire became more obvious.

'You know where that's going to lead?' he asked.

'I sure do,' I said, and smiled. He shook his head at me.

'You're trouble, Brooker. You tell me that you want to take it slow, then you rip my boxers off and now, you're encouraging me again. Just trouble.'

I laughed and then in a flash he grabbed me, pushed me below him, while holding the weight of his chest in his arms ... he was a big boy, no wonder his arms were so well built if he was constantly holding up his own weight.

'Tell me what that was about last night?' he said, quietly.

'What?'

'The missionary thing. Has someone hurt you?' he asked, scanning my face.

I felt my face go red. 'No. I just wanted to go slowly,' I said, again. It was the truth – I didn't need or believe in instant intimacy – I like a build-up. 'We don't need to do everything in our first sexual encounter.'

He breathed out, as if he was deciding if he believed me or not and then he rolled onto his side and pulled me against him, my back against his chest.

'Okay you can dictate the pace, Brooker, but I want to make you scream,' he said, seductively. Fuck he was sexy, hadn't I mentioned that?

I turned to face him. 'I haven't showered.'

'I don't care,' he said.

I didn't want The Russian to think me a prude, but I just had a psychological thing about it ... I didn't want The Russian going anyway below unless I was fresh from the shower – I wanted it to be clean and sweet. Missionary and hands were fine but nothing else – yep, I sounded like I had issues. Then, I saw my opportunity to sound sexy and not too weird.

'I'm saving it,' I said, 'for later.'

'Later when?' he frowned, pausing from exploring me to study me again.

I sighed and bit my lip with the intention of adding some drama and suspense to it. I was not manipulating him like Leesa, I was just trying to hide make my need to pace the intimacy until I felt secure with him –well that was what I was telling myself.

'I have this thing that really turns me on,' I started and I saw I had piqued his interest. He pushed himself further up on one elbow to look down on me. Meanwhile, his hand rubbed along my chest and stomach which was really distracting.

'Do tell?' he invited me.

'Saltwater. I love swimming in saltwater and then when we're dry, licking the salt off each other, feeling our skin after that immersion ... the smell, the taste. Weird?'

I swear his body hardened and his eyebrows shot up.

'Really?'

I nodded. It was true, weird but true. I loved being covered in ocean saltwater and I loved tasting it ... it was so, well, ocean-ish. I don't know where it came from, but I've always loved it. Even as a child when it wasn't erotic of course, I wouldn't wash off when I came back from the ocean, I just loved the salt on my skin when it dried. I loved the smell, taste and feel.

'So ...' I continued, 'after the gym and our ocean swim, I was hoping you might lick me and let me lick you, unless you think that's too weird,' I said, avoiding the truth a little and still managing to sound reasonably sexy. I hoped.

'Weird yes, but weird good,' he said. 'I'd be happy to lick the salt off you,' he said with a smile skirting his lips. 'But right now ...' he ran a finger over my lips and I grabbed his finger and sucked on it. With a grin, he slowly drew it from my lips and lowered his lips to mine.

'Brooker, your mouth can have me when I can have you,' he said, playing fair. 'But I'd love to see that gorgeous butt of yours,' he ran a hand over my butt cheeks, then rolled me over onto my stomach. I felt him rise above me and his body covered mine. He grabbed a pillow, placed it under my hips and reaching for a condom, slipped it on. Slowly

I felt him pressing against me. I was tight and a little sore from last night, and I gasped as he entered me.

He stopped.

'It's okay, it's very okay actually,' I promised him, and he continued to slip in slowly.

'Brooker, you feel so good,' he moaned.

I moaned my agreement; it was amazing feeling The Russian as a part of me and I began to move in motion with him, keen to feel him shudder and groan. He came with a wonderful growl of satisfaction, and then he lowered himself, burying his face in my hair.

We stayed cocooned for a few moments until he pulled out, removed the condom and disposed of it. He returned and hearing and understanding what I had said and without any attempts at sly play, he used those large hands to bring me to a new high for the morning.

When we had both been well and truly satisfied, he smiled at me.

'Morning,' he said and I giggled.

'Morning.'

Then he reached over and pressed the same button that opened the blinds and he pulled me into him. I gasped at the beauty of it. The sun was just beginning to rise over the water – to describe it wouldn't do it justice – this ball of pink, orange, red and yellow. Laying spooned together we had an uninterrupted view of it.

'That's what I wanted to show you,' he said.

'Wow, you get to see this every morning?' I asked.

'I do, but the view's even better today,' he said, kissing my neck. So charming.

I rubbed his arm as it wound around me, and lying in his embrace we watched the color show on the ocean as the sun lit the horizon.

Chapter 17

Just after sunrise we rose, got into our gym gear and The Russian grabbed a protein shake from the fridge for after our workout. I declined the offer.

'I'm going to need to keep my strength up,' he said, with a mischievous look in my direction. 'By the time I work your ass off in the gym, then swim and seduce you ... it's a long time until we eat.'

'A man must eat,' I agreed, 'especially a big man,' I said, with a suggestive glance.

He shook his head at me again. 'Yep, you're trouble, Brooker. I might have to have a word with your father. See if it's not too late to save you.'

'I think he'll recognize that you're the one corrupting me,' I said, narrowing my eyes at him. What a cheek, again!

We hit the gym and no one there cared who we were or what we were doing. That's what I loved about Archer's Gym – it was a serious gym. We worked out in rhythm. I was doing less weight but a good number of repetitions and The Russian was doing more weight, more repetition. I tried to match him for reps but came nowhere near him.

Then I went to do the rowing machine for a bit while he did a few other weight combinations. I don't bother with the running machine unless I'm injured and want a soft impact run; I prefer to run outside and enjoy the fresh air.

I finished and looked over at The Russian and he gave me a nod that he was done too. I headed to the girl showers, but not before he called me back.

'Nice workout,' he said, tapping my butt. He was glowing all over with sweat, and looked lean and taut – I swear I could have bounced off him ... hmm, weird thought, must try it.

'Thanks,' I said back to him. 'You too, although I thought you slacked off a bit on the chin-ups,' I said, just to rile him.

'Did you now,' he growled.

'I think you owe me ten in private,' I suggested.

'My chin has plans for later ... it's going to be seeing new sights,' he said, with a suggestive glance. 'I want you to know that as sweaty as you are now, I'd love to do you right here on the gym floor.'

I must have looked slightly alarmed because he added. 'Not that I would ... I'm not into exhibition sex.'

I breathed out. 'Phew, I thought you were going to go all caveman then and throw me to the ground.'

He moved toward me as if it was a good idea and I blocked him with a quick move behind the water cooler. I've had my share of defensive moves on the court and he would have to do better than that! Besides, there was no point tempting a growling, turned on lion ... there, anyway.

He grinned, 'Nice play.'

I laughed.

'I thought we'd give the showers a miss and go straight into the ocean,' he said. 'If you can drive home with me sweaty.'

'Brilliant idea,' I said. One of my pet loves was to swim straight after a run ... the cold water hitting the tired and worked out muscles, so cleansing.

We grabbed our bags and returned to the car. I followed The Russian's lead and spread my towel over the seat before getting into his Merc. The Russian opened the sun window as we drove and in a matter of minutes, we drove into his garage. We didn't even go into the house, we stripped off in the garage, put on our swim gear and took the towels from our bags. The Russian never took his eyes off me while I self-consciously put on my two-piece gold swimsuit. He was wearing boardshorts ... a sexy pair that sat very nicely on his hips.

I could only imagine what his ex wore to the beach ... I didn't know where that thought had come from, but I somehow felt conscious all the time of following in her shoes. I didn't have to imagine too hard what she wore, I had seen photos of her skimpy beach outfits, that is, when she wasn't swimming topless. My two-piece bikini swimsuit was more modest ... it had fabric covering all of the important parts and extra areas as well.

The Russian moved to the driveway and waited as I grabbed my towel and followed. I wrapped it around my waist.

'I was enjoying that view,' he complained and I gave him a look that said 'hold that thought'! He grinned, and pressed the buzzer to put his garage door down. Like an old married couple, he gave the keys to me and I stuck them in my beach bag and then he took my hand and we walked across the lawn and down onto the sand. Our first beach trip together!

It was only about nine o'clock and the beach was still uncrowded, mainly being used by boardies, joggers and early swimmers. We were both sweaty from our workout and the first impact of the water on skin was wonderful – cold but wonderful. The Russian took to the water like a dolphin, with powerful movements, while I dodged the waves and swam gently in the shallows. Then he strode through the waves towards me; I watched his muscles clench as he did that, thank God I was in cold water or I might have combusted.

The Russian pulled me against his wet chest and gave me a long kiss. I loved that he had no hang-ups about being affectionate or showing it; I wondered if being in a predominantly female household had helped with being in touch with his emotions.

'How good is this?' I asked, after I had detached myself from his lips to draw breath.

'So good,' he said.

'I want to sunbake a little and dry off,' I said, glancing towards our towels on the beach.

'Yeah, I'd like to see that too' he agreed. 'I'm going to swim for a few more minutes. I'll see you out there.'

'You wouldn't be delaying your exit to watch me do the walk, would you?' I asked with suspicion.

He grinned. 'Me? Guilty!'

I laughed and gave him a kiss and headed out, turning back once to see him standing there, arms folded in waist-deep water as he watched me. He grinned and turned to dive back under a wave. So gorgeous.

I lowered myself onto my towel to dry off. The air was warm even though it was early and I closed my eyes feeling on top of the world. It was not even ten yet and I had had great sex, a workout, a swim and all with the hottest man on the planet. Imagine what could happen by eleven a.m. I could smell the salt air, feel the breeze on my skin and the sun warming me; I think I might have dozed off and then I felt a sprinkle of cold water over me.

I opened my eyes to see The Russian lowering himself beside me.

'Dry?' he asked me.

'Mm, wonderfully,' I murmured.

'We can fix that,' he said, and rolled onto me, shaking his head and spraying water on me. I squealed and tried to push him off. He was freezing cold on my lovely warm body.

'Get off you big wet whale,' I whined.

He roared with laughter. 'Wet whale? Well that's fucking great. Not a shark, or a sleek dolphin ... a big, fat, wet whale. And just out of curiosity, how many dry whales have you seen?'

We were both laughing then.

'Get off, you're cold and wet,' I said, trying to push him off.

'Not until you pay me a compliment,' he insisted.

'Fine then, you're a sleek dolphin, now get off.'

'That didn't sound sincere to me,' he said, lowering his wet head and rubbing his hair on me.

'You're a gorgeous, fit, sleek dolphin, happy now?' I pushed him.

He grinned, and finally rolled off me. 'Wet whale,' he shook his head.

'You must have been the worst brother to grow up with,' I said, wiping the sand and water off me. 'I bet you made your sisters' lives hell.'

'That's my job as a brother, and now as a boyfriend,' he said.

He lay back beside me and sighed, resting his head on one arm.

'Boyfriend, huh?' I said, loving the sound of that.

He looked over at me, and just for a second, I saw a flash of doubt in his eyes. It was so out of character to see the super confident and laid-back Russian looking vulnerable that it brought home to me what I'd said. He'd already told me he had spent many years with a woman who had played around all the time – I couldn't cope with seeing images of The Russian playing around, so I couldn't imagine what that had done to him ... I was surprised he was up for a relationship at all.

'You think we're just doing all this and hanging out casually then?' he asked, keeping his voice neutral, but I could tell this was opening wounds. I put that to rest.

'Hell no. I love you saying the 'b' word ... boyfriend,' I said and let it roll over my tongue. I visually saw him relax, he exhaled, his chest falling. I rolled on my side to look at him and ran my fingers over him, tracing marks on his chest. 'It may be your job as my boyfriend to find ways to tease me, but it's my job as your girlfriend to ensure you are adored and well-serviced, and I think you may be in need,' I said. I ran my finger just under the waistband and felt him inhale.

'Big job,' he said.

'A challenge, but I'm just the girl for it,' I grinned. He took my hand from his waist and wrapped his fingers around it.

'Give me ten minutes to dry off and I'll launch that challenge,' he said, and kissed my hand. I lowered myself back down on my back and closed my eyes too, leaving my hand resting comfortably in his.

After ten minutes he sat up. 'I can't wait any longer, we have to go.' His hair was mussed up and full of sand and he looked super lickable.

'Don't shower,' I warned him. 'I want to taste the salt on you.'

'Quick,' He said rising. We saw three young boys running towards us.

'Russian,' they yelled.

'Hey, how are you?' he said, super friendly.

'Want to play soccer with us?' they asked.

He shook his head. 'Woah, don't think I could take on the three of you. You might show me up.'

'I'm the vice-captain of our school football team,' one of the boys said.

'Yeah, I could tell that,' The Russian said. 'This is my girlfriend Carly,' he introduced me.

I shook hands with each of the boys and they told us their names.

'We're just about to leave, but next time I see you here we'll have a kick, yeah?'

'Yeah, cool,' they said, and ran up the beach. One of them yelling, 'Mom, The Russian said he'd play next time!'

The Russian raised his hand and waved to the mother and she responded with a grin and a wave. He turned, picked up my beach bag and looked at me.

'What?' he asked as I stood smiling at him.

'You are so sweet.'

He growled in my ear. 'I'm so not sweet, Brooker, I want to have you writhing in front of me right now, begging to be allowed to come.' He snatched my towel off me and threw it over his shoulder. 'And don't even think of putting that around your waist. I want to see the view,' he said, tapping my butt.

I was so turned on but tried to play it cool; The Russian gave me a satisfied smile. I rolled my eyes at him and pushed my sunnies on to try and hide behind them.

'Do you always get what you want?' I asked, walking slightly in front of him as ordered.

'No, but I intend to in the next hour.'

*****

I barely got in through the glass sliding doors before The Russian was on me, and boy did he know how to make a girl swoon. He cupped my face in his large hands and gave me such a long passionate kiss, that I couldn't remember where I was for a moment.

'I needed that,' he said, as he pulled away. This man was so gorgeous.

'I can't remember my name,' I said, and he grinned. He reached up and lifted my hair off my neck and undid my bikini top. He threw it off and sand scattered over his floors;

neither of us cared. He wrapped his arms around me and, lifting me, he carried me into a room that I hadn't seen yet. I realized why when I found myself in the middle of a huge white leather sofa – big, round and like a bed with pillows on one side. So comfortable that you could have fitted at least six people on it ... yeah, we're not going there.

He stood in front of me and pulled his board shorts off. His body was covered in salt, sand and was so sexy; I wanted to applaud. He knelt down on the ground beside me on the leather sofa.

'Brooker,' The Russian said in his deep, sultry voice, as he looked into my eyes.

'Yes, Russian?'

'Stop thinking now. Yes?'

'Yes,' I said, and nodded and then he began to kiss me, lick me, kiss me … I lost track in a haze of passion.

'Mm, you were so right ... the salt is delicious.'

'Delicious,' I agreed, arching my back in pleasure. I heard him chuckle. Then I felt his hand moving down to my hips and I grabbed the leather sofa but had nothing to grasp.

His fingers and his tongue were magic. It was fair to say he was every bit as good off the ground as he was on it.

'That's ... so ... orgasmic,' I panted, arching in pleasure as we enjoyed the intimacy together. The Russian kept his own rhythm going and I came so hard, so full-on, that I thought he would have to peel me from the ceiling. As I wound down, he licked and kissed his way back up my body and just held me so tightly that I felt like I would be loved and safe forever. It was the most amazing sex I had ever had; it was the most amazing love I had ever made.

'I can't see you yet,' I said, blinking in his direction and eventually his features became clear again.

'Brooker,' he shook his head, 'you were right, worth waiting for that.'

'So worth it, best ever,' I muttered short sharp sentences, and then I felt and saw how pressing his need was. My eyes lit up.

'Your turn,' I said, pushing him onto his back and that's no mean feat. He laughed, caught unaware and I looked at his body like it was a buffet. He watched me with amusement as I was deciding where to start, and then I went for it. He was easily satisfied; his body was so sensitive to touch that it almost hummed impatiently as it waited to be discovered. He groaned as I teased him – getting closer, then moving away. I love doing that!

'Killing me,' he groaned.

'Mm,' I agreed keeping control and then I showed him no mercy and got to work finishing him off. Not long after he stopped me and pulled me up beside him.

'Stop ... you're killing me,' he said, with a satisfied look on his face.

I grinned. 'Love that salt.'

'I'm never moving from this house,' he said. 'Going to live beside the beach forever,' he continued. 'Might get a saltwater pool too ...'

I laughed and rested my hand on his chest.

'You're a surprise package, Brooker,' he said, and kissed the top of my head.

'I'm a very satisfied and hungry surprise package.'

'Me too, starving. Let's shower and go to brunch. Maybe

you should shower first or we won't get out of here,' he said.

I sat up and observed the room for the first time. The wall was covered in about half a dozen television screens.

'I study the game here,' he explained. 'Lucas is coming over tonight and we're watching the three games being played this weekend while we have a bye ... we've got two of those teams in the next month.'

'I do that too,' I said, 'good to study the opposition's strengths and weaknesses.'

'Want to stay over?' he asked.

'You're so nice to ask, thank you.' I knew he probably preferred to watch the games with teammates, it was a serious business watching plays, not like relaxing watching a sports game. 'I'm working,' I said.

He looked surprised.

'The Sports Daily is getting their money's worth out of me – I have to cover the men's basketball game at Lowe Stadium. I'd invite you to come but I'm in the media box and you're seeing Lucas,' I teased.

He smiled. 'All good. C'mon, we have to eat,' he said, pushing himself off the couch and offering me his hand. He pulled me up and against his chest, giving me a firm kiss. 'Shower,' he said, pointing to a room across the hall. 'I'll go get your bag.'

Again he watched as I walked out of the room naked, such a perve, bless him, and I heard him enter with my bag a few moments later. When I got out, I heard his shower go on in his ensuite. Within thirty minutes we had walked down to his favorite cafe and were ordering coffee, toast and eggs.

We sat at a sidewalk table and watched the world unfold around us. He wrapped his long legs around mine under the table.

'You know what I like about you Brooker?' he asked.

'Hell yeah, lots of things I imagine,' I said, and he smirked and shook his head at me.

'Okay, I give up, what?' I asked.

'I love that you are real. When you work out, you work out ... you sweat, you're not looking in the mirror to see if you look okay,' he said, reaching over for my hand. 'I love that you go to the beach and get wet. You actually swim in the surf, no make-up, you dunk yourself, get your hair wet. Love it.'

I looked at him surprised. 'Why, what do other girls do?'

'Don't ask, I don't want to spoil you,' he said, rubbing my hand.

I knew a lot of real girls, especially having been in sporting circles for years ... I never thought to do anything else. Our coffees arrived before our brunch, we thanked the waiter and sipped with appreciation.

'You know what I like about you, Russian?' I asked, licking cappuccino froth off my top lip. He watched me do it and smiled. It seemed like everything turned The Russian on.

'Tell me,' he said, with a glance at his watch, 'we should have enough time,' he teased, inviting me to praise him.

'Everything so far,' I said, and leaned over to kiss him.

*****

I went to work and The Russian watched the plays with Lucas. As tired as I was after work, I crawled into bed and knew sleep was impossible. I lay in bed with this stupid grin on my face and I went back over every moment with The Russian and then started again. I wanted to message him to say goodnight but I didn't want to risk waking him. Clearly The Russian was psychic because at midnight a message came through on my phone.

Brooker, you're keeping me awake!

I giggled like a schoolgirl and held the phone to my chest like a hug. Then I messaged him back.

Ditto, Russian, get out of my head. Even a natural beauty needs beauty sleep ... do you mind?

Then I waited with much anticipation and nothing happened. Oh well, maybe he did drift back to sleep. But no, ten minutes later another message pinged on my phone.

I'm thinking of every inch of your body.

I messaged him back: I can still feel you inside and outside of me.

I waited for the reply, and then it came.

Great, thanks for that. Getting up to watch TV. Brooker, you're trouble!

Then I slept.

Chapter 18

The next week flew by in-between catching The Russian when I could between his training and work schedule; my last week at *The Sports Daily*; completing my remaining sponsorship commitments for my team, the Suns, including promoting the end of season last home game which The Russian had bought the VIP seats at; and some commitments for the new job – it was fast and furious.

Saturday would also mark my last game reporting in the Saints' media box before I started my new gig, and the Saints were playing the Chicago Cats – not an easy team to beat. This game was different though from any other that I had reported at because for this game, The Russian and I were in deep like, maybe luuvvveee –yes, I had to say it like that. I'm now one of those pathetic over-the-top people who are smiling all the time and putting smiley faces on messages. And yes, I'd tried the name Carly Renwick out loud. It sounds so good!

I met up with my new fellow commentators – Suzie and Catherine – during the week as the station wanted to shoot some promos with the three of us ... that was fun. After the promos, we had lunch with our boss – my new boss – Karen, the Cable TV Head of Production. It was nice to relax with them as friends over lunch instead of glaring at them over a basketball as opposing team members. We reminisced about some of our more memorable games and then Karen went through the expectations for the season ahead. I was so excited to be on board that at home, I kept practicing around the house, trying to get my pace right and not talk too quickly; Josh must have wondered who I was talking to all the time! I spent time getting up to scratch with all the other teams' players and coaches. Luckily, because I was still a signed player, I knew of most of them.

On Friday the Saints were holding one of their pre-game press conferences which Sasha had to organize and *The Sports Daily* sent me along to hear what the coach had to say. The Russian wasn't on the roster for this conference – Lucas was always in attendance being Captain Fantastic, and this time he was joined by Buzz aka Damien Hall, the team's practical joker as I had already experienced. Buzz looked like an ex-marine, hence the buzz cut which I assumed had contributed to his nickname.

I arrived right at the last minute, thanks to the traffic, and saw The Russian's silver Merc in the parking lot. I didn't have time to go to the offices and say hi as I raced into the media room, in the building next door. I wasn't the last to arrive as one more journo came in after me, but the coach was just starting. I recorded him and jotted down a few things as well.

After it was over, Sasha indicated for me to wait a moment and then Captain Fantastic came past me.

'Hey Carly, how are you?' he said, stopping nearby and looking tall, handsome and glowing in his Saints' dress pants and open shirt.

'Hi Lucas, I'm great thanks, how are you?' I smiled back at him like a woman in love ... with someone else. He had a look on his face that said he knew.

'I'm very well, so is my Forward I believe?' he said, referring to The Russian.

'Really?' I asked, looking innocent.

'In fact, for a grumpy bastard, I've never seen him so happy. He even shouted me a coffee today,' Lucas said, a mischievous look on his face.

'Wow,' I said, eyes wide. 'What on earth has come over him? Have you spoken to the team psychiatrist about him?'

Lucas shook his head and looked alarmed. 'No one is brave enough to go into the dark spaces of The Russian's mind. At least I know you won't distract my player given your own sporting pedigree.'

'I'll do my best, Captain,' I said, saluting him and he gave me a wry look as he made a sound of disbelief and wandered away. I stuffed my notepad and phone in my bag and Sasha joined me.

'Hey Sash,' I said, 'all okay?'

'All is very good. I have a message from The Russian ... he said he'd text you but it takes so long with his 'big, masculine hands',' she did air quote marks and rolled her eyes.

I laughed. I could hear The Russian saying those words.

'Sure, is it above board?' I said, now a little worried.

She nodded and, doing a Russian impersonation, crossed her arms across her chest and lowered her voice. 'Tell

Brooker to see me before she leaves, I've got something for her.' Sasha said, and fell out of character. 'Got time?'

'Sure. I don't need to be at *The Sports Daily* for another hour if I include my lunch break,' I said.

'Good, if you give me a minute to lock up, I'll walk to the office with you.'

I helped her lock up and then we wandered over to the administration building, chatting about her designing business. As we walked through the office, Sasha introduced me again to her colleagues Kay and Alice.

'Of course we remember Carly from your last visit,' Kay said, smiling and giving me a small wave from her desk in the corner.

'And we've seen a fair bit of you since,' Alice teased, 'kissing The Russian, feeding The Russian, dancing with The Russian ...'

I sighed. 'Someone's got to do it.'

'Kay would have,' Sasha dobbed her in and laughed. Sasha could be wicked.

Kay went bright red and shook her head at Sasha.

'Don't you believe it Carly,' she turned to me. 'I'm a happily married woman with two children ... I just like to ensure The Russian is looking after himself ... purely maternal.'

The Russian must have heard me from his office next door and appeared in the doorway.

'Haven't you three got something to do?' he asked, looking from Sasha, to Kay to Alice. He reached for my hand and pulled me into his office. Eddie was sitting working on a spreadsheet.

'Hey Eddie,' I said.

He spun around and looked genuinely pleased to see me. 'Hi Carly, good to see you.'

'You too!'

'Ed's just leaving,' The Russian said.

Eddie looked surprised. 'Am I?' he glanced from me to The Russian. 'Ah, yes, I am just leaving ... got to go get some lunch? I'll be back in ...?' he hesitated.

'Thirty minutes,' The Russian said, and I giggled at the two men.

'That's right,' Ed said, grabbing his keys and wallet. 'The usual?' he asked The Russian.

'Thanks,' The Russian answered.

'Anything for you Carly?' he asked. So polite.

'Thank you, Eddie, but I've got to get back to work,' I said.

'Yeah, so go,' The Russian said, and pushed Eddie out the door. I could hear Eddie chuckling as The Russian closed and locked the door. He moved to the stereo and I thought he was going to turn it off, but he turned it up. 'Thin walls,' he said and leaned against the door, pulling me against him.

'Hello Brooker,' he said, smiling down at me.

I grinned back at him. 'Hello Russian.' I took in his handsome attire: work dress pants and open shirt, a tie hung over his chair. He was checking out my outfit at the same time: a black pencil skirt and fitted white blouse, along with reasonably high heel black court shoes.

'Don't you look sexy and all corporate,' he said.

'That's me, the sexy corporate journalist,' I teased him, 'able to drill all the way down to get a story.'

He leaned down and kissed me, slowly then hungrily, and I wrapped my arms around him to steady myself.

'I've missed you,' he groaned. God I loved how open he

was with his emotions. I'd never had that, and never for one moment expected it with The Russian.

'I've missed you more,' I promised him. 'I've had to take matters into my own hands so many times this week.'

He grinned and shook his head. 'Brooker, isn't that a sin? Will you need to say four Hail Mary's for that?'

Before I could reply he began to unbutton my shirt, revealing my white lace bra. I looked around quickly.

'Russian, we're in the office,' I said, alarmed while looking at the window and all the camera and security equipment in the room.

'We are indeed. The security cameras are not on in here, the window is frosted, the door locked.' He rubbed his thumbs over my bra and I drew a sharp breath; I tried not to moan too loudly. There was a knock on the door and I jumped.

'Ignore it,' he said.

'Russian, are you there?' A voice boomed. I recognized it as Captain Fantastic.

'He'll go away,' The Russian said.

I was torn; terrified that Lucas could get in and distracted by The Russian's hands and the scent of his hair and cologne.

'Russian?' Lucas said again, tapping on the door.

The Russian stopped, pulled away from me and sighed. 'I'm not here,' he called out in exasperation and I heard Lucas laugh.

'Okay, come and see me when Carly leaves.' I heard him stride off and I pulled my shirt around me, mortified.

'What?' The Russian asked, 'he can see me anytime, and don't worry, no one is seeing this part of you except me,' he said, resuming his touching of me. 'I've never had sex in my office,' he added.

'Really?' I asked. Now he had my interest, this could be a first and I had a thing for milestones. If it was memorable, The Russian would think about this whenever he walked into his office ... at least for a while. Suddenly I was inspired.

I began to undo the buttons on his shirt and I slipped it off. I then reached for his belt and continued my good form – well, that's what it would be called in sport circles. Besides, if we were going to do it in The Russian's office, I wasn't going to be the only one revealing skin.

His breathing was matching mine now and I moved my hand down his body, discovering his desire also matched mine and then I did something about it. The Russian tried to deliver but I ordered him to stay out of my way while I did my thing and he obeyed. Amazing.

I brought him to the edge and given we only had thirty minutes until Ed returned, I delivered. The Russian looked so hot when he lost control at my hand that it was almost enough to make me come.

'Wow, he said, getting his breath. 'Well, that's ruined me for the rest of the day. Can we just curl up somewhere now?'

'I wish. But I've got to go write up what your coach said at the press conference.'

'Not before I see you arched over my desk,' he growled.

'You can do me another time,' I said, and started to do up my shirt.

'No way, Brooker, I'm taking you here and now.' He read my concern. 'Relax, it's totally private, I promise you,' he reassured me, again. He reached behind me, unzipped my skirt and lowered it for me, and I stepped out of it. He lifted my shirt and his expression said he appreciated my white lace panties. Then he reached up under my white shirt and pulled my panties down and completely off.

'Good look,' he said, taking in my white shirt and high heels. Then he headed straight into my phobia zone. He lowered me onto his desk and wanted to go down below.

'Russian!' I hissed, alarmed and turned on.

'Shh, relax, don't think,' he said.

He pulled my hips towards him and then he rose, kissing me passionately and he put his hands to work. I relaxed immediately, thank God. I love this guy. I love that he understands, that he is sensitive. I love that he listened to me.

I struggled not to groan loudly in ecstasy and I think I used every Saints' name that I could remember from my Bible study days. I came in minutes, my body arching in pleasure and when I was spent, The Russian gently pulled me up and off his desk.

He tapped my butt. 'You're gorgeous, Brooker, the best part of my day. You can put your clothes on now, you hussy,' he teased.

I smiled, a love drunk, super chilled out smile and did up my shirt. The Russian reached down for my lace panties and, leaning down, slipped them over my legs and pulled them up ... there was something very sexy about being dressed and undressed by The Russian. I reached for my skirt hanging on the back of the chair and slipped it on, tucking in my shirt. The Russian zipped me up at the back, even though I could do it myself. He turned me around, as I patted down my hair and he looked me over.

'You'd never know except for the glaze in your eyes and blush on your cheeks,' he said. He pulled me closer and we just hugged. It was so good just holding each other for a few moments, and then he pulled away.

'I think I got all the information I need,' I teased him as if I'd been doing an interview.

'If you need anything clarified ...' he said, with raised eyebrows.

'Oh, I'm sure I will.'

'Tonight?' he said. 'Are you still coming over?'

'Do you really want me over before a game?' I asked, frowning at him. 'I get it if you want to just have a night on your own to prepare, I really do.'

He moved the chair out of the way of the door as I powdered my nose and straightened up.

'Brooker, you keep me awake when you're not with me, so if you stay the night, I might have a better chance of sleeping.'

I grinned at him. God, I loved that he'd said that.

'I'll think of a way to exhaust you before bedtime,' I said, brightening.

'Oh I'm sure you will,' he said, and opened the door to walk me out. 'I thought I'd cook up some pasta.'

'Of course,' I said, and he laughed. Carbs, carbs and more carbs. 'Sounds great,' I assured him. 'We've got two games to watch tonight.'

He looked over at me surprised. 'You want to watch them?'

I frowned. 'Of course. You have to watch your opponents' play and I need to watch them since I'm reporting on the

Saints game tomorrow. So here's my plan, tell me what you think ...' I said, lowering my voice, Lord knows we loved a plan – we were both methodical. 'Dinner while watching the games, some sort of physical contact to ensure you are spent – I have plenty of ideas – then bed to sleep at a reasonable hour. Simple.'

He put his hand on the back of my neck and pulled me in for a kiss, even with the door open.

'Love the plan,' he said, his eyes genuinely looking happy and I think relieved. Did he think I'd want to watch a romance movie or something?

He walked me out and luckily Alice and Sasha were out to lunch, but Kay was there; she gave me a knowing smile and wave.

'Good to see you again, Kay,' I said, on departing.

'Yeah, she's the best of the bunch,' The Russian said, with a wink in her direction. Kay blushed again. I wondered how many nights she had fantasized about The Russian being in her bed. Tonight, I'd be in his. Thank you, patron Saint of love, yet again!

Chapter 19

The speed of my life did not slow down ... the weekend and the week that followed were a blur; between servicing The Russian – tough gig, but I was the girl for it – reporting at my final Saints game which the boys won, thank goodness, and starting my new job, life was hectic. My first commentary game was on the Saturday afternoon when my team, the Suns, played the Minnesota Leopards. I really wanted The Russian to be there, but I was also relieved that the Saints had an away game and he wouldn't be back until Sunday afternoon. His presence would have made me twice as nervous, if that was at all possible.

It was so bizarre arriving at the Suns game but not getting changed with my teammates. Instead, I was in the commentary box and checking team names, player positions and organizing interviews. I was so nervous.

Many of my teammates looked up to wave to me in the media box and Aimee and Steffi snuck away to give me a hug for good luck. I wished them the same; I wasn't supposed to be biased, but of course I wanted the Suns to win! Suzie promised she'd take the lead with the commentary throws and let me follow and contribute; thank goodness she was one of those wonderfully supportive colleagues and not someone who wanted to see me fall on my face.

It was fifteen minutes until the game started, the stadium was filling up and Suzie and I went courtside to do our first cross. I checked my phone was off and saw a message there from The Russian.

Wish I was with you, but I know you'll be great. Go get them, Brooker!

He was adorable. I took a deep breath, nodded at Suzie that I was ready and we went live.

Suzie: Welcome to today's hotly-anticipated game between the Santa Ana Suns and the Minnesota Leopards on Suns' home soil. I'm Suzie Ellis and I'm delighted to welcome to the commentary team, Carly Brooker. Even though she hasn't officially retired yet, we'll take advantage of her Suns' knowledge!

Carly: Thank you Suzie and hotly-anticipated is right. The Suns and Leopards have met in the playoffs so often, that it's not surprising that a rivalry has developed.

Suzie: And it makes for a great game. From your personal history of playing against the Leopards, Carly, what do you think are the challenges to watch?

Carly: The Leopards' point guard Julia Walters against the Suns' Lia Cartwright will be a clash to watch out for, and the rivalry between Suns' center Aimee Ross and the Leopards' Brittany Burke should bring an extra edge to the game.

Suzie: The Leopards' chemistry seems tighter to me than the Suns', especially as the Suns have a few players out injured and are trialing some of their reserve team. Would you agree?

Carly: I think given the reserves train with the A-team, that there's little room for error in reading teammates' play.

Then, we were off air and the cameras panned to the teams running out onto the field. I did it, my first commentary cross was done and Suzie gave me a quick pat on the back on our way back to the commentary box. I breathed a sigh of relief. I heard the vibration of an incoming message on my phone and checked it quickly – The Russian must have been watching the game live from his hotel room.

You're a natural. xx

I texted him back. *First one under the belt. Thanks for the support. Cx*

The referee blew the whistle and the game began. The few hours flew by, and it was over before I had time to get my breath. I had survived my first game as a commentator, and not only survived it, nailed it! The relief was palpable ... I would be able to sleep and eat again now.

*****

Sigh ... you know when you think everything is going so perfectly, that absolutely nothing could upset you? Wrong. The Russian and I had our first fight ... and I hadn't seen it coming, and he wasn't even home, he was in Colorado at his away game.

The Suns won their game against the Leopards – woo hoo – and when I stopped trying to be professional and unbiased, namely after the game, I went out with the girls and their partners (those who had them) and we partied. It's funny because the whole time you are training, eating well and being competitive, you can't wait for the day you can pig out, drink as much as you like, and not worry about injuries. And then that day comes and you find yourself clawing to stay involved.

The girls and I drank a little, danced a lot, went over the game again and just had a great night. Earlier I had sent a message to The Russian to tell him I missed him and wished him goodnight. I promised I'd be watching the game the next day and cheering for him. Later that night, or morning as the case may have been when I got home, I looked at my phone and I had three missed calls from him. The last one had only been thirty minutes before and it was nearing one a.m. I didn't know whether to call back or not. He hadn't left messages and I didn't want to risk waking him or Captain Fantastic, with whom he was sharing a hotel room. I felt sick now ... had he been injured, had something bad happened, did he just need to talk because he was psyching out about the game or something?

I took my uneasy feelings with me into the shower. Josh was out, so I didn't have to tiptoe around while I showered, washed my make-up off and prepared for bed. I just got under the covers when my phone rang ... it was The Russian.

Relief coursed through me that he rang, but my stomach was still churning with anxiety about why he was calling.

'Russian, what's wrong? I didn't know whether to call you back this late or not,' I said.

There was silence on the other end of the phone.

'I've been trying to reach you for hours,' he growled.

'I was out with the team celebrating their win. I couldn't hear my phone in the club. What's wrong? Where are you?' I asked, swinging my legs over the side of the bed and striding out to the living area to pace while we talked.

'I'm on the balcony of our hotel room. Lucas is asleep in the room.'

'What's wrong? Why are you calling?'

'You tell me,' he said. 'I'm surprised you even answered.'

I stopped, confused. 'I don't know what you're saying Russian. What's happened?'

'Really? You're all over social media with some guy, several guys actually,' he said, his voice was dangerously low.

'What guys?'

'The guys you were tarting around with,' he snapped.

'Hold on,' I said, still confused. 'I was out with the girls, I didn't have a guy with me ... I grabbed my iPad, tapped in my password and checked out the feeds. Some of the girls had already posted images from our night out and there I was with Steffi, both of us planting a kiss on the cheek of our team manager who stood between us and was old enough to be our father; then there was a shot of me with Aimee, her cousin Roy, the coach and the coach's husband. Roy had his arm around Aimee and me; there was another shot with Steffi, me, Latoya and her fiancé ... they were nothing shots.

'They're not guys, well technically they are, but they're the team guys ... our team manager, the coach's husband, Latoya's fiancé ...' my voice trailed off as I heard the sound of overwhelming silence on the other end of the line. Was he seriously freaking out about this?

'Russian,' I started again, 'this is nothing more than if

you were out with the Saints and had some random group shots taken with the club's extended family.' All clubs had extended families of partners, kids, relatives and friends.

I heard him inhale. 'I told you Brooker, I wasn't playing this game; I'm not putting up with that shit again ... I've had years of it. If you want to fuck around, fine, but not while you're with me,' he said, and hung up.

I stared at the phone. What the fuck had just happened? In a matter of minutes I had gone from a huge high to the lowest of lows.

I looked at all the shots to see what he was seeing, but they really were innocent – especially when you knew the people in the shots as well as I did. Then I got angry. I didn't want to wake Lucas, but I guessed The Russian had his phone on silent, so I rang. He must have stayed out on the balcony because he answered after a few rings and I could hear the noise of the city behind him – I had been bracing myself for the message bank.

'Russian, we need to talk,' I said, in my most pacifying voice.

He made this grunting sound.

I felt scared and angry, they were competing with each other. I kept going. 'I know you're in pain and I know you've been hurt before, but you can't deflect that on me,' I said. Again, dead silence. 'I don't fuck around. I've never fucked around, I've never cheated on anyone and I won't do that, do you understand?' I asked. He didn't answer.

I continued: 'I'm not your ex-girlfriend, Russian, and you need to find a way to unload all that baggage you are carrying about her and these jealousy issues.'

I waited, neither of us spoke for about a minute.

'So let me get this straight ... you often go around kissing guys and letting them put their arms around you?' he snarled.

'Yeah, I do when they're friends. And when your female friends – Saints' partners, the office girls, old friends – do the same to you, I'll hide my jealousy and trust that you don't have feelings for them, and that your intentions to me are pure.'

He ignored what I said. 'That cousin of Aimee's was keen to get to know you last time we met, now you're all over him. Why don't you just follow him up and we'll call it quits?'

I knew he was baiting me and I knew he wanted an avalanche of assurances but that hit like a punch to the stomach. Now I was hurt and fucking angry. I snapped.

'I've got a better idea, Russian, when you grow up, give me a call ... if I haven't fucked off with the entire male basketball team by then,' I shot back at him, and then I hung up. I breathed out, put my phone down and burst into tears.

It rang straight away and I didn't answer. The Russian's name lit the screen and this time he left a message.

'Don't fucking hang up on me Brooker,' he growled, 'call me back.'

Fuck you, Russian. I put the phone on silence so he wouldn't stalk me for the rest of the night, what sleep hours remained, and I went to bed. But I didn't sleep, I cried, and stressed and went through all my actions in my head to see if I had been 'tarty' or led anyone on, or disrespected The Russian.

Then I decided to drive home in the morning ... it would

take me a few hours but I could get there in time to hear Dad give mass and then see what he thought about the situation. Dad's perspective would help – he was a qualified counselor as well as a reverend.

I glanced at the clock – it was nearly two a.m.; I would leave at seven to get home by nine and to attend Dad's nine-thirty service. My phone buzzed beside me a few more times and then, somehow, with pure exhaustion riding me, I must have slept a few hours. I woke and washed my face, my eyes were swollen, and I put on something conservative for church. I drove with the sun rising around me and headed home.

Chapter 20

I felt sick as I drove home and I knew The Russian would be feeling like shit too. I didn't want to ruin his game today but I didn't want to talk to him either before I had my head in order – there was no point in both of us getting angry again and hanging up on each other. We had to find a way to manage it because we wouldn't survive it, and I was hoping Dad would give me perspective.

I drove into the churchyard, which was also my parents' home while Dad served the parish he was assigned to; I was about fifteen minutes early. I entered the front of the church to catch Mom in the vestibule; I knew she would be there handing out the hymn books while Dad was preparing in the small room beside the altar. Her first reaction was as expected.

'Carly! What's wrong? What's happened?' she asked, pulling me into her to kiss each cheek.

'Hi Mom, sorry to drop in unannounced ...'

'Don't be silly, this is your home. Are you okay?' she said, cutting me off.

'I just needed a male perspective, no offense, and I thought

I'd see you and enjoy Dad's mass as well,' I said with a shrug, trying to keep it all super casual while my head thumped, my stomach churned, and I looked like death on legs.

We greeted a couple of parishioners and she handed them a hymn book. Mom turned back to me and shook her head, reading the situation immediately.

'Men,' she sighed. 'Nevertheless, your father will be delighted to see you, it will make his day.' She softened and squeezed my hand, 'makes my day too.'

'Thanks Mom,' I said, smiling at her. Mom didn't easily give affection, she was very stoic, so it took a lot for her to say that. Then Dad came out towards the altar area and saw me. He did a double-take, like he'd been caught in a time warp, and headed down the aisle, smiling and adjusting his church robes.

'My prayers have been answered,' he said, looking towards heaven. I smiled and shook my head at him while giving him a hello hug and kiss.

'Tell me you're staying for mass and lunch after?' he said.

'I am staying for mass and lunch after, if that's okay?' I offered, with a glance to Mom.

'Always,' Mom said.

'Wonderful, well today has just gotten better – a beautiful day, parishioners filling the seats and my two girls,' he grinned. It didn't take much to make Dad happy. Bless him.

'I'm going to go get a seat,' I said, leaving them both to their work, and slipped away. I was hoping I wouldn't see any of my childhood male church or school friends and get my photo snapped with them ... heaven forbid!

I selected a seat and slipped into a pew, knelt and

thanked God for good health, family, my new job, friends and for The Russian, and then Dad entered the altar to start mass. I joined in the hymns and prayers and enjoyed his sermon, which seemed to have been written for me that day – keeping the faith in each other and the world in modern times. I had full faith in The Russian, but he wasn't having any in me. I didn't know how to make him secure, I didn't know if I had to change who I was to make that happen or if I should change. I returned to Dad's sermon and then participated as best I could in the rest of the mass when I wasn't drifting off going over the previous night's argument in my head, again and again.

After Dad had seen off the last of the parishioners he joined Mom and me at home.

'You two have shrunk,' I observed.

'We're getting older ... that's what happens when you don't see us often enough. Next time you come home, we'll be a foot tall,' Dad joked.

I laughed. 'It's good to be home.'

'It's good to have you home. Now come on, let's get some of your Mom's prize-winning lemonade and chat.'

'Yes, get out of my kitchen while I work,' she said, bossing us. Mom got to fixing lunch while Dad and I moved into the lounge room to talk.

'We've heard and read a bit about your new boy, online of course,' Dad said.

I nodded. 'I will be bringing him home to meet you as soon as the season's over and he can get away.' Then I told Dad all about it; he listened attentively, sipping the cool homemade lemonade that Mom had made while I talked, and I finished by reminding him he only had my perspective.

He sat back and thought about my situation for a short while.

'I've had a few people in your situation; a number of couples that I've had to give counsel to,' he said.

I breathed a sigh of relief, I knew he'd be able to help me see the light in the relationship; I dreaded the day I wouldn't have my father's counsel. I relaxed back in my chair, tired of talking, tired in general and listened to my Dad, trying to remember everything he was telling me.

'You have to remember, darling, that Alex has been very, very hurt,' my father explained. 'He started off with a full trust bank and it has been completely diminished. Now he's coming into this relationship, but you don't have the benefit of a full trust account. You've got nothing in your trust account and you have to build it for him to trust you. The reverse of what most normal couples start with,' Dad said. 'He's asking you to prove you're worthy when you've done nothing to prove you are not.'

I nodded, totally getting the big picture.

'But,' Dad said, continuing, 'he's not doing it to punish you, he's protecting himself. Men and women are both victims of cheating, but their reactions can be quite different.'

'Do you think my actions were inappropriate?' I asked, 'please tell me the brutal truth Dad, I won't be offended.'

He shook his head. 'Your actions weren't flirtatious or meant to hurt Alex. You socialized with friends as you normally would, feeling secure in your new relationship with Alex. But you do need to help him rebuild his trust if you want to be with him.'

'How? I told him I am a one-man woman, that he was the only one, and he's already met my friends,' I said. I felt my phone vibrate in my pocket again, but Dad and Mom were very anti-phones when in company. I knew it probably was The Russian – his game was on at one o'clock and it was now nearing eleven-thirty.

'Alex is probably very confident in areas he can control ... you're not one of them,' Dad said. 'So now that he is falling in love with you, it's opened his wounds, he's feeling very vulnerable.'

'We both are,' I said, agreeing.

'Before we discuss steps to help the situation, there's a few things, darling, you need to be aware of for your personal wellbeing,' Dad said. 'You can give him the '*I won't cheat on you like your ex did*' speech, and probably have already?'

'I have,' I said.

'Yes, well, it will take actions not words to convince him, and seeing those photos of you with other guys, as innocent as they were, has just triggered all his concerns. He's not only been cheated on, but cheated on very publicly and had to try and look stoic. Each time she's returned to him, he's forgiven her or accepted her excuses and meanwhile his own self-worth has suffered.' Dad stopped to sip his lemonade.

'He's such a dynamic and confident guy though in every other aspect of his life. It's completely out of character, he doesn't act like he's affected,' I said. 'I guess she's really worked him over.'

Dad listened and thought some more. He continued. 'Be careful then, Carly ... you can't be explaining your actions – you shouldn't have to explain why you didn't text him back

186

immediately or why you didn't answer his call straight away, or who that man was you smiled at; that's not healthy either. You've said that you've fallen for each other very quickly; well, that speed isn't helping, because he's got nothing to hold on to ... no build-up, no history with you. Suddenly he's in deep and you might cheat on him or leave him.'

'Will we survive this?' I asked.

'Of course,' he said. 'Will he seek counseling?'

'I doubt it very much,' I said, thinking of my lion. 'He's very alpha.'

'Hmm,' Dad said. 'You may have to show more transparency than you normally would in a relationship, just until you are secure together – you know, tell him where you went and who was there, and make sure he knows those people. Give him a sign ... something that's uniquely his.'

'What do you mean?' I asked, putting my glass down and leaning back into my parents' old leather couch.

'Tell him that when you put your hand on your heart, you are thinking of him. So in those photos he saw, or if you are doing an interview, a quick placing of your hand on your heart will be a signal you are thinking of him in that situation. He'll be looking for it, it will make him feel more secure and safe.'

'That's cute,' I said, smiling.

'I'm full of cute ideas,' Dad agreed, and grinned.

'Tell Alex you deserve to start with a full bank account of trust and that it can overflow, it can be added to. So every time he feels safe or loved he tops it up. When he's feeling insecure, he has to think of how much is in the account already. Is there enough there for him to draw on?'

I nodded. 'Yeah, that's good too. Makes him stop and think of his actions.'

'Exactly.'

'But most importantly, and I've learned this lesson the hard way, and so have many of my counseling clients ... the time he invests worrying about losing you and whether you are cheating on him is driving you away, and he will lose you. So he must try and be in the now. Every time you or Alex get worked up, stop and breathe. Invite him to talk about it, remind him regularly of all the great things he is to you. We must all remember to do that,' he said, with a glance to Mom in the kitchen.

'Thanks Dad. You can say no ... but if I talked him into speaking with you about this, instead of a psychologist, would you talk with him?' I asked.

'Of course, darling. But be warned, I'll be asking him his intentions for my daughter as well,' he said.

I rolled my eyes and Dad laughed.

'Come on, let's not keep your mother waiting.' We rose and I linked my arm through his. I had some work to do with The Russian. I was prepared to do it – I wondered if he was. However, I had my limits ... I won't be called a tart or accused of fucking around when I didn't do that. I was drawing the line right there. We entered the kitchen and Mom announced lunch would be ready in ten minutes.

'I'm going to go and call Alex and wish him luck for the game,' I said, and excused myself. I felt more secure in my own head now that I hadn't done anything wrong – I just hoped he'd cooled down and thought about his actions too. I walked outside into the church grounds and checked the time – he was probably on the team bus on the way to the stadium now ... may be best just to text him.

I decided to check his messages first. I took the silencer off my phone and saw he had called three more times last night and three times since six a.m this morning. He'd left two messages in my phone message bank and both of those had been left earlier today ... that was probably a good thing. I was glad he hadn't vented last night; I wondered if he'd learned from experience not to do that.

I put the phone to my ear and listened to the first message that he had left about six a.m.

'Brooker,' he sighed, 'I need to talk with you, hear your voice. Call me.'

His voice was heavy with stress and weariness. I listened to the second message, which he had left about an hour ago when I had been in church.

'Please, call me.' That was it.

I checked the text messages and there was one there that he had sent about three a.m., and one this morning about half an hour ago. He mustn't have slept at all.

I dreaded opening the first one which he had probably written when he'd been majorly pissed off. I tapped on it and read:

Are you in bed alone?

For the love of God, thank goodness he hadn't left a stack of those; he'd have so much more to apologize for this morning! Seriously! I opened the text he had sent thirty minutes ago and read:

Where are you? Call, please Carly.

He'd used my first name ... I didn't know what it meant.

There was no apology. I decided to text him and I tapped out the words:

Play well today. I'll be thinking of you. Cx

That was good, it was generous given what had transpired. I took another long look at the words I had typed, took a deep breath and pressed send. Done!

If he was still angry, well, that was a peace offering and might help him put things on the back burner until the game was out of the way.

My phone rang moments after the text had gone off to him, his name flashed on my screen. Butterflies filled me, my stomach churned ... I truly felt terrified answering it. I thumbed across the screen, accepting the call.

'Hello.'

'Brooker,' he said, his voice was heavy, he breathed out as if he had been holding the weight of the world until I called. 'I'm sorry.'

I couldn't help myself, I started to cry.

I heard him swear softly under his breath. 'Babe, don't cry, I've been sick for hours about what I said to you ...'

I still couldn't say anything ... I didn't know what to say.

'I hate being the one to make you cry, don't cry,' he said again. 'I'm truly sorry ... where are you?'

'At Mom and Dad's.'

'You went home? Are you okay?'

'Yes. I drove home early this morning and went to Dad's service. Dad helped me.'

'You told him what I said?' he asked.

'Yes.'

'I'm never meeting him,' The Russian said, and I laughed

for the first time in over twenty-four hours. It felt good to have a bit of tension lifted.

'He's not judgemental and he's a counselor too, he has some good advice for us,' I said. 'And he's praying for your soul,' I joked.

The Russian chuckled. 'Thank God someone is.'

I heard a voice in the background.

'Where are you? Was that Lucas?' I asked.

'I'm out the front of the hotel, we're just getting our gear on the bus to go to the stadium. And yeah, that was Lucas,' The Russian said.

Lucas's voice came down the line again. 'Is that Carly?'

'Yes,' The Russian answered.

'Thank fuck for that,' he said.

I heard The Russian walking, putting some distance between them.

'Brooker, I'm a fucking idiot ...'

'But you're *my* fucking idiot,' I said, teasing him and he laughed ... that beautiful, rich, baritone laugh.

'We'll land about seven tonight, can I come over and see you then?'

'Okay,' I agreed.

'Or you could pick me up at the airport?' he suggested, 'Like some of the partners do.'

'Or I could pick you up at the airport,' I agreed.

'Russian!' I heard a male voice yell. 'Final call for the bus.' The Russian ignored it.

'Great. I'll text you the flight details later.' He breathed out again. 'Brooker, I'm worried that ...'

I held my breath. *Please don't say 'we're not going to make it', or 'we're not suited'* ... I couldn't take it.

The Russian continued. 'I'm worried that I don't know how to fix this and I'll blow it between us.'

'Russian,' I said, his name softly, 'We'll sort it, I promise.'

Lucas interfered again. 'For Fuck's sake, Russian, get on the bus!'

'I've got to go, they're all waiting.'

'What? You're the only one not on the bus?' I laughed. 'Go then, I'll be watching the game and sending you positive vibes.'

'Thanks for calling me back, I needed to hear your voice.'

'Russian!' I heard a chorus of voices that time.

'I'm fucking coming for Christ's sake,' he yelled back. 'Got to go. Text me later? See you soon?'

'Yes to both,' I said, feeling in love and happy again after that horrendous night of pain.

'Bye,' he said the word slowly and deeply, like he was drawing out the moment before disconnecting. He was walking at the same time; I could hear his movements.

'Hang the fuck up now and get in here,' Lucas said in the background.

I heard The Russian swear again and hang up, and I laughed. We were okay; we were going to be okay ... I hoped we were going to be okay.

I went back inside and felt so much better. Mom called out that lunch was ready and I walked through the hallway and living area to the kitchen, past the shrine that had been set up for my sister, my deceased sister ... the reason I hadn't been coming home very often.

Chapter 21

I was recording the Saints game at home – I know, such a dedicated sports journo, and perve – but I watched it with Mom and Dad as well, and then headed home just after. I got in around three-thirty with plenty of time to preen before I had to join the WAGS at the airport to pick up The Russian. I sent him a message to congratulate him on a brilliant game – maybe he should get stressed out more often – and he texted back the flight details and the cutest message about not being able to breathe properly until he saw me. It always surprised me when he put himself out there, romantically.

As I walked in the door and found the house empty – not sure where Josh was – my phone rang. It was Sasha.

'Hey Sasha, good game and another win,' I said in greeting.

'Great game. Makes my life so much easier when they win ... plenty of media coverage and it's all good,' she said. 'Not to mention the mood around the office is so much better. Speaking of which, what did you and The Russian discuss in his office the other day?'

I grinned recalling our misadventure. 'Oh you know, just the usual stuff – technique, the highs and lows of sport.'

'Uh-huh,' she said, unconvinced. 'Kay said the meeting appeared to go well. Anyway, I'm just checking to make sure you are okay.'

'Oh, that's nice, thanks. Why?' I wondered if The Russian had told anyone in the team about our fight, or maybe Lucas had spread the word.

'Nik woke The Russian up in the hotel corridor this morning. He was sleeping outside his room, Lucas kicked him out!'

'Oh that,' I said. 'We might have had a few words and some late night and early morning messages exchanged ... maybe he didn't sleep so well and Lucas kicked him out to get some sleep.'

'Mm, well, Lucas and The Russian aren't spilling, but I don't care about the details ... I'm not a gossip girl. I just wanted to make sure you weren't eating ice-cream and watching break-up movies,' she said.

'Sash, you're the best, thanks for caring. I'm just fine,' I assured her. 'Will you be picking up Nik tonight?'

'Yeah. Are you coming?' she asked, surprised.

'I am! Until then, and hey, thanks Sash.' We hung up and I decided to give the house a quick clean and change the sheets, just in case. I hear make-up sex is really good.

*****

I got to the airport about twenty minutes early and found the gate where *my* man would be arriving soon. I was pleased to see Sasha already there; I joined her and she introduced me to a few of the other girls, including Eddie's fiancée, Tiffany, and Laura who was Buzz's fiancée ... I'd heard they'd only recently gotten engaged. Laura was gorgeous with this wild red hair and green eyes.

Alice was there from the office too and she waved and came over with her friend, whom I recognized as Mia – Captain Fantastic's girlfriend. I was fit tall, but she was fit cute ... about five-foot-five, well-proportioned, with runner legs and slim hips. She had her shoulder-length brown hair tied back in a single braid.

'Hi Carly,' she said, 'I hear our boys shared a room last night ... well, for a while,' she grinned.

I shook her offered hand. 'Yes, The Russian must have been snoring and got kicked out!' We had a laugh and a chat about sports. She was keen on getting some physical therapy experience with my Suns team and I said I'd be happy to introduce her to the current physical therapy staff. She asked after my injury, which was kind, and she was genuinely interested. I could see what Lucas saw in her, she was calm but confident, in charge, and she inspired me ... she made me realize that maybe I needed to be firmer with The Russian. Close down his insecurity, not let him run away with it, and instead of trying to appease him I should try pulling him into line and making him see how ridiculous it all sounded. Seemed like a good plan anyway.

Then the plane landed and my heart rate increased. I looked over and saw a few journos and photographers waiting for the team. One of the photographers recognized me and gave me a wave; I waved back and prayed he wouldn't come over ... I needed The Russian to see me with the girls and waiting one hundred percent for him when he came through that door. I wondered how the super cool Russian was going to react. Sasha said he always avoided the spotlight with his ex Leesa, but I guessed she had always been in the spotlight. Would he kiss me publicly? Would he hurry me out of there, or treat me like I had always been part of the furniture and be super cool about it? My money was on the latter.

The doors opened and a few of the flight attendants came out, along with a handful of passengers. Buzz was out first and greeted us. He wrapped an arm around Laura and gave me a wink as they left, as though all was forgiven for his prank. Some of the Saints' crew followed, then the coach, and Lucas who gave Mia a wave and pointed in the direction of the journos. She nodded, knowing he had to give a quick interview first.

'Bloody journos,' she said, winking at Sasha, and then she remembered I was one too and rolled her eyes dramatically. 'I'm surrounded by them. Wow, it's going to be hard not to report the internal scoops you hear now, Carly,' she said to me.

'Tell me about it. I've had to separate my inside knowledge of the Suns from my job for years!'

Tomás came into sight, greeted us all and left with Alice, and then Nik and The Russian appeared. The Russian's eyes scanned the area and found mine, and he gave me a smile that would launch ships. He walked towards me, threw his bag over his shoulder and wrapped his spare arm around me, pressing me hard to him, our lips locked. It was so healing, his lips on mine, his skin against mine, just the feel of his strong body encompassing me, and he didn't stop kissing me. I couldn't believe it, in front of his teammates and everything!

'Geez, not in public you two, cut it out,' Lucas teased, coming over and giving Mia a showy kiss.

'Get a room, Russian,' Nik added as Sasha threw herself at him, and then we heard the sound of flashes and The Russian released me just a few inches, enough to draw a breath.

'So needed that,' he said. 'Hello, Brooker.'

'Hello Russian,' I grinned up at him, admiring his dark eyes and beautiful face. He looked exhausted.

One of the journos yelled out to us. 'Going to teach him to play basketball, Carly?'

'I don't think he's tall enough,' I replied with a wave. The Russian nodded at the journo, and hurried us along.

'We need to get home immediately,' The Russian said, slightly breathless. 'Let's go.'

He released me only enough so I could walk, tucking me into his body, ignoring the flashes of cameras. When we got to my car, he threw his bag in the back seat and sat back while I drove, annoying me by rubbing his hand over my leg, and anywhere else he could get access to before I hit him away for being distracting. We hardly spoke, we just wanted to be together, to be near each other.

Luckily, Josh wasn't home and The Russian hustled me straight into my bedroom, closing my bedroom door with his foot and knocking me onto the bed. When we were settled, he stopped and placed his forehead on mine.

'I'm sorry, forgive me?' he asked. It was so sincere and private, and I felt all his pain and anxiety and I hated Leesa for causing this beautiful man to doubt himself.

'You scared me a little,' I whispered and he pulled away to look at me. He looked ashamed. 'Russian, do you really think I'm promiscuous?'

He put his finger on my lips. 'Never, don't say it, don't think it. This is my problem, I know it ... when I calmed down last night and stopped panicking that I was going to lose you to some guy, I realized I was going to lose you because I had been such an asshole. Then, you were so far away ... I didn't sleep ... I couldn't reach you.'

'I'm sorry. I wasn't trying to hurt you by not answering – I was freaked out and I had to talk with Dad and look at my part in this, whether I was 'tarty'. I was also a bit scared to ring you back.'

He groaned and put his head on my chest. I ran my hand through his hair. 'Shh, we're all good,' I said, and then he started to kiss me, slow at first, but then our need kicked in; it felt desperate for both of us. He kissed me hard, his tongue angry and thrusting inside me, and mine giving as good as it got. My clothes were off in moments and I pulled at The Russian's Saints' traveling uniform shirt and pants, discarding them quickly.

Within seconds, he was slipping on a condom and pushing himself inside me. I dug my nails into his arms, I needed to feel him so badly and he had the same hunger, I could tell from the force of his thrusts.

'Harder,' I said, sinking my fingers into his skin, and he

forced himself in deeper until I cried out with the pleasure and pain of it.

He wasn't gentle and I didn't want him to be. I came with a needy desire and when I came down off the roof, he moved his hands under me and thrust harder. He looked so intense and gorgeous, and then I felt him releasing himself into me and I buried my face in his neck. I held him so tight that he'd have bruises afterward. Then he stilled, breathing heavily, and lowered himself beside me. We stayed that way, just holding each other for the longest time.

I think we were both almost asleep when The Russian forced himself up and discarded the condom. He returned and, lying on his back, he wrapped me against his body, and within minutes I could hear his steady breathing. My beautiful guy was wiped out from no sleep and the pressure of the game, but at least now he was there with me and we were going to be okay. I mouthed that I loved him because I did, and I watched him sleep. We'd have to work on the king of the jungle's Achilles' heel.

Chapter 22

The Russian's phone alarm went off at six a.m. and we both jumped awake. He grabbed it and groaned.

'You know I don't work Mondays because I work Saturdays,' I said, 'but I really appreciate the early wake-up call so I don't fall out of my routine,' I stirred him.

The Russian smiled and flipped me onto my stomach. 'Since you're awake, and I'm a morning person ...'

He lowered himself onto me and his hands slipped underneath me to the front of my body, where – with a few skilled moves – he had me fired up in moments.

'Come inside me,' I begged.

'Who's driving here?' he asked.

I laughed. 'You are, Russian.'

'That's right,' he said, in his sexy low voice.

I moaned with pleasure as he pinned me down so I couldn't even wriggle and played me like a violin. I tried to tell him how good it felt, but I couldn't get the words out and I wasn't even a morning person. I panted as I came down from my high.

'Come inside me, please Russian,' I begged him after I was perfectly sated.

'Yes bossy, Brooker,' he teased me. I heard him search for a condom, he slipped it on and keeping me pressed down into the pillows, he took charge.

'You are so tight,' he hissed between his teeth.

'Because I've just had a huge orgasm,' I said, stating the obvious, which got us both laughing. He started teasing my ear with his tongue just to annoy me and I squealed and wriggled stilled pinned underneath him. Then he pushed a little harder and took my breath away.

'That got your attention,' he said.

'You feel so good,' I moaned.

The Russian moved slowly and every now and then he stopped to get control. He started again and he drew a sharp breath, so I knew he was close and I let myself go with him. I was a quivering mess by the time he lowered himself on me.

'Fantastic,' The Russian muttered and I chuckled at his review. He smacked my butt. 'I love this butt, amongst other things.'

I turned around to watch him remove the condom, head to the bathroom and stride back to the bed. Great view. When he returned and slipped in beside me, I broached one of my new strategies to help our relationship.

'Place your hand on my heart,' I said, and he did, then lowered it. I rolled my eyes and he smiled and moved it back up again.

'You're no fun, Brooker,' he said.

'I'll give you fun in a minute,' I warned him. 'Mm, I just channeled my mother.'

'And mine, but without the Russian accent,' he said.

'*Babe*,' I said, using his term of endearment. 'This is our sign, to protect us and to show you that you are my only thought.'

He looked confused and ran his tongue over his lower lip as if he was going to be in trouble for something. I leaned in and kissed him quickly before continuing to explain.

'What I mean is ... if you see me in social photos, or giving an interview, or commentating, or even glancing your way in a crowded room, and I place my hand on my heart, even for just a minute, it's for you. It's me telling you that you own my heart.'

He smiled and with one hand, cupped my cheek.

'I love that,' he said, and sealed it with a kiss.

Then I remembered ... 'Why was your alarm set?' I asked, knowing he didn't have morning training and wouldn't need to get to the office until later.

'Ah yeah, that ... Tia's got a school recital this morning. She's one of the kids performing and being presented with an award. I promised her I'd come along,' he said.

'You are such a good brother, and such a good lover,' I added.

'That so?' he asked, raising an eyebrow and looking mildly pleased with himself. 'Want to come?'

'Not yet, I just had two orgasms,' I said, happily as I stretched out on the bed.

'Focus, Brooker, do you want to come with me to Tia's presentation?' he asked, a smile on the edge of his lips.

I laughed. 'Oh that, yes! I'd love to.'

'Really? You know it's going to be a bunch of five to ten-year-old kids making a lot of noise, and putting on a performance that only family would endure?' he said, frowning in my direction.

'It'll be fun,' I said, excited to be invited to a family event.

'Then get your butt into the shower. I'll join you in a minute,' he said, putting his hands behind his head and leaning back on the bed.

'What are you going to do?' I asked suspiciously.

'Watch you walk in,' he said. We were back on track.

*****

I selected a sundress with sandals to wear and then we swung by The Russian's place so he could grab a clean change of clothes. I avoided going near the bedroom where he was changing, in case he got distracted. We headed off again and got to the school in plenty of time – I was still driving and would drop The Russian home afterward.

'Been meaning to tell you that I like your car, Brooker ... it's a good size – I can fit in it – and it suits you,' The Russian said, admiring my white BMW Gran Coupé from the inside.

'Thank you, I think.' I wasn't sure why he thought it suited me. 'I love this car, I treated myself to it when I got my contract renewed. I figured I had a bit of security then.'

The Russian nodded. 'After you had your home loan sorted?'

'Of course,' I said, 'spoken like a man with a management degree.' He smirked at me, but looked approving as well. I pulled into a car park at the school hall that was a fair distance from the entrance, but clearly the elementary school concert pulled a crowd.

The Russian took my hand as we walked in and got lost amongst the crowd. School kids were running around, finding their families, showing off, doing normal kid things. However, it soon became obvious that we were being recognized. It was like a small whisper in the room, and the crowds parted as The Russian spotted his mother and we made our way towards her. Tia saw us and, with a squeal that would break glass, she ran over propelling herself at The Russian who gave her a hug. Then she saw me and jumped up and down. So cute. I gave her a hug before she raced back to the stage to prepare. I heard her saying to her friends. 'That's my brother, he's a Saints' player.'

One little girl next to her said: 'I saw his girlfriend on television.' Tia nodded. 'She plays sport too and she's a TV star.'

I chuckled and The Russian sighed. 'They'd be more excited if you were a Disney princess and I was the prince.'

'Aren't we?' I asked, looking a little disappointed.

We made our way towards his mother, Lana. She looked lovely – slim and sophisticated in a lemon dress with high strappy sandals.

'Carly, so good to see you,' she said.

'And you too Lana,' I said, as we exchanged cheek kisses.

'How did Dad get out of this?' The Russian growled.

'Work. But he did get to the last one,' Lana said. 'And since you're the boss at work, you'll have to come up with a better excuse next year.'

The Russian made a humph sort of sound, but I think he

would go to anything that Tia was starring in, he really did adore his little sister.

We found three seats and as I looked around, I couldn't believe the people sneaking looks at us, especially the mothers sneaking looks at The Russian. A number of people came and went as they greeted Lana and The Russian, and met me.

I whispered to The Russian: 'I think some of the cougars in the room are very upset you brought a date.'

The Russian put his arm around my shoulder. 'That's why I brought you, to protect me,' he joked.

Lana patted her son's shoulder. 'I'm so pleased you brought Carly. You are very lucky to have her, I hope you look after her.' She turned to me. 'You'll have to be patient with him Carly, he is a man.'

'He is that,' I said, agreeing and teasing The Russian.

'I hope he knows how lucky he is,' she said, smiling approvingly at both of us. 'He can be moody though and stubborn, but I'm sure you'll work wonders with him.'

'I'm right here, Mom,' he said, shaking his head and pointing out the obvious.

Then the concert began and I felt like part of the family. The Russian held my hand the whole time ... bliss. But he was right – if I hadn't been in love and just happy to be sitting in each other's company, the ninety-minute concert would have been agony!

Chapter 23

After I had dropped The Russian home I spotted the coffee van, the very same one that visited the Saints office ... *Wendy's Caffeine Hit*. It was written on the van. Too good. I followed her until she pulled up outside a grocery store, and I raced to catch up with her.

'Wendy,' I called. She stopped and looked around. Wendy was probably in her late forties, with bleached blonde hair and a small, wiry build. She looked like she had worked hard all her life.

'You don't know me,' I said, coming up beside her, 'but I'm Carly, The Russian's girlfriend.'

'Ah, The Russian,' she said, her face softening ... hmm. 'One of my favorite customers. Good to meet you, Luv.'

'And you. This is going to sound strange, but Sasha from the Saints' office ....'

'The media lady?' Wendy asked.

'That's her. Well, we're trying to work out how The Russian beats her to the top of the queue each day and we were wondering if he asked you to message him when you were near.'

'Ah,' she said, and waggled her finger at me, 'I'm like a doctor ... I don't reveal anything about my patients' coffee habits.'

I grinned at her. 'I get that, I'm a journalist. But maybe, just maybe, we could do a deal. Perhaps you would like some tickets to a Suns or Saints game, or .... some merchandise ...'

'Hmm,' she rubbed her chin thinking. 'Very tempting.'

I pushed a little harder. 'In fact, we don't even need you to reveal what is going on – if anything,' I added hastily. 'Just once, if you could send Sasha a message first so she could race out to meet you ... just the once would be enough to beat him at his own game.'

She laughed. 'You girls, that's funny.'

I grinned at her. 'Why don't I leave you my number and maybe text me when you've thought about it?'

'We girls do need to stick together,' she said, handing over her phone as I put my number in.

'Thank you, Wendy. Hope to hear from you,' I said, with a smile.

'I'm not saying I have a system with The Russian, and I'm not saying I don't, mind you,' she said.

'I hear you,' I agreed, 'you'd make a fine reporter.' I said and gave her a wave as I walked away. Everything had a price ... my first boyfriend, a salesman, had taught me that one.

After I had gotten back in my car, I then got a phone call from Serge, my PT. He was sick and had to cancel my appointment. He was trying to get someone to take it ... I had an idea. I told him about Captain Lucas's live-in-lover and PT, Mia, who ran her own business on the side and told him Mia was keen to do some casual Suns physical therapist work; here was her chance. Serge said he was fine with it, so I rang Sasha who asked Alice for Mia's phone number. I waited for Sasha to text through Mia's number, called her, and she booked me in that afternoon at 'their' place at three-thirty. Done!

*****

It was easy to find Lucas and Mia's place ... it wasn't far from The Russian's, and wow, another amazing place! There was security at the bottom of the hill and my name was on the list to come into the gated community. I drove up and parked on the street in front of the house. Mia was at the front door before I got there, dressed casually in what looked like running gear – sports shorts and a tank. We gave each other a hug; I could look over her head while I was doing it – I must have had a foot on her.

'I am so glad you called,' she said, 'we should have swapped numbers at the airport. Come on up.'

I followed her up the stairs and stopped to admire the view – it was a glasshouse with floor to ceiling windows showing off the stunning ocean views from every angle. Everything was white and the beach literally started at the front door.

'The Russian's place is pretty good too,' she said, 'the same view, further along.'

'I know,' I agreed, 'I don't think you could ever tire of it.'

'I can't imagine not seeing this view now, I'm spoilt for life. It's this way,' she said, heading down a short hall. I followed her as she went into another large, clean, white room set up with all the gear she could possibly need. 'This is my PT room; Lucas set it up for me. Mind you, he's my biggest client.' She at least had the good grace to blush when she said it.

'Does he let you work on the other guys?' I asked, curious.

'Never,' she said, and rolled her eyes. 'Nik suggested it once and Lucas almost increased Nik's need for physical therapy. So I don't push it. I've got plenty of other clients and I prefer females while I work here alone.'

'Makes sense,' I said.

'Change into whatever makes you comfortable, but I suggest just your underwear so I don't get any cream on you, and you don't sweat on your clothes,' she said, and added: 'Don't worry Lucas is not here and he wouldn't walk into this room without knocking anyway.'

I went into the dressing room and stripped off my shorts and shirt, returning to lay on the table as she directed.

'Well, I'm very pleased poor Serge is sick, sorry Serge,' Mia said. 'You're the first Suns' player I've worked on.'

I braced as she began to work over my leg and knee. It was much better, but with the pressure the physical therapists applied, there was always an element of pain.

'Speaking of that,' I said between sharp breaths, 'I spoke with Serge and he'd love to hear from you if you want some casual Suns' work.'

'Really?' she asked, 'fantastic, thank you!'

'Pleasure,' I said with a groan, and Mia laughed.

'I do have something that will be a pleasure,' Mia teased. 'After we finish this session, the Saints' boys should be training on the beach out the front. We could have a drink and watch? Purely on a professional basis ... physical therapist, journalist ...'

Visions of The Russian working out on the beach flooded me. 'What a brilliant idea,' I agreed. 'Brilliant.' I closed my eyes and tried not to think about my injury, while Mia worked her wonders.

Thirty minutes later Mia declared us done. I could hardly move; I think I was plastered to the table.

'I'm stuck here,' I moaned and Mia laughed, helping me up.

'Do you want to shower?' she asked.

'No I'm good, thanks. Really appreciate it, Mia, especially on short notice.'

'Happy to do it. I'll just go wash my hands and then we can watch the boys suffer ... um, I mean, work out,' she said, with a smile and a glance at the clock.

I pulled my shorts and top back on, and, grabbing my bag, slipped out some cash to give her. She walked in seeing me holding it.

'Don't worry about it,' she said, graciously, 'I'm happy to do it.'

I knew she didn't need the money, but I insisted on paying her.

'I won't feel like I can ask you for more PT in the future if you don't let me pay,' I said, and slipped the dollars under her desk paperweight near the door. 'Besides, the club reimburses me, so don't give it a second thought.'

'Thank you, I'll send you a receipt if you can message me your email address,' she said. 'Come on, let's get a drink.'

I followed her from the white PT room back down the hallway to the front of the house. She entered the kitchen, opened the fridge and offered me a drink.

'I'm having a diet cola, want one?' she asked. 'Or I have juice, water, normal cola ...'

'Diet cola is perfect, thanks.'

She handed me two glasses, grabbed the cans of diet cola and stuck a bag of pretzels under her arm.

'There's something wonderfully decadent about eating and drinking while you watch the boys work out. Kind of like payback for all the times they annoy us,' she said with a grin.

'Well, The Russian and I are fairly new together, so he hasn't annoyed me too much ... yet.'

'Just wait until they lose a game,' she said, heading to the balcony. Then she remembered I was a professional athlete. 'Oh sorry,' Mia's eyes widened. 'You'd know what that's like of course. I don't mean to dismiss the sense of frustration and disappointment, it's just that they can be unbearably grouchy for days after.'

I sat in a tall, white leather chair opposite Mia with our drinks between us as we looked over at the beach. The chairs were deep but high, so we could see over the balcony edge with an uninterrupted view of the sandy beachfront and crashing waves.

'No apology necessary,' I said, 'I've been known to be a bit unbearable to live with myself on those days!'

We both extended our bare legs to catch some sun and then Lucas drove into the garage below. He looked up to see us and gave us a wave and a surprised look in my direction.

'Good day, gorgeous?' he asked Mia.

'Very good,' Mia said, leaning over the balcony. 'I've just been doing some physical therapy on my client,' she said, with a nod in my direction.

'How's the knee?' Lucas asked.

'Getting much better, thanks,' I said.

'Well enjoy watching us suffer,' he said, with a smirk in our direction as he grabbed a workout bag from the trunk of the car and headed straight down to the beach.

'Oh we will,' Mia said just to me, and we both giggled.

Then the Saints' boys started to arrive. We were so close I could hear the coach and trainers ordering them to get a move on, and my heart rate went up as I spotted the beautiful, tall, dynamic presence of The Russian.

'They hate the beach workout,' Mia said, with a smile. 'Did the Suns do it?'

'Once a week,' I said. 'It's agony, but good if you've got injuries. Running in the water helps, as you know.'

'Personally, I love it, you must come by again around this time,' she teased. 'I'm sure we can find something to do even if you don't need PT!'

'We would look much more the part if we were sitting here sipping Martinis,' I said.

Mia's eyes lit up. 'Oh yes. We should have a WAGS cocktail party on beach training day.'

'Won't the coach be cheesed off if we're sitting up here distracting them?' I said.

'Then we won't distract them of course,' she said, with almost an evil grin. 'Besides, they should be focussing on the task at hand.'

'Agreed,' I said, expecting to get a cocktail party invitation anytime in the next few weeks. A little red sports car pulled up and Alice alighted, waving up to us.

'Hey,' she said to us as Mia buzzed her in down below.

She was obviously on the gate VIP list since she'd driven straight through. She came upstairs in her business wear.

'Look at you two workout gals,' she said, eyeing off our sportswear. Alice gave Mia a kiss on the cheek and did the same for me, which was very sweet.

'How did you get an early mark from work?' Mia asked, narrowing her eyes, as she jumped up to grab a drink for Alice.

Alice slid onto a chair beside Mia and let out a long breath as she watched the guys run out of the surf. 'Marvellous.'

I giggled beside her like I was part of a secret Saints watching club.

'The boss, Jim, is away today, so while the boss is away, the mice play,' she said, accepting the drink and thanking Mia. 'Besides, I've done my share of weekend game days to steal back a few hours.'

The Saints were wet, their bathers were wet, their chests were wet and their tanned torsos gleaming.

I sighed. 'So good.'

'So good,' Mia repeated and nodded.

'You could sell tickets to this,' Alice suggested to Mia.

'Enterprising,' she agreed. 'But we're going to have a girls' cocktail party instead, right here, one training afternoon just for the WAGS. It was Carly's suggestion.'

I shrugged. 'I can't take all the credit, I drew inspiration from out there.'

'You're working wonders on The Russian,' Alice said, 'he seems sort of calmer. Sasha has worked with him for much longer than me but she said he is definitely happier. She keeps dropping your name to get a reaction.'

'Really?' I grinned, pleased to be working some magic on him. 'What sort of reaction?'

'He gets this lovey-dovey look on his face ... I think it is very sweet but you know how Sasha loves to stir him.'

'Ha, that's funny,' I said, laughing. 'But it's early days yet, I'm sure he'll go back to being his usual self in no time.'

I was pretty sure that Lucas hadn't told The Russian I was up here with Mia, perhaps he thought The Russian would know I was coming over for PT, but I hadn't spoken to him since I had left Tia's concert this morning. I watched him with the team. He truly was a beautiful looking man.

The trainer ordered them to hit the sand, and the Saints players all lay on their backs; they seemed to know the routine.

'Here comes the abdominal core circuit,' Mia said.

'I remember it well,' I said, subliminally wincing and Mia grinned.

The countdown began and the guys began on the crunches. In between repetitions, the trainers demanded the guys plank, I could feel the burn. Mia and I both groaned; Alice was more of a yoga girl. Watching The Russian plank was so sexy; his arm muscles just bulged and his core was so tight, even better when his body began to shudder with the pressure and he dropped his head to control his body ... so sexy.

Mia fanned herself, not taking her eyes off Lucas.

'We can always go for a cold swim after,' she suggested, with a glance towards the plunge pool in the corner.

'We might need to,' I agreed. Next came the push-ups ... those arms, that tight butt ... and then the boys stood to begin sprints and The Russian grabbed a towel to wipe his face. So frigging sexy again. Lucas came up beside him to do the same and must have given me away because The Russian looked up towards the balcony and right at me. He gave a slightly discernible smile; we both knew it was best not to look too happy at training ... you'll be worked harder. He kept his gaze on me as he reached for a bottle of water, drinking and spilling some of it over his chest ... fuck me now, seriously.

Then I swear he worked out even harder after that, like he was making sure I got the show of my life.

*****

Lucas ran up the sandy front yard of his beach mansion and into the house, coming up the internal stairs. On the beach out the front, the Saints had finished their session and were dispersing. He came out to us on the balcony and wrapped Mia in a bear hug.

'I've been sent up to get you girls for a swim. C'mon, surf's up,' he said.

'Eww, get off me,' Mia tried to wriggle out of his grip. 'You're sweaty and awful.'

'You like me sweaty,' he said, kissing her as she wriggled.

Who wouldn't like him sweaty? He was something else: his blue eyes looking so blue, and his pin-up boy looks.

'I only like you sweaty when I'm sweaty,' she grimaced. Lucas released her, pulling her up from the chair and tapping her butt.

'C'mon, orders from The Russian and Tomás, get your gear off and report to the beach.'

'Aye, aye, Captain,' I said, rising from the seat into action.

Lucas gave me a smile and raced back out of the house again.

'Do you need swimmers?' Mia asked me.

I shook my head. 'No thanks, I've got swimming, running and gym bags in my car ... you never know.'

'I thought you would,' she said. 'Alice?'

'Can I wear that red two-piece suit?' she said.

Mia rolled her eyes. 'I'm giving it to you, as long as you leave it here so you're always covered when you drop in. You always liked it more than me.'

'Yes!' Alice said, going to change. She gave me a grin. 'I'm a bit partial to shopping.'

'It's her middle name,' Mia said, following her to get the swimsuit.

When we were changed, we headed to the beach, where The Russian emerged long enough from the surf to drag me in with him. Sexy beast.

*****

Twenty minutes later, I came out of the surf before him and headed over to get my towel. I didn't realize Lucas was behind me until he called my name.

'Hey,' I said, shaking the sand off my towel before it stuck to me.

'Can we talk a minute?' he asked.

'Sure,' I said, looking around. Mia and Alice were still swimming. If Lucas was going to ask me not to distract his forward before a game, there was going to be trouble.

'I just wanted to check you were okay,' he said, toweling down.

'Oh,' I said, surprised. I wasn't expecting that. 'I'm fine, why?' I frowned at him.

Lucas cleared his throat, clearly uncomfortable. 'The Russian told me what happened, sort of, between grunts and shrugs, you know,' he said, not doing much better than The Russian did I imagine. 'He was really worried he blew it with you... he's a good guy...'

'I know,' I said, cutting Lucas off. 'I know he's a good guy, and you're a good friend to speak for him.'

I spread my towel out and sat down. He did the same with his towel and lowered himself beside me. I saw him glance quickly to the surf to see where The Russian was before continuing.

'I want to give you some context, but you never heard this from me and you can't ever tell him you know, unless he shares it with you,' Lucas said.

I groaned.

Lucas frowned. 'It's important. If you understand what's happened, you might cut him a break when he's an idiot. Besides, it's my job to look out for the guys ... well I'm trying to step up in that area.'

I grimaced. I can imagine it would be hard given that most guys keep everything bottled up.

'I don't think I want to know,' I said.

Lucas shrugged. 'I just don't want him to blow a good thing.' He looked uncomfortable using that term. 'You know what I mean.'

'I do,' I said, and thought about it for a few moments. 'Okay, thanks, best you tell me then.' I could feel my stomach clenching, not to mention my heart.

'It'll stay strictly between us?' Lucas asked.

I nodded. 'I promise.'

Lucas drew a breath and began. 'Leesa has pretty much ruined his ability to trust in any relationship.'

'I know about Leesa,' I interrupted. I saw The Russian, Mia and Alice leaving the surface.

'Did you know she got pregnant, with The Russian's kid?' Lucas didn't stop. 'Then she had a big night out when she was a fair way along and miscarried.'

'Crap.'

'It gets worse,' he said, hurrying up his story. 'When The Russian left her, she tried to kill herself. Since then she's been seeking security from every man she can, by the looks of it. It's done his head in.'

I didn't have time to take it all in or ask questions as the rest of our group dropped down beside us. I nodded my thanks to Lucas and looked over at my man. What was I supposed to do with that information? It did explain why he hadn't just walked away from her sooner. In fact, it explained a lot; that would put me off having a relationship for a long time. Let's not even begin on the trust issues.

I wondered if he would ever tell me. Wow, he had been through some pain. And I couldn't mention a word of it to him.

Chapter 24

I might have been too smug too soon about beach training ... my coach called to say since I was given the all-clear by Serge to play in the last game of the season, I had better get more serious about my training, and the beach session was going to be one of the sessions. Wait until I tell The Russian, he'll have one of those grins on his face like I got what I deserved for watching him sweat it out. Nevertheless, I was kind of looking forward to getting back to training with the girls.

My new boss, Karen, was totally supportive of me leaving each day at four-thirty to get to training by five p.m., and when I entered on Tuesday, the Suns' girls cheered. It felt great to be home again. I started slowly under the guidance of Serge, but really enjoyed it, especially being with Steffi and Aimee again. And that was when I heard the news ... a joint beach session had been organized with the Saints!

When the coach announced it, everyone turned to look at me, but I was just as shocked.

'I didn't do it!' I said.

'No, Maria in marketing has organized it,' Coach said,

with a noticeable edge to her voice ... I don't think Coach was particularly happy about it, but the Suns' girls were.

'Are any of the Saints still single?' Aimee whispered in my ear.

I gave her a nod. 'Three in the firsts and half a dozen in the reserves.' That brought a smile to her face.

Coach continued. 'Anyway, we'll have some media there and supposedly it's good for both teams to promote our end of season games and next year's membership campaign. Strike while the iron's hot, apparently.' She handed over to Lenny, one of our trainers.

'Now, we won't be trying to match them to the point of risking injury, will we?' Lenny asked.

'No,' we all said in unison, but we were all thinking we wanted to whip their butts.

'However ...' Lenny continued, 'it's a good opportunity to push yourself just that little bit harder and I'm sure they'll be doing their best to look good. So, tomorrow, Laguna Beach at five, our usual time.'

'And be prepared for the usual training session,' Coach stepped in. 'This is not a social visit, we will be training.'

'Sounds pretty social to me,' Lia said, nudging Aimee and me. 'Are you sure you had nothing to do with it?' she narrowed her eyes at me.

'First I've heard about it,' I assured her. I caught the eye of the Suns' marketing guru, Maria – she was sitting in the grandstand looking pretty happy with herself – and she gave me a nod. Hmm, I'd get to the bottom of this.

When training was over, I had a chat with Serge about going a little harder next time and then I caught Maria before she left. I was about two feet taller than her, I swear, and she took a step up on the bleachers to talk to me eye-to-eye. She had short, cropped brown hair, and little features.

'I can't take credit for the idea,' she said, before I had even opened my mouth.

'Ah, so it's not necessarily taking advantage of The Russian and my situation?' I asked, tongue-in-cheek, not that I minded. All publicity was good publicity for sports clubs, especially if it encouraged people to play the game, buy a membership or attracted a sponsor.

'No, but that certainly helped the situation. The Atlanta Furies women's team just did the same stunt with their opposite male team ... sure, they both play basketball, but I thought, why limit ourselves to that? Why not have the Saints versus the Suns – two local teams both heading into the finals?'

'Why not?' I agreed, with a smile.

'Sex sells, Carly,' she said, tapping her nose. 'Anyway, must run, you're looking good out there.'

'Thanks, Maria,' I said. I was sure I was looking good if I could bring in a dollar ... but it was a small price to pay to give something back to the club.

*****

The next afternoon we arrived in our squad bus for the joint training session, and the Saints were already on the beach in their training gear. There was also a good smattering of media with cameras and photographic equipment, and I guess it was no surprise most of them were keen for that shot of The Russian and me training together ... no pressure!

The Suns' girls were dressed in our training shorts and tanks with our swimsuits underneath. The Saints' boys wore pretty much the same, except many of them had their tanks off already – show-offs. The Russian still had on his tank ... I'm sure it was for dramatic effect, so he could rip it off later and thrill me.

I spotted Mia; she was working with the PT guys, so not watching with a cocktail from her balcony. She gave me a return wave and smiled. Then the two coaches called the teams together and welcomed us, telling us they would take it in turn to run the drills. They suggested we paired up and The Russian grabbed me even though the team's defender, Jackson, had cozied up next to me and asked if I wanted to partner. The look The Russian gave him could have frozen the ocean; Jackson grinned and quickly moved on. I noticed Aimee wasted no time partnering with him; he was single.

It truly was the battle of the sexes, but somewhat predictable. Given the size of The Russian and some of the boys, we were lighter and faster with the sit-ups, but the boys had more arm strength when it came to push-ups. The Suns' girls were more flexible than the Saints' boys, but the guys were pretty good on the cardio ... they had bigger chests and lungs and they used them against us. The planking was pretty even and no one wanted to give in first, but in the end the coach called it over ... thank the Lord for that; my stomach was caving in. I collapsed to the ground as soon as Coach called it over and groaned.

'You're a pussy, Brooker,' The Russian teased me.

I glanced up at him from my flat out position with my cheek pressed to the sand and grimaced.

'I'll give you pussy in a minute, Russian,' I threatened, then I realized what I had said.

The Russian grinned. 'That'd be great.'

'I so walked right into that,' I groaned.

He pulled himself up, and me along with him. Snap, crackle, pop went the camera flashes. Lucas was getting a fair bit of attention too as he was partnered with our tallest and most athletic player Karley, and she wasn't giving him an inch – Lucas so tall and fair, Karley so tall and dark ... rather beautiful they were. I glanced towards Mia, but she was totally unfazed, which was totally healthy.

Then the two physical therapists from the Saints and Suns pulled Buzz and me out of training just to do some work on our injuries, which meant The Russian and Latoya – who had been partnered with Buzz – got together. I knew The Russian and Buzz had a history of mutual dislike – too much testosterone – but I didn't realize that it would cause a problem.

Buzz and I were lying next to each other on the tables, sharing a few laughs, and my PT, Serge, and the Saints' PT, Andy, joined in. I then noticed The Russian was watching me, and I swear his dark eyes had green in them. This was not good. Man, this guy was so insecure. I was lying face down, but I lifted myself up a bit and, ensuring I had his attention, I moved my hand to my heart. His brow furrowed as he realized what I was doing, and then he smiled at me. I thought we were okay. But no ...

True to his reputation of being the club fight boy and stirrer, Buzz read The Russian like a book and began to act upon it. I could feel Buzz running his eyes over me and then he leaned over to make a joke, as though we were sharing an intimate secret. He placed his hand on my arm.

It was like the beach exploded; The Russian was pulling Buzz up from the PT bench by his throat and Buzz struck out, getting in a few good pummels to The Russian's rib area.

The Suns' girls screamed and huddled out of the way, and Saints' players seemed to emerge on the two men from all sides. Lucas and Nik were at the core of the fight, trying to pull the two men apart without much success, while the PTs and management were blocking the media to stop taking photos. I joined the Suns' girls, scurrying away, keen not to be caught in the crossfire.

The players managed to contain the scene but not before the media had a few good shots, and you can guess the headline for that one.

'You're a fucking stirrer, Buzz,' Lucas said, pushing him backward. Buzz grinned, not taking his eyes off The Russian.

'If I had one less ounce of self-control,' The Russian hissed at him.

'Yeah, what would have happened?' Buzz taunted him.

'Let's just say your season would be over,' The Russian threatened.

Several of the Saint's boys continued to stand between them. I could tell their coach was seething.

'Russian, Buzz, hit the water and cool down,' he ordered them, 'And if either of you makes contact, you're on the bench this weekend, and I mean it.'

The Russian wouldn't look at me; maybe that was a good thing, especially as everyone else was sneaking glances in my direction.

'Let's get back to work,' our coach called and everyone got back in position.

I saw The Russian and Buzz emerge from the waves a few minutes later and the coach took them aside for a dressing-down. They re-joined the training session five minutes later. The Russian still wouldn't look at me. I didn't know if he was angry with me, embarrassed or angry with himself.

At the end of the training session, we formed two lines like we did on game days, and all moved along shaking each other's hands. It had been fun except for that incident, and it made training more interesting for the day. When I came to shake hands with The Russian, he held my hand a bit longer. The training group broke up.

'Come back to my place?' he asked.

'If you can drop me back to my car at our clubhouse later?'

'Sure,' he happily agreed.

Lucas came over. 'You two want to come up for a drink?'

'Ah, thanks ...' I said, with a glance to The Russian.

'But no, thanks buddy,' The Russian said. 'I've got to show Carly something ... very important. High-security stuff.'

Lucas grinned. 'Yeah, I'm sure she needs to see that.'

*****

A few of the Saints and Suns stayed for a dip in the ocean and then after, The Russian and I walked back to his place. I think his streak of jealousy must come with a desperate need for reassurance because we'd barely gotten inside the door before The Russian set upon me. His strong hands pulled me close to him and he kissed me like a man needing oxygen. We didn't make it to the bedroom, luckily he had that huge circle couch; I was on my back on it, with my swimmers pulled down past my knees and off before I could say 'take me, Russian'.

The Russian made this guttural sort of sound as he moved back up my body, and then removed my swimsuit top. Sand was all over us – gritty lovemaking, we didn't care, I just as greedily pulled off his shorts and swimmers. I began to run my tongue over his defined six-pack, and I could tell it was appreciated. The Russian was primed. But then he stopped me, and pulled me up close to him; his eyes were full of pain ... enough to stop primal needs and make him reach for me.

'What is it?' I asked and touched his face. He didn't speak immediately, but I could see him carefully putting his words together, not wanting to be naked emotionally and physically.

He swallowed. 'About earlier ...'

I stopped him, putting my finger on his lips.

'It's okay. We got through that intact, didn't we?' I asked. *Please say we're okay, please. I didn't want him to give up on us before we had really started.*

He nodded slightly, barely noticeably.

'I fucking hate it when it happens,' he said, and took a deep breath.

I nodded. 'Buzz is playing you. You know I'm not even remotely interested in him, don't you? You can trust me, Russian.'

He didn't say anything, just watched me with his guard up.

'I trust that you can be the man I need, Russian, and I can be your woman, who won't hurt you, but will protect this,' I said, placing my hand on his alpha heart.

He made a small sound in his throat, as if he was swallowing all those doubts, and then his mouth met mine and our love filled up all the empty places in us both. The Russian was craving me as much as I was craving him, and I didn't tell him, but I was as terrified of losing him as he was of me – my heart would never take it, I'd never recover. Instead, I trusted in the moment and hoped it would last forever and that everything would be okay.

But something bad that I never expected was to come, testing us both.

Chapter 25

I knew this day would one day come, my last professional game. I felt emotional and terrified that it wouldn't be one of my better games. I didn't want to go out like that ... I was scared my knee would give away. I desperately wanted to play well for the team, and because The Russian was going to be in the audience with his friends.

'I'm so nervous, it's insane,' I said, trying to shake myself out. I was in the kitchen at The Russian's place on Saturday morning, having another glass of water before I left.

He came up beside me, took the glass from my hand and turned me around.

'I understand, but let's look at this. You've played games that have been more important,' he reminded me.

I nodded, feeling the security of his arms as he stood in front of me, looking delicious in his low slung jeans and a white t-shirt, which really set off his tan and muscles. I was in my Suns' uniform, ready to go.

'You're right, we've had semi-finals and finals that have been more important.'

'So,' he continued, 'what's the worst that could happen?'

He pressed his body against mine, and I was temporarily distracted by his erection pressing against me.

I thought about his words. 'The worst that could happen is that I have a really dud game and it's my last game ever,' I said, breathing out.

'You've got enough medals and tin on your shelf not to need this game to prove your worth,' The Russian reminded me. 'Just go out there, look flashy and confident, give it your best, remember what you've loved about playing and take a bow at the end,' he said, and kissed me on the top of my head. 'Besides, you look very hot in your uniform.'

I smiled and moved closer to hug him.

'You're right, thank you. I'll focus on the moment and the competition, rivalry, fun ...' I said.

'That's my girl.'

I pulled away. 'You'll bring my ...'

'...bag. I'll bring your bag and change of clothes,' he said, assuring me again.

'And you've got your tickets and ...'

'VIP passes, I've got them,' he assured me.

'And you know our sign?' I asked.

The Russian took my hand and kissed it, placing it on his heart ... very old fashioned and sexy.

'I know it,' he said, and smiled at me.

'What?' I asked.

'So this is what you're like before a game. I get it,' he said. 'Now go, see you there and don't forget to enjoy it.' He saw me down to my car and gave me another kiss.

I drove off full of butterflies – excitement, nerves, and a tinge of sadness as I'd never get to play with my Suns' teammates again. But at least I'd be at most games reporting from the commentary box ... that was almost as good. I also knew that at the end of the season, some would be retiring or traded or be dropped – nothing stayed the same for long in professional sport – the Suns I knew wouldn't be next season's Suns.

I wondered which ten friends the Russian would be bringing ... well, nine plus himself. He wouldn't tell me. Maybe his family? Maybe some Saints, maybe some friends I hadn't met yet? Then I pulled into the Suns' home ground for the last time as a player, and into the players' parking lot. I looked at the car that pulled up beside me, and Steffi was at the wheel. She waved enthusiastically and we walked in together.

'So good to play together again,' she said, wrapping an arm around my shoulder. We could easily reach each other.

We entered the very familiar dressing rooms and got into our usual routines. Our opposing team, the Seattle Sky, were already there and milling around their area as well.

Coach entered and we all quietened down for her update.

'Carly, if you can do a media interview on court fifteen minutes before the game, Latoya at half-time, and Lia and I will do post-game,' she said.

I nodded my understanding and Coach went on to give us a briefing and updates on player changes for the opposition. I was pumped, so were the other girls, and in the stadium you could hear the fans arriving. It was going to be big; the noise was already drifting into our changing rooms. When Coach finished, Aimee and I snuck out to have a quick look, and the place was pumping. The merchandise booth had a huge queue, membership sales for next year had a few people signing up and there were stacks of fans in our colors and those of the opposition, getting food and drinks, or photos with our mascots.

I heard some cheers and a lot of noise from the entranceway – what was going on? Then I saw them ... The Russian had brought his big gun mates from the Saints and they were heading to the VIP area.

Aimee nudged me. 'Friends in high places, huh?' she teased. 'Now we know who The Russian invited to share his VIP box with.'

'Great, like I wasn't nervous enough,' I said. 'So much easier playing in front of fans and strangers!'

'While being broadcast around the nation,' Aimee reminded me.

'And there's that,' I agreed, 'but you forget about the cameras when you're in the heat of the moment.'

'Mm,' she nodded. 'I bet you'll forget The Russian and his friends are watching the moment that whistle blows to start play.'

I watched as Lucas and Mia entered, along with Eddie and Tiffany, and moments later Nik and Sasha entered with Harry, the youngest Saints' team member, and another guy whom I didn't recognize, but he must have been a friend of Harry's. I was sure Sasha was looking forward to going to a sports game and not having to work for a change.

The media cameras went from our court over to the Saints, and kids swarmed them for autographs. Security held the kids back from the VIP area, but Lucas and Nik went out to sign some shirts and caps for the kids, and a few other body parts for female fans. There was no sign of The Russian ... I hoped he was okay, I hoped he was still coming. Of course he'd be coming, why wouldn't he? I was getting as bad as he was.

'There's your boy,' Aimee said, and I looked in the direction she was looking.

There was my beautiful Russian – dressed for the VIP area in a black button-down shirt, with gray pants and black shoes. His short back and sides haircut highlighted those high cheek bones, accentuating his strong chiseled jaw.

'Gorgeous,' Aimee muttered. 'Who's that with him?'

'Uh-huh,' I said. 'That's Tia, his little sister, she's ten.'

So cute the two of them together, and he was so protective of her with his hand on her shoulder. They were in the merchandise line and she was picking out what Suns items she wanted, The Russian was listening patiently. He looked up and his eyes scoped the area, seeing Lucas over in the stands and giving him a wave. Then he looked towards our dressing room, and his eyes finally landed on Aimee and me hiding against the wall; his eyes locked on me. He smiled and I think I orgasmed.

I smiled back and both Aimee and I gave him this starstruck wave. The Russian leaned down and whispered something to Tia and she looked in our direction, trying to find us. When she saw me, I got a huge grin and exaggerated wave as she jumped on the spot with excitement. The Russian shook his head and I laughed. It had taken only a few minutes before the crowd realized who he was and he started getting mobbed in the line. He moved Tia in front of him and again glanced in my direction. I waved and, grabbing Aimee's arm, we disappeared back into our Suns' allocated rooms. As we walked down the hallway, Maria from marketing passed me and stopped, her eyes wide with excitement.

'Carly, you're a legend,' she gushed.

'I haven't played yet,' I said, confused.

She waved her phone at me. 'Social media is going berserk! Our game is trending everywhere ... there are pictures of you girls arriving and the Saints arriving, and it's all over everything. We've had a huge jump in membership sales ... like this is the place to be.'

'That's great,' I brightened. 'Good for the club.'

'Good for the club,' she repeated, rolling her eyes as though I had discovered gold and thought it was tin. 'It's huge. We've never sold this many packages before the start of a new season ... you're making my job easy. Promise me when you're commentating Suns games next year, you'll bring your friends,' she said, cocking her head in the direction of the VIP area.

'Ah, I'll do my best,' I said. Then I remembered I had to do the media interview and raced back out to the entrance of our run, with a few minutes to spare. The TV crew was there waiting. It felt odd being interviewed by Catherine, who was one of my commentary team buddies in my new job.

'A big day for you and it looks like you've brought the crowd with you,' Catherine said, holding the microphone over to me.

'A very exciting day,' I agreed, 'and the Suns are wrapped to have this turnout, thanks to all our fans, followers and other local teams that are supporting us,' I said without blatantly mentioning the hunky row of Saints and their partners sitting opposite, or that The Russian had paid some obscene amount to purchase those seats.

'The Suns and Sky are no strangers on the basketball court,' Catherine continued. 'Last time you played them the Suns lost 53 to 55. Got some tricks up your sleeve today?'

I smiled at Catherine. 'It was a tough game and the time before we beat them by an equally slim margin ... so I think that today the fans will see two well-matched teams, both trying desperately to win. And yes, always a few tricks up our sleeves.'

'Well, enjoy your last Suns' game and congratulations on a stellar career. Ladies and gentlemen, Carly Brooker,' Catherine said to the camera and the audience.

I nodded my thanks, gave a wave to all, and jogged back into the run, but not without a quick glance to my heartbeat in the VIP area. Our eyes locked for those few moments and I recharged. I returned to the changing rooms for my final rah-rah, psyche up, pre-game session with my girls. Game on.

Chapter 26

Aimee was right – from the moment the whistle blew, I was completely in the game, and it was fast, furious and rough. I don't know where the time went, but it flew. Our first two-quarters were great and I've no doubt the excitement of the huge home crowd and playing together again helped; I know I was super pumped. I took a few hits and a few dramatic falls and slides; in my peripheral vision I could see The Russian bracing, as if he wanted to come on court and save me. Luckily, Mia was sitting next to him, being the voice of reason I imagine. When I did get the occasional breather to look at him, his eyes shone with love and I just soaked it all in. Tia on the other side of him was decked out completely in Suns gear and was her own cheer squad. It looked like she had made friends with the kids next to her, and they were having a great time –that's what it was all about.

As for my knee, I could feel it – I knew I would be lucky to see this game out, my days in the 'Sun' were definitely over. Aimee was having a blinder of a game, Steffi was out early with an injury, but I thought she was going to be okay to come back on later and the girls were just knitting together tightly. It was so good to be back, even if I only had one more shot at it.

At halftime the Seattle Sky were trailing us by 10 points, which was great, but we didn't want to get complacent. Coach delivered one of her shortest halftime speeches – I don't know what had gotten into her, maybe she was happy with how we were progressing! She did however hit the nail on the head with her choice of words:

'Look around at what this team is made up of,' Coach said, and we all looked into each others' faces. 'Some of you won't be here next season, some of you will finish your careers today, but this team is made of passion and loyalty.'

We all agreed and I tried not to get misty-eyed. Coach continued. 'This is our last game of the season as a complete team before we head into the final series, and yes, while we've already secured our place in the finals, think about this game ... how do you want to go out?' That was the perfect motivation ... we all knew how we wanted the game to end, how we wanted it recorded in history.

I heard later that security had had to rescue The Russian and Tia from crowds to get them back to their seat when Tia had wanted to go to the toilet. Luckily, there was no shortage of ladies prepared to take her in as The Russian waited some distance outside. Next time, Mia took Tia ... yep, three trips she made ... way too much to drink and I imagined Lana was going to give The Russian a serve for the sugar hit later.

We were back on for the final half and I felt the overwhelming significance of it for me. I had been playing since I could walk, it was all I knew. I was so grateful for the commentary job ... I couldn't imagine the grief I'd be feeling today if I was going to leave the game for good. Sure, I might have gotten to report on the game with the newspaper or online, but now, I'd be traveling to the games again with the girls from all different teams. The whistle blew.

The Sky came back as determined as we were, and we lost some ground to them. At one stage they were leading. I felt the perspiration pouring off me and saw the battle-hardened faces of my teammates.

I remember reading the press clippings days after the game, and one in particular that said 'Brooker took over like a woman giving her all. As the Suns clung to a 55-53 lead in the last quarter, Brooker turned up the heat, and with the support of her team, the Suns took out victory with a five-point lead. Carly Brooker said goodbye to her on-court basketball career in style.'

It didn't seem like that at the time; I was just playing hard like everyone else – determined to win this final game. I don't remember the noise of the crowd or being distracted by The Russian or the Saints right on court in their VIP seats. I just remember playing fluidly with my team for that one last time, and I loved it.

As the final siren sounded, we leaped for joy – we had done it, we had won. Our fans went crazy and so did we, hugging each other. We were in the finals for sure, but I wouldn't be playing them. This was enough for me. We shook hands with the Sky and then we did a lap of the court, thanking our fans. As I got to the VIP seats – despite being super sweaty, and let's face it, stinky – The

Russian gave me a kiss and hug that had the professional photographers and everyone with a camera phone around us going berserk. Tia gave me a hug too as she wrinkled her nose.

The Saints boys pecked me on the cheek and shook hands with the other Suns' girls as they passed by and I thanked Mia, Tiffany and Sasha for coming along.

'It was great,' Sasha said. 'I think I'll try and get a job as media manager for the Suns and drop the Saints.'

'Hey!' Nik said.

She shrugged. 'You're right, the scenery won't be as good for me.'

I laughed and thought there was no way I could say that comment to The Russian. It might push him over the edge. The Suns and I headed back for the presentations and as I came up to get a huge bouquet of flowers that the team had bought for me, I was walking with a slight limp. My body was cooling down and the injury was kicking in. But it had held up through the game, thank you knee, thank you body! Thank you, God!

Afterward, as I hobbled with the other girls down to the race, the Russian and Tia came over to the run and I gave Tia the flowers and asked her to give them to Lana. I wouldn't be going straight home, and I was sure she would enjoy having them in the house.

'Will you come over tonight when you finish celebrating with the girls?' he whispered in my ear. The Russian had been invited, but it would be game day for him the day after, so he had to stay home, eat carbs and watch the other teams play.

'Only if you're okay with that ... I can see you at the game tomorrow,' I said.

'I need you there so I can sleep.'

'I won't be late,' I assured him, gave him a quick kiss so we didn't make a circus of it, and leaned down to accept a hug from Tia. I waved them off. This time, there would be no social media shots of me with guys in our group ... we were not going there again.

I followed the last of the Suns' girls into the run, to shower, get some PT and celebrate. My coach walked beside me, her hand on my shoulder.

Chapter 27

The Suns' girls had only had a drink or two before they went onto the colas and water – their season wasn't over yet. I had a wine or two and moved to non-alcoholic drinks too ... supporting my team unto the end. It was only nine-thirty but I was wiped out – the day had been full of highs and lows and my knee was giving me a little bit of grief. I was keen to get to The Russians but I knew I would never have this day again. At least I wasn't the first to pike though, Steffi and her boyfriend, Wilson, had left half an hour before and Aimee was looking ready for bed.

I made my way around to each of my teammates to thank them, and to wish them well for the rest of the season. We were all a bit teary. Finally, Aimee and I left together and Aimee was okay to drive, she hadn't touched a drop, but I had left my car at the clubhouse and was going to hail a taxi to The Russian's house. Aimee wanted to drive me but it was completely in the opposite direction, so I assured her I was fine and saw her off. I turned to wait at the taxi rank when I heard my name called. I wheeled around to find Ken – my resident stalker – leaning on a car and smoking a cigarette. The hairs on the back of my neck stood up. I normally didn't worry about my stalkers but The Russian had put me on alert.

'Hi Carly,' he said, 'I thought it was you.'

'Ken, hey, what are you doing here?' I asked, keeping my distance. He leaned back on his car, an old taxi that looked like it had seen better days.

'I just finished work,' he said. I then noticed his uniform. '... just finished for the night.'

'Oh, of course,' I said, with a glance to his car. I breathed a sigh of relief.

'Yeah, she's not as fancy as some of the cars in the rank,' he said, 'but she's loyal and served me well,' he said, and patted the car door he was leaning on.

'Right. Well, I'm just finished for the night too ... I was celebrating with the Suns,' I said, and I waved my arm in the general direction of where some of the team was still hanging out.

'Yeah, I heard it on the radio. Congrats on the win and great game,' he said. 'Need a lift?'

'No, I'm good, but thank you, I'm sure you've had enough driving for the night and just want to get home.' I started to head towards the taxi rank.

'One more job isn't going to kill me, besides, it'd be an honor ... the car just won't be as new as some,' he said again, nodding to a couple of taxis in the rank.

I looked over and there was a line of people a mile long, waiting, and two taxis loading up. It would take at least another half-hour to get a ride.

'C'mon,' he stubbed out his cigarette. 'It's on the house,

a gift for your end of season game, and let's face it, you've given me plenty of entertainment over the years. I've enjoyed watching you play.'

'Thank you,' I said. I didn't know what to do now. I felt churlish turning him down when he was clearly a bonafide taxi driver and I might have scored him if I queued at the taxi rank anyway ... but it was all a bit weird.

He went around and opened the passenger door of his car, and then returned to the driver's side, slid in and started the car. He put the taxi's 'occupied' light on. I went around to get in, slipped into the passenger's seat and thanked Ken. I gave him the address.

'That's my boyfriend's place,' I said, making it known. 'He's expecting me about ten.'

'The Russian, hmm ... big lad,' Ken said.

'Yes.' I agreed and left it at that. At least we headed off in the right direction. Then I noticed I had no door handle. *Holy fuck, there was no door handle!* Had he taken it off when he'd opened the passenger door? *Fuck, fuck, what do I do now? Stay calm, we're heading in the right direction ... it might be nothing; it might just be a broken door handle. What you'd expect in an old car, I'm being silly, really.*

But if I wasn't ... I could see the headlines now: *Suns' Player Attacked by Stalker*, or *Why Did She Take the Ride?* Not to mention all the warnings to kids – *Stranger Danger ... if it can happen to Carly, it can happen to you!* Yeah, no wonder I was a journalist, I was writing my own death headlines.

'So, long day?' I asked, trying to stay calm, and sound normal.

Ken shrugged. 'I started about midday, so not too bad. I noticed you're limping a bit there ... just got through the game, huh?'

I nodded and smiled. 'My knee just had one more game in her. But yeah, it's feeling stiff.'

He moved his hand over and grabbed my knee, I jumped a mile high.

'I've always liked you, Carly, you know that,' he said, and gave me a lecherous smile.

'Thank you Ken, you've been a great supporter,' I said, and taking his hand I tried to push it off my knee but he gripped tighter, then inched his hand further up my leg.

I couldn't believe this was happening to me, I couldn't believe I was going to be a woman who was assaulted, maybe more ... fuck, what was I supposed to do?

'Ken, you know I have a boyfriend,' I said, my voice shaking, 'and he'll be really mad if I'm not home soon, or if he hears I'm in trouble.'

He smirked, his eyes not leaving the road, but his fingers spidered further up my leg.

'Stop!' I shouted, startling us both. 'Stop and let me out, Ken.'

He kept driving but his hand didn't move any further up my leg ... I could see he was thinking. I slowly reached down to the floor for my bag.

'Leave it there,' he snarled.

'Then get your hand off me,' I said. 'We've been friends for a long time Ken, don't ruin this now.'

'You were mine before he came along,' he said. 'He's got no right to you.'

I swallowed, following his strange logic.

'Ken, pull over please. I want to get out now.'

He then took a left turn instead of a right and my heart raced, I think I was going to be sick. There was no one on the road near us, I couldn't even signal for help, and we were getting further out of the built-up area. I reached down and grabbed my bag, and his hand swung from my leg to my face, hitting me hard. I was used to getting hits in the game, but I was unprepared for this, I felt the blood rushing from my nose.

My mind was screaming alerts ... I was more shocked than hurt, but I grabbed for my bag again, reaching in for my phone. Ken grabbed my bag and threw it into the back seat. I turned my back to him and swiped the screen. Ken's fingers dug into my shoulders and he yelled, 'Give me the fucking phone!'

I hit The Russian's number, and thank God he answered on the first ring. His smooth voice welcoming and unprepared for my needs.

'Help, Russian!' I screamed.

Ken pulled over sharply and I hit the side of my head against the window of the passenger seat. He stopped the car, grabbed me and I kept yelling to The Russian.

'I'm in a taxi, Ken ...' the phone fell to the ground and Ken pulled me towards him, sticking his tongue into my mouth. I spat and bucked and tried to push away, but he was so much bigger. I was strong, but I couldn't get away from him, he was just bulk. I was pressed hard against the door; the door that wouldn't open. I started bashing at the window, trying to break it. I could hear The Russian calling out to me and then he stopped. I knew he would be getting help.

Ken pulled his tongue out of my mouth and yelled. 'Fucking stop that, bitch,' he said, and pushed me back hard against the seat. I turned around to see if the back seats had door handles and they did. *Thank God!* I shoved Ken with all of my might – years of pushing weights had to help – but I could only push him so far; I was trapped in the front of his car just by his bulk and the small amount of space we had. He grabbed me by the back of my neck and I scratched and hit him like a cat. He pushed my head onto his leg, and I heard him undoing his zip. He was going to force me onto him. I grabbed at his crotch and squeezed until he screamed and released my neck. I drove a fist into his throat and dived into the back seat.

Ken was gasping for breath, but his arms flailed, trying to grab me as I was half in-half out of the front and back seats. I pushed through, opened the back door and stumbled out. I ran, I didn't have my phone or handbag and I didn't care. I pulled off my high heels, abandoning them and just ran back towards the turn-off and the main road. My knee buckled and I stumbled but kept going.

I ran as fast as I could and I prayed my knee would hold up. My chest was tight with anxiety and trying to breathe at the pace I was running. I kept going, in the dark, feeling the hard road on my bare feet. I felt like I had been running forever, all the time my hearing was finely tuned, expecting the sound of Ken's car any moment. I knew he wasn't fit enough to chase me on foot.

I kept glancing back and then I saw some headlights – he was coming after me. I left the road, ran into the thin scattering of trees along the side of the road, and threw myself flat onto the ground. His headlights wouldn't pick me up now.

That didn't stop Ken; he was driving really slowly up the street and had put on the large spotlights on both sides of his taxi sign. They shone into where I lay, but above my head. I stayed put, trying not to make a sound, praying that I would be spared. I stayed that way for what felt like hours, but it wasn't. Eventually, his car passed me and went out of sight. I pulled myself up, staying close to the edge, in case he swung back again.

Then I heard a siren, a police car, but I still couldn't see it. Had they picked him up further along the road? I started limping up the road in that direction. I could have cried with joy as The Russian's car came into view. I waved him down, he pulled over, hurried from the car and grabbed me. He held me even though I tried to pull away, just to breathe. He released me long enough to check me over. I guess I didn't look that good with the blood down my front and dirt over my clothes from laying flat on the ground.

'I'm okay, just got a fright,' I said, still in shock. I knew I was shaking, but I was operating on adrenalin. 'He's in his car, that way,' I pointed to the way The Russian had just come from. 'I hit him in the throat and ran.'

'They've got him. You're bleeding, limping ...' The Russian was saying.

'I didn't encourage him, he was a taxi driver ... at the rank,' I started to justify myself, something I would never have done before my relationship with The Russian.

'Christ, Brooker, don't even think that, it never occurred to me,' The Russian said, looking shocked. 'None of this is your fault.'

'I lost my shoes back there somewhere, my phone and bag are in his car,' I said, still raving.

'It's okay, Brooker ... Carly, shh, take a breath.'

I nodded still breathing fast, my eyes darting around like I expected Ken to come back. But, everything was quiet and still except for my breathing. The Russian continued to support me, watch me ... he probably expected me to become more hysterical any minute.

I shook my head. It had been such a great day and night up until then. A car's headlights lit the road and I pulled closer to The Russian. A security van sped our way and braked suddenly on seeing us. Eddie and another guy in a security uniform jumped out.

'You're safe,' Eddie said, exhaling.

'Thank you, yes,' I said.

'The cops have arrested him,' the other security guy said.

'Thanks, Jack,' The Russian said, and stroked my back with his hand. He left me momentarily to go to his car, and came back with a towel.

'What happened?' Eddie asked.

I told them the story as I wiped my bloody nose on the towel. I told them that I should have gone with my gut instinct, but it had seemed kind of churlish when he was a taxi driver, there with his taxi.

'Did he hurt you, or ...?' The Russian couldn't say the words.

I shook my head. 'He tried, but he didn't get that far. There were no door handles in the front,' I said, my voice starting to crack as the realism of the situation began to hit me. 'How did you get here so quickly?'

'You didn't hang up. We tracked your phone,' The Russian said. 'Eddie, can you take Carly to my house and ...'

'No way,' Eddie said.

It seems they all knew The Russian too well. 'You're not going near this situation Russian, not for a minute.'

I could hear The Russian's teeth grind with anger. Every muscle in his body was hard and flexed, on alert and ready to pound someone.

Eddie – the voice of reason – continued: 'Carly is safe now and you can't ruin your career for a guy who'll get his day in court.'

'He needs to get more than that,' The Russian hissed.

Eddie continued. 'You need to get Carly home, and Jack and I will catch up with the police and let you know what's happening. The cops will need you to make a statement Carly, but it can wait until tomorrow if you are sure there's no, um, samples that we need?' he asked as discretely as possible.

I felt The Russian bristle with anger beside me.

'He didn't touch me, but he tried,' I said, looking up at The Russian.

'If I see him I'll fuckin' ...' The Russian began and I put a finger on his lips.

'Sorry,' he said, releasing a long breath of frustration. 'Let's get you back to my place.'

He thanked Eddie and Jack and watched them head off. He lowered me into the passenger seat of his car, locking my door. As soon as he came around to the driver's seat I began to shake ... delayed shock, I guess. He turned the heat up in the car and held my hand. We drove on for about a quarter of a mile before we came across the police car, Ken's taxi, and Eddie and Jack with their security van. Ken was leaning against his taxi, surrounded by the men.

It must have gotten too much for The Russian, because he suddenly pulled over.

'Lock the doors,' he said to me and before I could stop him he was out of the car and rushing at Ken. Eddie saw it unfolding and he and Jack tried to cut The Russian off, but it was like trying to stop a charging lion. Ken started screaming for his life and then one of the police officers bundled him into the back of the car, while the other officer blocked The Russian.

Eddie and Jack stepped in, and it took the three of them to restrain The Russian. Eddie and Jack pushed him back towards his car; I hadn't locked the doors, there was no need to. Eddie opened the driver's door and he and Jack shoved The Russian in, which was no mean feat given the strength of ten men he seemed to display.

Eddie hissed at him, panting heavily. 'Don't fucking try that again, Russian. Take Carly home, we'll deal with it.' He looked over at me. 'Sorry, Carly.'

The Russian started the car, his jaw locked and his eyes never leaving Ken who sat huddled in the back of the taxi, somehow managing to make himself look small.

'Seriously, get out of here,' Eddie said, closing the car door and blocking The Russian's view of Ken. I placed my hand on The Russian's, and he turned as if noticing I was still there. He swallowed, and the men stepped back as The Russian pulled the car away from the scene. When we returned to the main road, I completely broke down – all the stress and fear pouring out of me.

'Carly, babe ... it's okay, you're safe now,' The Russian said.

I couldn't help it, I was suddenly terrified.

'I hate to see you cry, what can I do?'

'You're here,' I said, between sobs, 'I'll be okay.'

*****

The Russian didn't know what to do; he rubbed my back as I leaned over in the seat, and when we got home, he helped put me to bed. I heard him on the phone with the Saints' team lawyer, asking him to work with the Suns' team lawyer to keep this out of the media; I was hoping they'd succeed.

I slept fitfully and each time I woke, I was wrapped in The Russian's arms, with him murmuring the words that I was safe now – he didn't let me go all night.

Chapter 28

The next morning, I insisted The Russian stuck to his normal pre-game routine and I put on my brightest face – I was fine, really fine ... a little jumpy maybe, but that was to be expected. Eddie called early to let us know that Ken had been charged, and not surprisingly, had a few other similar charges and complaints in his history. Eddie also had my phone, handbag and my shoes as well, and he would get them back to The Russian today at the game. The other piece of information that The Russian told me, after I had been prodding him to know all the details, was that Ken hadn't been working that night – he had followed me from the game to the club and had been waiting for me. Super creepy.

My man, The Russian was a rock. I just looked at him and felt better, and if he had at all been protective before, now he was truly over the top. We drove together to the game, The Russian in his team training gear, looking super sexy and in control. I knew he kept glancing my way ... I think he was waiting for me to have a repeat performance of the previous night and a total meltdown.

When we arrived at the Saints' stadium, he insisted on walking me to my ticketed seat from Russian's ticket allocation, but I wanted to drop into the media box first and wish my replacement good luck. When we got there, he managed to obtain a promise from Sasha that she would walk me to the WAGS area ... so sweet and over the top! I don't know how he thought Sasha was going to save me from any evil – she was slighter than me – but I guess there's safety in numbers.

He greeted the journos, casting a look at a few that he thought were going to put me over their shoulder and run off with me – yes, we were working on it – and then he pulled me aside before leaving. I could see some of the journos subtly watching us from the corner of the media box.

'Are you going to be okay?' he asked, his brow furrowed.

'I'm going to be just fine. What could possibly go wrong?' I said, and he made this grunting sort of sound. 'Really, I've been fine for twenty-four years, so one weird night isn't a life sentence,' I said, assuring him.

'That weird night could have been a lot worse if you hadn't been able to reach me. Thank God I wasn't in the shower or asleep!'

'Play well,' I said, pushing him out the door of the media box and towards the stairs. I followed him out. 'I love you.' OMG, I just said that. Out loud. I had been thinking it and then I just blurted it out.

The Russian stopped dead and turned to look at me. His came in close to kiss me but instead moved to whisper in my ear.

'I love you, Brooker.' He pulled away to look at me again and grinned.

'Go!' I said, returning his happiness with a silly grin of my own.

'Geez Brooker, you're bossy,' he said, walking away.

'You don't know the half of it buddy,' I told him, folding my arms across my chest, and watching that great butt disappear down the stairs. Yep, that was satisfying. I went back in and Sasha gave me the third degree.

'What's going on? Has something happened? The Russian's being all over-the-top protective!' she frowned.

'Confidentially?' I asked her.

'Of course,' she nodded, and pulled me back outside the media box.

'One of my stalkers attacked me last night,' I said. It was the first time I had said the words and it made me shiver. I rubbed my arms.

'Oh my God,' she hissed, 'did he hurt you?'

I shook my head. 'No, but he scared the shit out of me. I managed to get through to The Russian and he brought the police, Eddie and his team. The guy's been arrested ... I'm not the first complaint, allegedly.'

Sasha shook her head. 'Fucking men.'

As she said it, Nik appeared at the top of the stairs, hearing her comment.

'Who? What's happened?' he asked, in his clipped German accent, a deep frown on his forehead.

'Not you, gorgeous,' she said, and kissed him. 'We're talking about bad men.'

'Oh them,' Nik said, looking relieved. 'Can't stay, I just

slipped out on my way from PT into the training room.'

'They're right next to each other,' I said.

'I know, so it was a fair slip,' he agreed.

'I've got to go talk to Dan,' I said, looking for a way to give them some privacy and spotting the journo from radio *K-Talk* inside the media room, 'Have a good game, Nik.'

'Thanks, Carly,' he said, not taking his eyes off Sasha.

I left the two cute lovebirds and went back into the media box before Sasha rejoined me and escorted me to sit with the WAGS for the first time as The Russian's girlfriend.

*****

'You really don't have to walk me up here,' I said to Sasha as we entered the VIP and partners area.

'Are you kidding me? Like I'm going to have grumpy bum giving me a hard time on Monday morning,' she said, and snorted.

I laughed, thinking of The Russian holding court in the office. We got to the grandstand we needed and Sasha walked straight in, wearing her Saints' uniform; she greeted the security guy. I flashed my VIP pass, but he recognized me and congratulated me on my game last night. *So kind.*

Mia and Alice were both there, along with their younger brothers whom I met – Alice was in her Saints' uniform, so I was guessing she had been working earlier or was still on the job. Then Eddie's partner Tiffany arrived, along with Buzz's fiancée, Laura. Tiffany and Laura insisted I sit next to them, which was great ... I really liked Tiffany, and Laura was a lot of fun. The two of them together were a bit outrageous and outspoken, which was just what I needed – a distraction.

'You know our boys don't like each other,' Laura nudged me, '... so we should become best friends.'

'Men,' I shook my head and they both laughed. Then the coach's wife, Elizabeth, came over to greet us and I met her for the first time. She would have been in her fifties, and so striking. I had heard she was an ex-model and she still had the classic good looks and grooming.

'Ah,' she said, smiling at me as she took my hand. 'I heard that The Russian had lost his heart and I can see why.'

'Thank you,' I said, delighted to hear word traveled fast.

'Congratulations on a very impressive last game too,' she said. 'I was allowed to watch a bit of it when all the other soccer games had finished,' she said, with a roll of her eyes.

I laughed.

'I know the feeling ... I'm always torn between sports, but living alone I usually control the remote,' I told her. We spoke for a few minutes and then, Elizabeth went to sit with a friend, and Tiff, Laura and I went up to the bar to grab a drink. We got back just in time as the boys began to come out on the oval. I looked out for my guy ... I was so excited to be able to watch the whole game without reporting on it.

The Russian, like all the players, had his own dedicated fan group and his fans were a mix of all ages, especially young kids and females keen to get his attention. There were banners with his name on them, and as he did the lap of the ground with the team, the kids ran along the edges calling out to him and other players. As he came around to my side, his eyes sought me out in our grandstand and when he found me, I swear his chest deflated as he relaxed and exhaled. For me it was the opposite – my heart rate went up and my body went on alert. Mm, funny that.

The Saints were playing the New York Reds and the last time they had played them, it had been a draw. Both teams were determined not to let that happen again, although it was a bit of an occupational hazard in soccer.

'That's a fine butt your man has there,' Tiffany nudged me, and Laura burst out laughing.

'You can't say that,' Laura said.

'Why not?' Tiffany looked horrified. 'I can admire the view.'

'It is a fine butt,' I agreed, 'there are quite a few fine looking butts down there.'

Laura shook her head. 'Carly, do not encourage her. Tiffany, you look at your own man's butt.'

'Oh, I've seen Eddie's butt many a time and I never tire of it,' Tiffany began. As if he knew we were talking about him, Eddie looked straight up at us and gave Tiffany a quick smile.

'Ain't love grand?' I said.

'It will be if they win,' Tiffany said.

'Hell yeah. When they lose, Buzz goes into this deep funk ... takes all my skills to lift him out.'

It made me think about my own performance in relationships, after the Suns lost games. Sometimes you forget to think about the partner and what they go through too.

The game began and the crowd really got into it, and so did we. It was so much fun to be watching instead of working, to see The Russian's moves, watch him in action, watch his concentration and the way he read the play. It was great to see the other guys playing as a team too, especially now that I was getting to know them all personally. Plus, I got to watch The Russian for the whole game and not have to give equal time to all players ... bliss.

The game started off fast and full-on as if both teams decided it was the first half that was going to win the game. We – being the Saints – got an early goal and we went berserk, so did the fans. It was nicely fed to Tomás who put it away; we all congratulated Alice as if she had kicked it herself. Just as the Reds looked like they were going to increase their assault, my man The Russian counter-attacked with venom, redirecting the ball and feeding it to Captain Fantastic, who moved it back down to the Kaiser – Nik, Sasha's man – and in it went for a goal. We were so excited that nothing could have ever provided the high we were on.

The boys were looking good out there, and my guy, in particular, was looking gorgeous – determined, sweaty, in-charge and mine. Mm, I would have loved to do him right there, right then. I opened my bottle of water and took a cooling sip ... better. The Saints had a 2-0 lead going into half-time, and as the boys left the field, Laura and Tiffany dragged me back to the bar. They were such a bad influence.

I made sure I was back in place before the team ran out again, and right from the start the NY Reds were in trouble. Thank goodness – I know it's great for the fans, but I can't stand a tense and close game when I'm emotionally involved ... it just kills you. The Saints had it all over the NY Reds; in fact, it just looked like the visitors lacked imagination. In the heat of the moment the referee pulled out the yellow card for one of the opposition who was playing against Buzz – I heard Tiffany mutter 'thank God it wasn't Buzz'.

It was all downhill from there for the Reds; the Saints brought it home and sealed the result with a fantastic display of team effort – Lucas, The Russian, Harry and Tomás were all involved in that final goal, and the Saints booked their place in the finals. At the final whistle, the huge crowd was on its feet cheering the Saints who had taken the game 4-1 – a big score for soccer.

It was going to be a great night, and tomorrow, The Russian was going to meet my parents.

Chapter 29

It was my turn to pick the music and I put on one of my favorites; The Russian gave it a nod of approval. We were doing the drive to my parents' place for Monday lunch. I know, traditionally people have Sunday lunch, but we both work or play on Sundays and I have Mondays off. The Russian took the day off too, leaving Eddie in charge and Sasha gloating she'd get to the coffee van before him for once. We were almost tempted to swing by for a coffee on our way, just to beat her and see her reaction ... ha, that would have been worth it. Oh, I forgot I was supposed to be on her side when it came to the coffee van!

I glanced at The Russian as he drove ... so handsome. He was wearing a collared black shirt with his jeans and Dr Martens – plenty of rubber on those soles to make a quick escape I imagine. Feeling my gaze, he looked in my direction.

'I'm not nervous!' he said, again.

'Are you sure?' I teased him. 'Not even just a bit?'

He scoffed. 'Parents love me. I'm charming, handsome, a good prospect ...'

'Modest,' I added.

'Modest,' he agreed. 'I'm big enough to look after their daughter and successful enough to give her a good life. Although I failed on one of those of late.'

I leaned over to run my hand along his arm, up to his shoulders, and massaged his neck.

'Don't say that,' I said, 'you can't be with me twenty-four hours a day, and I was stupid getting into his taxi ... let's not go there.'

'If you keep doing that we'll be going somewhere else very shortly, and it's got nothing to do with your folks,' The Russian said, as I kneaded his neck.

I laughed and drew back a little to keep my hand on his shoulder.

'So, tell me all I need to know about your family in five minutes,' The Russian said.

I puffed my cheeks out and expelled the air slowly.

'Okay. Mom's the straight-shooter, tough one. She organizes Dad, the church, me, the neighborhood, anything she can. She's pragmatic and she won't fall instantly in love with you, no matter how adorable I think you are, or you think you are,' I said.

He scoffed. 'We'll see about that.'

I didn't mention that she had never liked any of my boyfriends. They all fell into categories: too smart, too rude, too disrespectful, too lacking in ambition, not good enough for me, and on it went. I didn't want to make The Russian be anything but himself around her. I thought about Dad and filled The Russian in.

'Dad is a gentle, kind man with a typical sort of dad

sense of humor. His parishioners love him because he is compassionate and open, and he can be very serious when he needs to be, and very over-protective of me.'

'Hmm, great,' The Russian said. I could only imagine what was going on in his mind. 'Are you closer to him?' he asked.

'Definitely. Mom is not big on affection. But that's okay, I know she's there for me and she's proud of me ... I think,' I said.

'How could she not be? So am I going to meet any brothers or sisters that I have to charm as well?' he asked, tongue-in-cheek.

'No,' I smiled and shook my head at him.

'That's fine, I've won over the most important family member,' he said.

'That you have,' I agreed. 'But ... don't mention the incident the other night to them, please.'

'Our great sex? Hardly!' The Russian said, keeping it light.

I rolled my eyes. 'No you big head, the taxi incident.'

The Russian smiled. 'I won't. But can I ask why?'

'Because Mom is pragmatic and Dad is over-protective. I'll get a lecture on personal safety from Mom who'll say it was my fault for putting myself in that situation, and then Dad will start calling me every second day. I've left home, I like it that way,' I said.

'You've said that several times now since we've met. Clearly as an only child you must have felt smothered or something ... but don't worry, I won't leave you there.'

I was going to correct him but then the road to the church came into view and I had to give The Russian directions. As we turned into the street, I felt a warm familiarity seeing the church and my parents' house.

He placed his hand on my leg and I jumped. I realized where that reaction came from.

'Sorry,' I said.

'It's okay ... it will take you a little while.'

I swallowed; my heart was racing as the thought of that night came back to me. I tried to not think about it.

'This is nice,' The Russian said, admiring the church and its grounds.

I guess it did look nice ... quaint, even a bit old worldish. I pointed to the best place for him to park and he swung the car in and turned off the ignition. He took a deep breath. I knew he was a little nervous, and then he confirmed it.

'Your Dad's going to want to have a chat with me isn't he? About this whole trust issue and his little girl?' he turned my way.

'Only if you want to talk about it,' I said. 'Dad wouldn't force anyone to talk about personal stuff unless they wanted to, but he has some experience in his area.'

The Russian nodded, looking more uncomfortable than ever.

'Come on,' I said, opening the car door, 'come and meet my parents.'

*****

As we came up the path, the front door opened and Mom and Dad came out. They were about the same height, both thin, and I noticed Mom had dressed up a little ... that was nice. Dad was in his traditional white business shirt and black pants, a little cross clipped to his collar.

I walked in front, taking The Russian's hand. My parents kissed me and they both shook The Russian's hand. He called them Mrs Brooker and Reverend respectively, but they insisted on Kathleen and Michael. We both towered over them.

'Well, I never thought we'd meet someone taller than our Carly, sometimes we wonder where she came from,' my father joked, looking up at The Russian who smiled and relaxed a little.

'Both of my parents are tall, so I'm legitimate,' The Russian joked.

I couldn't believe it, but I swear my Mom smiled a charming smile at him. I looked from her to The Russian and back to Mom again. Unbelievable ... must've been the big lion aura; he was such an alpha. We followed them both in and I gave him a look.

'What?' he asked innocently.

I could smell a roast, Mom had cooked my favorite – probably everyone's favorite – and Dad paused on the way through to answer the phone.

'Unless they're dying, Michael, tell them that you are unavailable until after two,' she said, and Dad nodded.

The Russian chuckled. I guess that had been pretty funny, but normal for us.

'What can I do to help, Mom?' I asked.

'Nothing, I'm organized,' she said, as if I had ever doubted it. 'Why don't you show Alex around the church and yard, and then when your father is off the phone, we'll have lunch.'

She gave Alex a warm smile as she said it. *What the—?* He'd be gloating about that all the way home ... *sigh.*

I took his hand as we went on the grand, but very small, tour. What was funny for me – funny weird – was that I'd never taken a guy home, and I'd entered my house a thousand times, but now I was looking at it through The Russian's eyes. I went through the back of the house and showed him Mom's prized vegetable and herb garden, and on the other side her prized flower garden. Ever practical, she fed us and supplied fresh flowers to the church. The woman was wasted organizing this small church community; she should have been working for the United Nations.

I then took The Russian through the churchyard and into the church. He admired the stained glasses windows, which were truly beautiful, and the intimacy of the small church.

'When was the last time you went to church?' I asked him.

'You're asking me in here?' he said. 'A lightning bolt might come down from the ceiling and strike me dead if I answer that.'

'Yeah, you're probably right,' I agreed, teasing him.

He tucked me under his arm and we went back to the house. I took him through the side entrance, and I was so used to the shrine for my dead sister that I had completely forgotten to warn The Russian. One room was done up as if she had never left, and along the hallway was photo after photo of a girl who looked like me ... dark hair, almond-shaped eyes and lightly tanned skin. Photographs from her birth to teenage years, her last photos were her sixteenth birthday.

His eyes took it all in before he looked to me, a thousand questions written on his face.

'This is my big sister, Claudia,' I said, introducing them. 'She's three years older than me.' I lowered my voice. 'She died when she was sixteen ... eleven years ago now ... heart disease ... she was born with a defect.'

'You didn't think to mention this?' The Russian asked, and stroked my hair as he looked from Claudia to me.

I swallowed. 'We both have things to learn about each other ... some secrets, I guess,' I said.

He didn't answer. I pushed him a little and said almost in a whisper, 'I know that you almost had a child of your own, once ...'

I watched as his eyes glossed for just a moment as he fought his emotion and the resurfacing of that inner pain – I caught him in an unguarded moment and he wasn't prepared.

'Ancient history,' he said, and cleared his throat.

I turned back to look at the photos of my sister and me together; she was beautiful, feminine, petite ... so not like me. I don't know why I hadn't mentioned her to The Russian. I had created this other life, and it didn't include the sadness at home, and the fact that my mother hadn't always been as cold as she was now; or that from the age of thirteen she had forgotten me, her living daughter. I knew this wasn't uncommon ... I knew a lot of mothers reacted to grief in this way ... I read a lot about it, and I couldn't expect more from her, this was how she was coping. And this was how I coped – by pretending my worlds were divided.

'Okay, we don't need to talk about this,' The Russian said,

reading me and I suspect wanting to avoid revealing any more of his own secrets.

I nodded and then heard Dad calling us.

'C'mon, let's lunch and go,' I said, maybe too hurriedly, which drew another look of consternation from The Russian.

*****

Lunch was smooth sailing, and Mom was particularly charming to The Russian; all I could think of was that she had been worried no one would ever have me, and she didn't want to scare him off ... hmm. She kept trying to overfeed him as if he was bound to starve to death in my company. Then The Russian surprised me, again, and Dad too.

'Michael, I was wondering if I could have a word with you ... even though it is Monday and probably your day off,' The Russian joked.

Dad looked delighted. 'There's no sleep for the wicked ... or me either,' he said, with a wink in my direction. Such a daggy dad. The Russian thanked Mom, praising her cooking, which she lapped up, then Dad and The Russian excused themselves and went into Dad's study while Mom and I cleaned up. I would have loved to be a fly on the wall ... he was definitely getting grilled on the way home.

'He's very nice, Carly,' Mom said, giving her approval.

'Yes, he's very level-headed and not at all star-struck,' I agreed.

'He has lovely manners,' she continued.

'His parents, especially his Mom, are quite strict. He has

three sisters, I said, filling her in while I was trying to keep one ear towards Dad's study. It was hopeless, not a sound escaped.

I saw my mother's lips thin and I knew a lecture was coming.

'Don't scare him away now, Carly,' she started. 'Just try and be a little bit less of a tomboy and more of girl, like your sister.' Here we go. Like my sister, the beautiful, feminine and dead one.

'You don't have to compete with him, or be so independent,' my mother continued, 'let him feel like he's the man and let him occasionally win – at sport, or give him the last word ... you know what I mean.'

I didn't actually ... did she mean that I was so competitive that I wouldn't support or empower The Russian, and what was she basing that on – all her observations of my relationships or a very young relationship with my sister which had never really had a chance to develop?

I just sighed and nodded; I wasn't up for the fight. Dad and The Russian didn't emerge for half an hour and by that time Mom had caught up on my life and I on hers. The Russian had barely gotten out of the study before I was thanking them, and he followed my lead and we were out the door.

We were driving away and I gave them a wave, and breathed out. I could feel The Russian stealing looks at me as he drove.

'What was that about? In a hurry?'

'I love my parents,' I said. That's all I said. It was complex and The Russian living in his much-loved family cocoon probably wouldn't get it.

'Babe, I think you better talk to me,' he said, glancing my way.

'Thanks for coming,' I said, 'nothing to talk about. Hope it wasn't too painful.'

'On the contrary, your parents are lovely, plus, I told you your Mom would love me ... mothers always do.'

I groaned and The Russian laughed.

'It appears I'm good with the Brooker women,' he continued, the big head.

'I've never seen her like that, you worked your charm indeed,' I conceded. 'What did you talk about with Dad?' I cut to the chase.

'I was just direct with him. I told him I knew he knew that I had trust issues, but I was working on it and that you were trustworthy, the problem was mine,' he said.

I leaned closer so I could put my hand on his shoulder.

'Thank you, that's sweet.'

'It's true,' he said, with a shrug. 'Of course I told your Dad that I was an exceptional catch as well, and his daughter was very lucky ...'

I playfully hit his shoulder and he continued.

'I told him we had so much in common and were supportive of each other and our lifestyles and careers, and that I wish I had met you years ago,' he finished.

'Really?' I said, my voice soft and full of gratitude. 'And you couldn't even tell him you saved my life because I banned you from it, but I'm grateful for it.'

'There's a way you can pay me back,' he said, his face serious.

'Does it involve my tongue?' I teased.

'You're smart, too, Brooker, that's what I like about you.'

I laughed and thought about his words ... how we were alike, and I agreed.

'We do have a lot in common,' I started. 'For example, we're both tall, both play in the forward position, both play for 'S' teams – Saints and Suns, both like the gym and the beach, need our exercise ...'

The Russian agreed. 'Both gorgeous, and good in bed,' he added.

'That we are,' I agreed, teasing him. 'What time is your training?'

'Five o'clock,' he answered. 'I'm sure we can fit in a bed workout beforehand.'

'I'm counting on it,' I told him.

We drove along in comfortable silence for a while, and then The Russian broached the topic.

'Were you close to your sister?'

I shook my head. 'We were at an age that didn't make us close; I was thirteen, probably a pest, wanting to be her and wear make-up and clothes like Claudia had in her closet. She was sixteen and wanted her privacy. She was close to Mom, I was close to Dad. But I wish I had her around now though, I miss her and the relationship we could have had.'

The Russian nodded. 'I would have loved a brother, not that I don't love my sisters, but at least playing in a team has given me plenty of team brothers. So, is that why you don't like to go home ... because of the memories?'

'No,' I said, being honest with him. 'Claudia and I were two teenagers living in the same house who barely knew each other. We were absorbed in our own young lives – schools, friends, etc. I don't go back because I hate the shrine. I hate the fact that Mom can't be close to me for her own reasons and that Dad has to be too close and clingy. I can't breathe there.' I said, my hand involuntarily going to my chest.

The Russian reached out and took my hand in his. He kissed it and held it against his chest. I loved that man.

Chapter 30

The Russian and I were in different States this weekend ... him playing, me commentating. It was kind of exciting though. We sent each other messages and pics, had FaceTime, and we had no repeat performance of the last time he had been away and Lucas had made him sleep in the hallway. My colleague, Suzie, and I were both in Missouri to cover the Suns versus the Missouri Mystics first finals game, and we had separate hotel rooms. The Russian was in Ohio to play the Columbus Cats and he was sharing a room with Lucas, again.

Suzie and I went out to dinner and then she caught up with a friend for drinks while I declined the offer to join them, returned to the hotel room and showered. I slipped into bed with my ebook, waiting to hear from The Russian. After nine he FaceTimed me.

'Hello gorgeous,' he said, looking gorgeous. 'Where are you?'

'In bed, alone, in my hotel room ... a big bed too. I'll just have to take matters into my own hands while I think of you,' I said.

'Sorry, what was that Lucas?' he said.

'What!' I hissed, mortified, and he laughed.

'Just kidding Brooker, he's in the shower.'

'Russian, you'll pay for that,' I threatened him, breathing a sigh of relief.

'What are you wearing?' he asked. I scanned the phone down my front where I wore a white lace and somewhat see-through camisole. The Russian groaned.

'Well that's hardly fair ... I have to share a room and now you've got me hard and I can't do anything about it,' he complained.

'Poor you,' I said, smiling at him. Yep, two could play at that game. 'Can I see it?'

He thought about it; the Russian wasn't much for exhibitionism.

'No, just take my word for it. If I had my own room,' he said, again with a glance to the closed bathroom door.

'What do you think Lucas is doing in there?' I asked. 'I bet he's on the phone having a similar conversation with Mia.'

'Mm, maybe. Did you bring your pink toy with you?' he asked.

I gasped. 'How do you know ...'

The Russian roared with laughter. 'I don't, but now I do.'

I think I went three shades of red. 'This conversation sucks,' I said, trying to hide my embarrassment, especially since The Russian had gotten me again. He softened.

'I'm sorry babe, you're right. I forbid you from servicing yourself, that's my job. You will remain horny until I can deliver,' he said.

'Forbid, huh? Are you sure Lucas is in the shower?' I asked, trying to look over his shoulder in the screen image.

'Can't you hear that bad singing?' he asked. 'Ready for tomorrow?'

'I should be asking you that, but yes, I'm looking forward to my next commentary job. I've done my homework, so I'm feeling good about it. And you, sorted for the Cats?'

'Yeah, all good,' he said.

The Cats were on the bottom of the ladder, and The Saints towards the top, so I knew they weren't going to struggle that hard for a win tomorrow.

'Friday night, it's our anniversary,' The Russian said, 'will you come over for dinner at my place?'

'Really? How romantic ... what anniversary?' I asked, confused.

'One hundred days,' he said, 'since our first date. I'm officially counting your Ball night as our first date.'

'Russian, how romantic of you,' I said, thrilled. Now he looked uncomfortable.

'So, will you?'

'I'd love to, thank you.' Then the bathroom door opened behind him and Lucas appeared. I could see his naked chest, but the rest was blocked by The Russian's head. I was guessing and hoping he had a towel wrapped around him.

'Hi Carly,' he called out.

'Hi Lucas,' I called back.

'So, got to go. Love you,' The Russian said in a quiet voice.

'Love you too,' I said.

'You've got my security team's number—' The Russian started before Lucas interrupted, talking in the background.

'Love you Carly, miss you, want to kiss you,' Lucas said, imitating The Russian.

'Hang on a minute,' The Russian growled and put the phone down.

I was laughing so hard that I could only just hear the commotion in the background ... some kind of tackling, then the door slamming, a lot of knocking. The Russian came back on the line.

'Sorry about that,' he said and sighed.

'What did you do?' I asked.

'Threw him out.'

There was more thumping on The Russian's hotel door, and even I could hear Lucas yelling out. 'C'mon Russian, let me in, love you buddy!'

The Russian must have moved the phone away from his mouth because the next thing I heard was him giving Lucas a mouthful.

'Fuck off, Captain. You can come in when I finish.'

He returned to me. 'The crap I have to put up with,' he mumbled. 'So you've got—'

'—I have your security team's number; I don't think anything is going to happen to me in a different State,' I said, reminding him that I wasn't at home.

'You've got fans and followers everywhere, doesn't hurt to be prepared. Don't open the door, even if they say it's room service,' he continued.

'But what if I order room service?' I asked, teasing him.

'Then ... don't.'

'Right,' I said. 'I love you, thank you for worrying about me.'

The knocking started again and Lucas hollered. 'Are you finished yet? C'mon Russian, share the love.'

'I'm going to kill him,' The Russian said. 'Talk to you tomorrow, miss you.'

I hung up, chuckling as I imagined the scene between the two of them. I wished he was in the big bed beside me. One hundred days, huh, how sweet. He never stopped surprising me – but given what was to come, that was an understatement.

Chapter 31

Before I left for our anniversary date, The Russian messaged me to remind me to lock my car doors on the drive over – I know he worked in security but he was certainly practicing it on me. I decided to be very girly for our 100 days date anniversary – Mom had made me self-conscious that I wasn't feminine enough with The Russian, not that he had ever said anything. I think he liked me challenging him and working out with him ... sweating and all that stuff.

Regardless, I had bought a dress just for the occasion – it was retro in style, with a sweetheart neckline, sleeveless, and a rose print all over it. It was fitted to my waist and then ballooned out in layers. It even had a little bit of tulle underneath the skirt to give it some body. I matched the red roses in the dress with a pair of strappy red sandals and wore my hair down for the occasion. I felt pretty hot, very girly, and I ventured out for the ultimate verdict.

Josh applauded. 'Beautiful, where did you get that?'

I did a turn for him and sent the skirt swirling. 'From Vintage Girl,' I said.

'Made for you, it really suits you,' he said.

'Thanks, Josh, that's a relief. Mom has me worried that I'm not displaying my femininity,' I said. Josh had met my Mom and Dad and knew my history.

'Don't be crazy,' he said, opening the fridge and grabbing some cola. 'You're all woman.'

'You're good for me,' I said, giving him a kiss on the cheek as I grabbed my overnight bag and car keys. 'Now, I promise I won't be back tonight, so you've got the place to yourself.'

'Thanks, but you're always welcome to come home. We've got nothing to hide. Spencer and I are just going to get takeaway and watch a movie.'

He saw me out and I headed to the car, looking in the backseat before getting in to make sure it was all clear, and locking the doors when I got in, thank you, Russian.

One hundred days ... as I drove to The Russian's place for our one hundred days anniversary dinner, I couldn't help but smile the whole way. Seriously, I must have looked like an idiot to anyone who pulled up at the lights beside me. The few dramas we'd had during that time had been nothing, were not by any means insurmountable, and the highlights had been many. I had never, ever, been so happy – I just felt blessed with his love and my new career.

The Russian must have seen my car headlights and met me as I drove into his garage ... more security stuff, Lord knows who could have been hiding in there – a pussycat, or rat perhaps! He opened the car door for me and gave me his hand.

'Wow, look at you,' he said, his eyes running over me.

'You like?' I asked.

'Absolutely,' he said, and spun me around under his arm

as my skirt billowed out. Then his arm found my back and he pulled me in close for a kiss.

'I've liked every single thing you've worn and haven't worn since we met,' he said. I swear he was well trained; he knew all the right things to say to a girl. He leaned down slightly to kiss me hello; my high heels made us almost the same height, give or take an inch. He looked pretty gorgeous himself in his dark fitted jeans, a grey-marl T-shirt and an open navy shirt over it. He had a navy pair of Converse All Stars on his feet ... the man could dress himself.

'I like this too,' I said, admiring his clothes, 'warrants closer inspection.'

'You think?' he said, his lip curling into a small smile.

He reached into the backseat and grabbed my overnight bag, and then the moment was ruined.

'Russian,' a female voice said, and we both turned to see his ex-girlfriend Leesa walking towards us. Thank God I was dressed up and felt my best, because as usual, she looked Boho stunning – she wore a white lace top and a matching long white skirt; a tan belt and tan ankle boots; and a gorgeous tan-colored floppy brimmed felt hat. Her long blonde wavy hair was loose and fell around her shoulders.

The Russian clearly wasn't expecting her as his eyes narrowed and his entire body stiffened next to me ... no, I don't know if that part stiffened, but I hope not!

'Leesa, what are you doing here?' he asked, in a low voice.

'Interrupting something, clearly,' she said, glancing at me and my overnight bag. 'Hello ... Carly, isn't it?'

I nodded and gave her a small smile. 'Hi Leesa.'

She knew very well who I was and I wasn't going to play the same bitchy game.

The Russian hadn't moved, he stood frozen with my luggage in one hand and the other arm around my waist.

'I don't wish to be rude, but we're busy here,' he said. 'Just passing through, are you?'

'Can I talk with you alone?' she asked, not making eye contact with me at all and giving him the most seductive look she could. Hell, it worked for me and I'm straight. Anger washed over me; I had so been looking forward to tonight and even though I felt sorry for her, enough already!

'No,' The Russian said, and I looked sharply at him. *No* ... he was saying *no* to her outright and upfront. I turned back to her ... it was a bit like watching a tennis game. 'We have to go now,' he said, 'so take care and thanks for dropping by.'

I swear she was an actress, her eyes welled with tears and I felt The Russian soften next to me; he hated tears. No doubt she knew that, and she had played that card a few thousand times.

'Why are you in town?' he asked.

'I flew in to see you.'

'When?'

'Last night. I'm staying with a friend of Daddy's ... an actor ...'

'Of course,' The Russian said. 'Well, we have to go Leesa, we've got plans. Do you need me to call you a taxi or have you got a car out there?' he said, pointing to outside his gated property.

Then she changed. Miss Vulnerable went out the window and Miss Bitch appeared.

'You know what Russian? I don't need a fucking thing from you. I don't know why I'm even here begging you to see me. What the fuck? Who do you think you are?' she screamed.

The Russian moved in front of me.

'That's enough,' he growled, 'I'm sorry your trip here was a waste of time, but let's try to finish with some sort of respect for each other.'

'Fuck you,' she said – actually, she almost hissed it. 'You'll be sorry you broke up with me. When your career is over, you'll be nothing—'

'—right, well, thanks for that,' he said, interrupting her speech. He put my overnight bag down and moved towards her. The Russian took her arm.

'Don't fucking touch me,' she snatched her arm away from him. 'I'm leaving.' She walked a few paces down the path and then turned back. 'Have you told your new screw that when the team wins you're going to screw her all night, but you can't get it up when the team loses? Has she enjoyed that yet? She'd better hope the Saints have a good season. Or how ...'

The Russian's growl was as loud as his movements were fast, and he had her arm again. I heard him saying something about her father and doctor, and thanks to Lucas, I knew the context of that statement. The Russian had her down the driveway in moments and then she pulled away and strode off. He webbed his fingers behind his head as he stood and watched her depart; my heart went out to him.

That had been horrid, the whole thing was nasty. I could only imagine what their fights must have been like in the past ... Leesa working him up, The Russian losing it and having to channel his anger and frustration somewhere, always worried what the consequences might be if she was fragile. We, as a couple, were so not like that.

I saw her leave in her car and The Russian, his head lowered and his shoulders slumped, came back to me.

'I'm really sorry ...' he began.

I shook my head. 'Don't say it, it's not your fault. And just for the record, I don't feel like sex if my team loses either.'

The Russian chuckled. 'What if the Saints lose?'

I shook my head. 'Nope, I'm bound to have no libido either.'

He cupped my face in his hands and kissed me.

'Thank you,' he said. 'Have you got your phone on you?'

'Sure,' I said, rummaging through my handbag and handing it over to him, confused as to whom he was going to ring now. He punched in a number and then I understood.

'Charlie, it's The Russian ... yeah, good, thanks, and you? Good ... listen, can you please ensure that Leesa Hart is not given entry anymore please? Thanks, that would be appreciated ... no, under no circumstances. Yep, that's it, thanks.'

The Russian hung up and gave me the phone back.

'Gated security,' he explained, and then exhaled. 'Can you take a beach walk in that dress? I just need to let off some steam.'

'It's perfect for the beach,' I said, and while he raced inside and grabbed his keys and locked up, I removed my sandals. We put my shoes and bag back in the car, I locked it and The Russian slipped my keys into his pocket. He reached for my hand and we walked across his front lawn and entered the sandy edges of the beach. He kicked off his Converse trainers and left them on the edge of his property, and then, taking the small drop to the sand, he reached up for me, put his hands around my waist, picked me up and deposited me beside him. He took my hand again and we walked.

He was right; the beach was very therapeutic and the dark of the evening was calm and cool. I tried to break the tension.

'Your three-course meal won't be burning in our absence?' I teased him.

He smiled and kissed the top of my head. 'No. Lucky for you that it is all done and just ready to be served. Best meal you'll ever have.'

'Your mom again?'

'Ye of little faith,' he clucked. 'Just the dessert. I did the starters and the main is from Scarpio's,' he said, revealing he had organized dinner from one of the best restaurants in town. 'I didn't want you to run away screaming, and I figured there's only so many nights I can feed you pasta.'

We walked along for a while and let the tension fall from us; it was magic, such a beautiful night, and The Russian was right ... by the time we got back to his place forty-five minutes later, everything that had happened was forgotten, and then something happened that I would never, ever forget, ever.

Chapter 32

Carrying my bag again, The Russian led the way upstairs, unlocking his house. He swung the door open for me and I entered and gasped. I now knew why he had wanted to go on the beach walk first. The room was filled with roses – filled completely.

He grinned with delight seeing my reaction.

'Happy anniversary,' he said.

'Oh Alex,' I sighed. I stood in my rose-print dress, looking at the bouquets all around the room.

'There's one hundred ... one for every day we've been together,' he said, leaving me for a moment to put my bag in his room.

There were one hundred – ten bunches with ten in each and the scent and the sight was breathtaking. I didn't move as I took it all in, and then I moved from one bunch to the next, touching them, studying them and inhaling.

'I don't know which is my favorite ... the red roses are divine, but the yellow are magnificent, and the white ...' I swanned from one bouquet to the next. The room was like a glorious florist shop, and behind the bouquets, the glistening ocean water reflected the moonlight. I would never forget this moment.

The Russian leaned on the back of his sofa, his arms folded watching me. 'You don't have to pick a favorite,' he said, indulging me. 'They're all yours and the florist said they'd collect and deliver them to your place tomorrow if you'd like, or you can leave them here and visit them.'

'Oh Russian,' I said, again, and inhaled a pale lilac bunch. I moved over to him and wrapped my arms around his body. 'Thank you, that is the most amazing gift I have ever received.'

'The pleasure is all mine,' he said.

'I need a photo,' I said. 'Of me in my rose dress surrounded by your roses.' I grabbed my phone again and gave it to The Russian. I slipped my red shoes back on and made him take at least half a dozen shots – a wide shot with all the roses in, closer shots to show off the roses and a selfie of the two of us in front of the red roses.

'Thank you,' I sighed, 'I'm blown away. And I bought you sports socks,' I said, and The Russian laughed.

'That's a perfect gift,' he nodded. 'Very thoughtful ... I like practical presents.'

'Me too,' I agreed. 'But this is unforgettable.' And then something even more amazing happened. The Russian pulled away from me and dropped to one knee.

I gasped, taking in his pose, the roses around us, the moonlight, the moment. He pulled a small black box from behind the vase of roses where I stood and opened it. There was the most amazing diamond ring I have ever seen – huge, an emerald-cut center diamond, with a band adorned with round brilliant-cut diamonds.

'Brooker ... Carly,' he said, 'in one hundred days I have loved you in one hundred ways, will you marry me?'

'Russian,' I said; I knew my eyes were wide and my heart was pounding and I didn't want ever to forget this glorious moment. 'Yes, yes, absolutely yes,' I said, and then I cried.

The Russian rose and slipped the ring onto my finger. He picked me up and we kissed ... long, deep, passionate and I drank him in. Then he put me down.

'I got it from Tiffany's, but if you don't like it they said you could pick out something else,' he said.

'Are you kidding?' I asked, 'it is the most stunning ring I have ever seen, thank you, I love it.' I extended my hand to look at it and the glistening diamonds on my engagement finger.

I looked up at him and saw his delight. I cupped his face.

'I had no idea you were up to this. I love you, I love how special this is, thank you, Alex,' I said, using his real name to make the moment more intimate.

'Thank you for saying 'yes', Ms Carly Brooker-Renwick? I'm trying to be as politically correct as I can and my sisters thought that would be what you would go for.'

'Did they? Did you tell them? That's cute ... I think – since we're going to be together forever – I like Ms Carly Renwick better,' I said, and The Russian showed me his appreciation for that comment, picking me up and twirling me around.

When he put me down, I bounced up and down. 'I'm so excited, Russian, we're engaged.'

'Yeah, I noticed,' he teased me. 'I'll get us a glass of champagne, before you do more damage to that knee. We'll go to the balcony,' he said.

I just wanted to tell everyone in the whole world and share my happy news with my best friends, but that would have to wait as The Russian returned with the champagne. We went to the balcony, stood on the edge looking over the beach, and he popped the cork – love that sound. The Russian filled our glasses and we clinked.

'I love you,' he said.

'I love you, forever,' I added. We sipped and just stared at each other, being in the moment. Knowing that we had found each other, that we both wanted the same thing, and that we'd be together forever now. I was engaged; I was loved by The Russian and he saw his future with me. I teared up again.

'I didn't think you would say yes,' he said, 'given some of my performances to date.'

'Are you kidding?' I said, grinning at him like I was high. 'In a hundred days you have been my first thought of the day, my last thought, and every other thought in every waking moment.'

He smiled and I leaned in to kiss him ... a slow, champagne tasting kiss. We pulled away and I looked at my ring hand again ... I was engaged!

'Think we should announce it?' I asked.

'You're a girl, I know you'll be keen to,' he teased.

'I'm engaged to the most gorgeous guy on the planet, and I've just experienced the most romantic proposal ever ... hell yeah, I'm keen,' I said. 'But we should tell our parents before social media,' I said.

'My family knows, the girls helped me pick out your ring, and Tia is desperately waiting, well hoping, for an invitation to be a flower girl,' he said, rolling his eyes. 'Your parents know too.'

'That's what you were talking about with Dad?' I asked.

'I didn't ask for your hand in marriage,' he said, holding up his hands in defense, 'I know modern girls don't need to be given away from one man to the other ... well, Nikki and Ana said that, and Tia just went along. Mom agreed.'

'Thank God for that,' I said, because I seriously would have been pissed about that. I'm a stickler for my independence.

'I just let your dad know that I intended to propose and that I hoped they would support us, which he was happy to do.'

'So my fiancé, we probably should both call our parents though, and then we can put our announcements up,' I said, and grinned, liking the sound of the word 'fiancé'. 'And then we put our phones on silent so the rest of the night is ours.'

The Russian agreed.

*****

I went inside to get my phone from my handbag and The Russian grabbed his from the kitchen. He dialed his parents; they wanted to talk with me, and so did his sisters, which was really sweet. They were so excited for us, even though it had only been one hundred days. When eight-year-old Tia came on, I put her out of her misery.

'I was hoping that you could do me a big favor and be my flower girl?' I asked and I swear she screamed so loud that my ear was likely not to be fully functioning again for a week. Finally, the phone went back to The Russian who asked for the dog, Brodie, since he was the only one who hadn't gotten on the phone. I laughed and after hanging up, we called my parents. Mom was congratulatory but cautious, like she couldn't allow herself to be truly happy because her other daughter would never have a wedding. *Sigh.* Dad was wonderful and of course wanted to perform the ceremony. While The Russian spoke with Dad to receive his congratulations, I quickly called Josh, Steffi and Aimee. I told them I couldn't talk but wanted them to know first, before they saw it in my news feed. So exciting!

We then quickly prepared an announcement each.

'What have you got?' The Russian asked, grinning at me like I was an excited kid in an ice-cream shop ... I was much more excited than that.

I showed him the photo I had just taken of my hand with the huge rock on it – seriously, that ring if sold could fund the elimination of polio worldwide – one of my ambitions, but that was another story. Behind my photographed hand and ring were rows of roses. I wrote 'Breathtaking proposal ... in one hundred days, I've loved you in one hundred ways.' My hashtags were #engaged and #forevertaken.

The Russian grimaced. 'You can't give away my proposal ... the guys will bag me for the next ten years,' he said.

'Do you seriously think it is not going to get out there?' I asked him. 'Hell, the first question every journalist and female will ask is how did he propose?'

He rolled his eyes. 'Okay, but I may have to go undercover.'

'I won't do it if you don't want me to,' I said, studying him, 'we can keep it our secret.'

'No, go on ... tell everyone you've got the best, most

romantic fiancé in the world, they won't be surprised, I'm sure,' he said, his lips curling into a small smile. Such a big head.

The Russian got me to help him with his message; he used the selfie of both of us in front of all the roses, with just one hashtag - #shesaidyes.

'Ready?' I asked.

'Ready,' he agreed and we pressed 'post' and put our phones on silent. I put mine down and picked up our champagne glasses, handing The Russian his glass.

We looked at each other, just basking in the happiness of the moment. We clinked glasses and enjoyed the delicious bubbles, the quiet, the moment.

'There's a lot we don't know about each other,' I said, softly.

'Good huh?' he said. 'We've got all the time in the world ... unless, you're worried you don't know me well enough?' He frowned.

I shook my head. 'I know all I need to know.' I assured him. 'We are cut from the same cloth, you and me – made for each other.'

Then he took my glass off me, took my hand and we went inside where we made slow romantic love ... touching every part of each other with renewed tenderness and passion, and being in that moment of subliminal joy.

*****

Later that night – and it was late – good thing The Russian didn't have Saturday morning training, we lay in bed and laughed at some of the responses to our announcement.

Sasha: OMG, need a wedding dress? So thrilled for you! So is Nik ... except I think he's trying to work out ways to out-propose The Russian. Ha. Tell the Russian he's a big softie.

Lucas: WTF? You've raised the bar Russian. Damn U. Oh yea, and congrats

Tomás: Is this because I can tango and showed you up? Congrats U 2

Mia: OMG, OMG, so happy for you two! What a perfect couple!

Spencer: Josh told me the great news. I knew you were perfect for each other. We love him. Give him a hug from Josh and me.

Sure boys! All the Suns' girls had sent me beautiful notes, and there were so many missed calls from journos and friends. We put our phones down and returned to each other.

'Goodnight my fiancé, thank you for the most amazing night of my life,' I said, leaning on his chest and forgetting that Leesa had even come by earlier. I knew she would be in pain now, and I was sorry for that, but it just wasn't meant to be for her.

The Russian enveloped me in his arms. 'Goodnight my fiancée. Thank you for making me the happiest man to walk the earth.'

*****

First thing on Monday morning, my day off, and after The Russian had headed into work at the Saints' security office, I got a surprise text message from Wendy, the coffee van lady.

'Congratulations, Carly, to you and The Russian. My engagement present for you ... send me Sasha's number and I'll let her know when I'm arriving today, before The Russian knows.'

Ha! I texted her back Sasha's number and my thanks and delight at her present. I then quickly sent a message to Sasha to put her on alert. Victory! I knew Wendy must have been texting The Russian and giving him the heads up! I'd love to see The Russian's face when Sasha was finally in front of him in the coffee queue. Yeah, I knew I should have been on his side, but this was girl power, or coffee power, and if The Russian thought I had forgotten to crack this easy case wide open, he didn't have me pegged for much of a journalist.

About nine-thirty I got a message from The Russian.

'Okay fiancée of mine, please explain ... Sasha is in front of me at Wendy's coffee van. Not happy.'

This was followed not long after by a funny selfie sent by Sasha of her in the front of the queue with The Russian standing behind, his arms folded.

I messaged The Russian back. 'Goodness, how did that happen? Maybe, girl power! Remember, this girl loves you.'

Chapter 33

Six months later ...

We picked the non-season to marry – of course – so we could party, the players could relax, and neither of us had overwhelming work commitments. We had our wedding at The Russian's house ... the ceremony in the front yard, with the beach behind us, and then the reception spilled into the house. Helicopters flew overhead and security had a job at keeping the public and media out of the street, and letting the guests through.

Steffi and Aimee were my bridesmaids and we had selected champagne satin for them, which suited them both beautifully and complemented the ocean background. Of course Tia was stunning as the flower girl, and so important – The Russian couldn't wait for her part to be over so she would calm down a bit ... so cute.

My dress was amazing, thanks to Sasha: a fitted, natural satin backless gown, featuring French Chantilly lace and roses, hand-stitched by Sasha herself. It had taken her months to make and we made it financially worth her while, given the other work she'd had to put on hold to do it. I was hoping the publicity would let her design full-time now if that was what she wanted to do.

The Russian was breathtakingly beautiful, with his short back and sides, towering form, beautifully cut tuxedo, crisp white shirt and trimmings in champagne to match the bridal party. I could have jumped on him then and there and had my way with him. His two groomsmen were Captain Fantastic, Lucas, and his high school best friend, Matt, who had flown back from London, where he had been posted, to stand beside him, and meet me!

I didn't know how I was going to get through it. Dad stood at the front of the garden in the archway decorated with white roses, ready to marry us.

I took a deep breath, followed Steffi and Aimee and walked myself up our makeshift 'aisle' in the garden. The look The Russian was giving me brought tears to my eyes. I was so in love, so lucky!

All I wanted to hear were the words, and finally, Dad said them, and The Russian and I breathed ... 'I now pronounce you husband and wife. You may kiss your husband.'

THE END

Author acknowledgments:

I hope you liked The Russian's story and thank you to all the readers who requested he get his own book, I was keen to write it! Thanks to my romantic school friend who proposed to his girlfriend after 100 days and inspired The Russian to borrow that exact proposal. Thank you also to everyone who has loved my other Saints' – Lucas, Tomás and Niklas – and their ladies, Mia, Alice and Sasha. It has given me the enthusiasm to keep writing. As always, special thanks to my German 'translator and sub-editor' – Becky Strahl from InkEaters blog. Catch Becky's exiting and hot debut novel, *Shattered,* and her blog at: http://inkeaters.blogspot.de/

Finally my thanks to the Atlas Productions' team for loving the Saints and bringing them into the world.

And to The Russian himself … I wonder where you are these days, and if you knew this girl from the office next door was mad for you once upon a time.

About the author:

Ally Adams is a journalist who lives in coastal Victoria, Australia, with her husband and furry friends. She is a literature major, romance reader and writer. Connect at:

Facebook: https://www.facebook.com/allyadamswriter
Website: https://www.allyadamsbooks.com/

Sign up for Ally's 'love letter' newsletters for latest releases, free chapters and beta reader requests.

THE SAINTS TEAM SERIES

BOOK 1

TEAM

Lucas

ALLY ADAMS

Also in the *Saints* series:

Team Lucas

Just let me get my fill of you and I'll deal with the fallout if it happens... when it happens.

Mia Carter never thought getting suspended from her part-time job for having attitude could be the best thing to ever happen ... maybe.

When Lucas Ainswright—one of the world's biggest sporting stars—needs a minder, it just so happens that attitude is what is needed to keep Lucas in line.

Now Mia's job is to manage the sporting world's bad boy and keep him at the top of his game for the season. Game on!

THE SAINTS TEAM SERIES

BOOK 2

TEAM

Tomás

ALLY ADAMS

Team Tomás

Tomás Carrera has had to be responsible all his life. Growing up with a single mom and as the eldest of five siblings, Tomás missed out on a childhood of his own. Now his superstar soccer status has provided for his family and allowed him to let his hair down... and that's just what he's doing.

Signed to the Santa Ana Saints, Tomás is catching up for lost time with fast women, a fast Ducati motorcycle and a bevy of adoring fans. That is until he loses his heart to Alice and is torn with wanting her and his independence.

THE SAINTS TEAM SERIES
BOOK 3

TEAM
Niklas

ALLY ADAMS

Team Niklas

In his hometown of Berlin, Germany, Niklas Wagner is a superstar and when the Saints pay the big bucks to sign him up and bring him to Santa Ana, California, Nik takes a shine to his new life. When he meets the Saints' media officer, Sasha Saxon, sparks fly literally.

But Sasha is not your average girl – by day she is a journalistwho looks after the media for the national champion soccer team and at night she designs for her personal fashion label. She has big dreams and they don't include a boyfriend. Nik has never had to chase the girls but now he has met his match – Sasha is about to lead him on the biggest chase of his life.

www.ingramcontent.com/pod-product-compliance
Lightning Source LLC
Chambersburg PA
CBHW031219120726
47905CB00002B/397